THE INVITE

IRINA SHAPIRO

Storm

This is a work of fiction. Names, characters, businesses, places, events and incidents are either the products of the author's imagination or used in a fictitious manner. Any resemblance to actual persons, living or dead, or actual events is purely coincidental.

Copyright © Irina Shapiro, 2026

The moral right of the author has been asserted.

All rights reserved. No part of this book may be reproduced or used in any manner without the prior written permission of the copyright owner. This prohibition includes, but is not limited to, any reproduction or use for the purpose of training artificial intelligence technologies or systems

To request permissions, contact the publisher at rights@stormpublishing.co

Ebook ISBN: 978-1-80508-967-4
Paperback ISBN: 978-1-80508-969-8

Cover design: Lisa Brewster
Cover images: Shutterstock

Published by Storm Publishing.
For further information, visit:
www.stormpublishing.co

ALSO BY IRINA SHAPIRO

A Tate and Bell Mystery

The Highgate Cemetery Murder

Murder at Traitors' Gate

Murder at the Foundling Hospital

Murder at the Orpheus Theatre

Murder on Platform Four

Murder on the Prince Regent

The Carnival Murders

Murder on Devil's Ridge

Wonderland Series

The Passage

Wonderland

Sins of Omission

The Queen's Gambit

Comes the Dawn

The Hands of Time

The Hands of Time

A Leap of Faith

A World Apart

A Game of Shadows

Shattered Moments

The Ties that Bind

The Summer Solstice

The Winter Solstice

The Christmas Gift

Echoes from the Past

The Lovers

The Forgotten

The Unforgiven

The Forsaken

The Unseen

The Condemned

The Betrayed

The Broken

The Lost

PROLOGUE

The sunrise was breathtaking, fiery bands of fuchsia streaking the lavender sky and frost glittering on the pale blades of grass like minuscule bits of ground glass. The lake was calm, the still surface mirroring the vibrant colors of autumnal trees and the quickly brightening sky. On the shore, nothing stirred. No lights came on in the stunning waterfront properties, and no sounds of voices or passing cars disturbed the peace. A lone dove freewheeled over the lake, and colorful leaves silently fell to the ground and drifted on the surface of the water.

It was absolutely lovely, the north shore of the lake reminiscent of a charming painting. A rustic lodge, a wooden dock, and a sweet little rowboat just waiting to be taken out seemed a natural part of the landscape. The only thing out of place was the body that floated on its back on the calm water of the lake. The hair rippled like thick fronds of kelp, and the eyes that were covered in a gossamer layer of frost shone like diamonds in a face that was as pale as the moon.

And then a wail of anguish pierced the quiet morning, shattering the silence into a million jagged shards.

ONE
SERENA

The email appeared in Serena's inbox at 2:47 p.m. on a perfectly ordinary October afternoon. It was from SexyLexie69@gmail.com, and the subject line read:

>Don't miss this amazing opportunity

It had been drummed into Serena that she should never open any email that looked like it might be offering penis enlargement or Eastern European mail order brides. At best, it was a fishing expedition that might take her to some porn site or offer a questionable product. At worst, it could be a Trojan horse virus that would wipe out her hard drive, or a scam that would somehow open an electronic door into her most private documents, like the passwords folder that was actually called Passwords. Serena knew she should delete the email immediately, but this communication wasn't spam. She knew that for a fact, and, if she deleted the email, she'd spend the whole night lying awake, obsessing about what it contained, tension mounting as she envisioned all sorts of scenarios, each more worrying than the last.

Normally, Serena wouldn't even check her personal email

during the workday—her office had a strict no cellphone policy during work hours—but today, she had taken a mental health day from work. She had a few vacation days left and had every intention of using them before the end of the year. She had spent the morning the way she liked best. She'd slept until nine, had a light breakfast, then at ten she'd headed over to her favorite spa, where she'd enjoyed a fifty-minute deep tissue massage, followed by half an hour in the sauna and a cool shower before her mani/pedi appointment. Afterwards, she'd dropped into a boutique she frequented on Lexington Avenue and bought several tops, all on sale and very reasonably priced. She'd been craving tom kha gai soup for days and had picked some up on the way home. Serena had intended to check her email and social media and browse Pinterest for inspiration on a new project before binging several episodes of a new romcom that had dropped on Netflix on Tuesday. Absolute bliss!

She had hung up her purchases and set the container of soup next to her laptop, to be savored while she surfed the net, but, even though the spicy, coconutty aroma had made her mouth water only a moment ago, she'd suddenly lost her appetite, and this email wasn't doing her mental health any favors either. This was not a message she had ever expected to receive. Serena's hand hovered over the mouse for several long minutes before she finally clicked on it. There were seven names in the addressee bar—Serena, her husband Noah, four of their closest college friends, and Vince Howard. She had no idea why he'd been included since he was never really part of the group, but at the moment Vince was the least of her concerns. Trepidation mounting, Serena read the message.

Guess who's back!

I know I sort of dropped off the face of the earth these past few years and you're all really mad at me for not returning your calls and texts, but I'm back now, and I want to make it up to you and finally catch up in person. I have so much to tell you all, and, of course, I have yet to congratulate the newlyweds. So, I rented this gorgeous lake house (photogenic pictures attached) so that we can have a long-overdue reunion and enjoy each other's company without all the usual distractions.

You all lead super-busy lives and are probably trying hard to think of a good reason not to come, but this is an all-expenses-paid weekend at a stunning location and with your closest friends. So, no excuses, come join me at Witch Lake for Halloween weekend. I promise it will be memorable.

Love you and can't wait to see you,
Lex

Attached were four pictures. Three were of a house, perched on the shore of a dark, still lake and surrounded by woods on three sides. It really was very charming. There was a sizable deck, equipped with a Weber grill, a hot tub, and Adirondack chairs grouped around a firepit. A private dock jutted out over the lake, and a pretty rowboat was tied to a post, the oars laid across the seats and ready to use. The fourth image was of Lexie, and Serena examined it closely. Lexie wore a sun hat and retro shades and held up a tropical drink, possibly a mojito, in a toast as she grinned into the camera.

Serena's teeth began to chatter, and then her whole body started to shake, tears streaming down her pale face reflected in a screen that had gone dark. This was it, the end of everything, and there was absolutely nothing she could do about it. Serena bolted out of her chair, and just made it to the bathroom before she vomited into the toilet. Beads of sweat had formed on her forehead, and the smell of soup that drifted through the open door made her retch again and again. She sank onto the bathroom floor and pressed her forehead to the cool tiles, her knees drawn up to her chest and her eyes squeezed shut, as if she could block out the image of Lexie's smiling face.

On the desk, her cellphone trilled, ringing mercilessly until the call finally went to voicemail, and Serena knew precisely who was calling.

TWO

NOAH

Fuck me! Noah thought as he read and reread the email from Lexie. He was screwed on so many levels, he didn't even know where to begin. And he had about thirty seconds to figure out what to do. Serena wasn't the sort of person who read an email as soon as it dropped into her inbox, but she would have opened this one immediately, just as he had. And she'd be expecting him to react. If he didn't call her right away, she'd think something was up, and if he did, she would think he was desperate to preempt her outrage and only be angrier. From this moment until they either went to the reunion or didn't, Serena would be watching him like a hawk, searching for signs of guilt, regret, longing, and pain. And he was feeling it all at levels he hadn't experienced in years.

This would be the ultimate test, and there was really no way he could pass. He wasn't good at hiding his feelings, and the two women who'd known him his entire adult life would be able to read him like a book—a short, cheesy romcom that jumped the shark and turned into a horror story worthy of Stephen King. *Carrie* sprang to mind. What he really wanted to do was talk this over with Remy and Richie, but he didn't have time for a lengthy conversation, and they probably wouldn't even pick up during business hours. Richie might be with a client or in court, and Remy had a photo session booked for this afternoon. Still, Noah was desperate for support, so he fired off a group text and prayed that at least one of them would respond.

What the fuck do I do?

There was no need to explain. The guys would have seen the email and would know, if not fully understand, what he was feeling. Panic was at the top of the list. Why had Lexie had to send a group email and make the names visible? If she had bcc'd him at least, that would have bought him some time with Serena. He could claim he'd never got the email and that Lexie had obviously sent it only to Serena. Surely, after everything that had happened, Lexie owed him that much—but it seemed she no longer gave a shit how he felt. The girl who'd been so sensitive and careful of everyone's feelings was going in guns blazing. And the obvious questions were, why? And why now?

The replies from Noah's friends popped up almost immediately.

> REMY
> You go to the reunion
>
> RICHIE
> Take cover, bro

> Not really an option

> RICHIE
> Catch something deadly? No, wait, you already have, and you married her
>
> REMY
> Richie don't be a dick
>
> RICHIE
> Just trying to lighten the mood

> Not helpful

> RICHIE
> Look, you'll have to grin and bear it man

> **REMY**
> I second that

> Why?

Again, there was no need to explain what he was asking. They knew Noah wasn't asking why he should go to the reunion.

> **RICHIE**
> Guess we'll find out
>
> **REMY**
> Was bound to happen sooner or later

Remy was right. Noah had always known he'd have to face Lexie one day; he just hadn't thought there'd be an audience when he did. There was still so much between them—hurt feelings, words left unsaid, and, most of all, questions that had never been answered. Noah would have preferred to confront Lexie alone, but he really had no choice. She'd issued a public challenge, and, if he refused to go, Serena would think he still had feelings for Lexie and was afraid to see her, especially now that he was married to Lexie's best friend.

But if he displayed even a hint of eagerness to attend the reunion, Serena would assume he was desperate to see Lexie again. Noah was anything but desperate, at least not in the way Serena might think. Lexie had ripped his heart out and had brought him so low that, for a time, he'd actually wished he was dead. She'd been his first love, his soulmate, his future. Lexie had been straight as an arrow, a girl who didn't play mind games, sulk, or put him through endless trials designed to test his loyalty. She had never hurt him in all the time they'd been together, until that final text.

God, to be dumped by text less than a month after he had proposed. What a cliché. Wasn't there an episode of *Sex and the City* where Carrie was dumped via a Post-it note? Lexie had had a lot to say about that and had pronounced the dumper—Noah couldn't recall which loser it had been; there'd been so many—to be beyond redemption, his cowardice and lack of respect for the woman he was in a relationship with unforgivable.

And then Lexie had done the same to him, firing off a short dismissal and then refusing to answer any of his calls or texts. And now she was back, and she clearly didn't feel an ounce of remorse for the way she'd treated him. She was probably pissed at him for moving on with Serena. And he had convinced himself he had moved on, until he lay sleepless beside his unsuspecting wife, feeling like he'd been buried alive. He loved Serena, of course he did, but not in the way he'd loved Lexie. What he felt for Serena was calm, and safe, and carefully curated. What he'd felt for Lexie had been raw and wild and true. And he had foolishly assumed she'd felt the same about him.

Dear God, Noah thought as he selected Serena's number and pressed the call icon with a shaking hand. *Please help me get through this!*

THREE

REMY

"Well, that was a bolt out of the blue," Remy said when he met Richie for a drink that evening.

They settled in a corner booth at their favorite bar in Chelsea and ordered the usual, Coronas with lime. It was their tradition to meet on Friday nights, to pregame for the weekend, but neither ever had more than three beers, since they couldn't afford to get drunk. Remy usually worked on Saturdays. As a freelance photographer, he had to be available whenever a gig came up, and Richie coached his little brother's special needs baseball team on Saturday mornings and couldn't afford to be hungover, not when he was responsible for twenty-six kids with various disabilities.

Noah used to meet them from time to time, but he'd joined them only twice since he and Serena had gotten married just over a year ago. They'd seen it coming; had known Serena wouldn't stand for Noah hanging out with his single friends. She imagined that Remy and Richie did nothing but cruise for one-night stands when they went out, but mostly they just used the time to unwind and unpack their stressful weeks. Noah could have done with a time-out, today of all days, but he'd be signing his own death warrant if he left Serena hanging when she'd probably been stewing for hours and needed Noah to run home and reassure her that everything would be fine, and they would survive Halloween weekend.

"Noah is going down!" Richie announced with solemn finality as he raised the bottle to his lips.

"Is that your professional opinion?"

Richie was an assistant DA with the Manhattan District Attorney's Office, and he usually had an opinion on everything, even if he had no clue what he was talking about. But in this case, Remy had to agree. Things didn't look good for their golden boy.

"What the hell was Lexie thinking, setting that whole thing up?" Richie asked as he punctuated the question with a WTF gesture.

"You going?" Remy asked.

"Hell, yeah. I'm not going to miss an all-expenses-paid front-row seat to a gladiatorial match between Serena and Lexie. Hopefully, with a couple of rib eyes grilled medium rare and a bottle of some very fine Cabernet thrown in to accompany the event. I wouldn't say no to some mashed potatoes, or pasta, too," he added wistfully.

Richie had been on a low-carb diet for several months and dreamed of potatoes and refined flour the way some people dreamed of sex with a Hollywood star or winning the lottery. He allowed himself low-carb beer, hence the Corona, and the occasional glass of wine, but he had been fanatical about his diet and exercise regimen and had lost twenty-five pounds since April, when his latest Tinder flame had dumped him because he was fat, refused to wax his chest, and hadn't looked hot enough in her Instagram photos to make her ex jealous.

Richie was anything but fat. He was solid. The kind of guy who wore his peasant genes well and would appeal to a less superficial girl, one who actually liked him for his keen mind and great sense of humor. He was also the best friend a guy could have, and Remy thanked his lucky stars that he had met Richie at a time when he'd really needed someone to prop him up. He had been completely alone in the world for the first time in his life when he'd walked into the college dorm room he'd been assigned to share with a complete stranger. But for the first time in a long time he had gotten lucky, because that stranger was Richie. And then Remy wasn't alone anymore.

"What about you?" Richie asked as he side-eyed a plate of nachos the server had just carried past and breathed in the aroma of deep-fried tortillas and piping hot queso before his shoulders drooped in defeat.

"Yes, if only to referee the fight," Remy replied.

"There will be a fight, won't there?"

"I hope not. Serena doesn't deserve this. She'd been in love with Noah forever, but she never made a move. Not ever. She was loyal to Lexie until the end."

"That didn't stop her from offering Noah the sort of understanding and comfort he couldn't refuse when Lexie left him."

"He was in pieces, man," Remy reminded him.

"I know. I really felt for him. He'd just made the final payment on the ring when Lexie sent him that text."

"That ring cleaned him out. He wanted Lexie to have a ring she could be proud of."

Remy paid attention to such things. Maybe it was because he worked in fashion, or maybe because he'd been impressed with how much effort Noah had invested in choosing just the right ring, and how sure he'd been of his decision at just twenty-two. Remy had envied him then, thinking Noah had it all figured out. But Noah's life had imploded when he'd expected it least, reminding Remy how fickle and unpredictable women could be. He thought he might want to have a family one day. He'd be a good dad, but he wasn't sure about marriage. Couples didn't need a government-sanctioned contract to be happy. Marriage was an outdated, impractical, and stifling construct that made people feel trapped. If two people were happy together, they didn't require validation. And if they weren't happy, they didn't need the added pressure of feeling shackled. If Remy was ever lucky enough to find a woman he could love, he'd willingly enter into a committed relationship. But marriage? He didn't think so.

"What did he do with the ring?" Richie asked.

"I don't know. I never asked." Remy drained the last of his beer and shook his head. "He bought a new one for Serena."

"He must have traded it in."

"It's not a used car," Remy replied.

"No, but diamonds don't depreciate," Richie said matter-of-factly. "I can't even imagine what Serena must be feeling right now."

"Mad as hell, probably. She's not going to take this lying down. She'll fight for her man," Remy replied. "Do you really think Lexie has staged all this so she can get Noah back?"

"Either that or she wants to show everyone that she's over it and has no problem hanging out with his new wife."

"Rich, does Noah know?" Remy asked.

"Know what?"

"You know what."

"No, and don't you dare tell him," Richie said, with a look that warned Remy this could result in grievous bodily harm.

"How do you know Serena hasn't told him? She's just the sort to confess before the wedding. You know, start with a clean slate."

"Serena wouldn't do anything to jeopardize her chances with Noah, and I wasn't going to ruin it for her. He was welcome to her."

"Was he?" Remy asked carefully.

"I was never that into her, and she definitely wasn't into me. It was just sex."

"Noah will lose his shit if he ever finds out you two hooked up," Remy observed.

"Which is why he'll never find out. *Will he*, Remy?"

"Not from me, he won't."

"That's right," Richie said. "You're taking that secret to your grave, bro."

The server brought another round of beers, and they raised their bottles in a silent toast. What happened behind closed doors stayed behind closed doors. No one needed to know.

FOUR

REMY

Remy had always been Team Lexie. He knew what she'd done to Noah was low, but she had to have had her reasons. Lexie was always on the level. No artifice, no guile. She said it like it was and was always there for anyone who needed her. She'd been there for him. Maybe that was why they'd bonded the way they had—because of their parents, or the lack of them. Remy had always figured he was the luckier one of the two. His mother had been Pixie Durant, the model who had graced the cover of every fashion magazine for about two years before overdosing on heroin and choking on her own vomit. Remy never knew who his father was, and he doubted Pixie did either. From what he had read online, Pixie hadn't minded the casting couch—or any couch—one bit. Remy used to wish he'd met his dad, just once. Just to see what the guy looked like. To know what kind of man he was.

When he was little, Remy thought his dad was from France because of his name, but then he discovered that Pixie used to tell everyone she was French. There was a French-Canadian ancestor somewhere up the family tree, but that was the extent of their French heritage. Pixie probably named him Remy to keep the pretense going, then had promptly handed him off to her parents and never looked back. Remy didn't remember her at all. But he did remember Grandpa and Gran. They were good people—God bless their simple souls—and they'd done their best, but they couldn't love him any more than they could understand their wayward daughter. To them, Remy had been an embarrassment. The kind of shame you prayed over in church and explained away to your friends with tight smiles and mumbled excuses because you knew they called your grandkid a bastard and thought your daughter was a drug-addicted whore.

Remy thought that was bad, but then life did him one worse. His grandparents died while he was in middle school. Grandpa had been a lifelong smoker who'd disabled every smoke alarm in the house because they kept going off. One night, he fell asleep in his La-Z-Boy with a lit cigarette. The ash landed on a folded newspaper on top of the old shag carpet and the wooden house went up like a tinderbox. There wasn't much left to bury. If Remy hadn't been at a friend's house for a sleepover that night, he would've gone up in flames with them. Instead, he was handed over to Social Services and spent the next six years in foster care.

Lexie had been through the system too. Her parents were teenage druggies who left her at a fire station when she was just a few days old. By the time she landed at Quinnipiac University on a full scholarship, Lexie had survived twelve different foster homes. But she'd made it. She got her degree, and she got them—a group of friends who met freshman year and swore they'd always stick together. And they'd mostly kept that vow... sort of. They hadn't all been in the same room since graduation.

The girls were bitter about Lexie's desertion, but, although Remy missed her more than he cared to admit, he understood Lexie's need to break away and take the time to figure out who she was before making lifelong commitments. She'd seen her chance and had taken it, and, if the last three years were any indication, it was that Lexie had no regrets and had not missed the people she'd left behind.

But now Lexie was back, and this reunion promised to be interesting. Very interesting indeed.

FIVE
NOAH

When Noah got home, the apartment was silent. All the lights were turned off, and at first he thought Serena had gone out. Then he found her in the living room, sitting in the dark, her silhouette bulky in an oversized sweatshirt and her arms crossed over her chest. The New York skyline was visible through the window, the lights bright against the pitch-black sky of the October evening. There was enough ambient light for Noah to see once his eyes adjusted from the brightness of the LED lamps in the hallway, and he slowly entered the room, hesitant to make any sudden moves.

A bottle of Jack Daniel's stood on the coffee table. There was liquid at the bottom of the glass, but the bottle was three-quarters full, so Noah hoped it was just a prop and Serena hadn't been guzzling whiskey since the afternoon. But anything was possible. She hadn't answered any of his calls or texts, and he thought he'd caught a whiff of vomit when he'd first walked into the apartment. Never a good sign, since Serena was rarely sick.

To ask her if she was all right would probably upset her, so Noah got straight to the point. "I'll do whatever you want, Ree," he said desperately.

Serena stared at him, her eyes unnaturally dark in a face that was deathly pale.

"You want to go, don't you?" she wailed. "You can't wait to see her."

Noah did want to see Lexie. He realized it only after the news had settled and the feelings he'd buried when Lexie didn't come home came rushing back. But he wanted to talk to Lexie in private, with Serena preferably in another state, maybe a different time zone.

"I will do whatever you say," Noah repeated stoically.

The safest course of action was to let Serena decide. That way she could feel like she was in control, and maybe it would help her to deal with this unexpected situation. Watching the emotions pass across his wife's face, Noah could tell she was truly torn. More than anything, she wanted to decline and find a way to avoid seeing Lexie ever again, but, if she refused to go, she would be as good as admitting that she was afraid and insecure in her relationship with Noah, and Serena would never cop to that, as it would be so glaringly obvious at the reunion who was a no-show. Short of someone close to them dying suddenly, no excuse would be good enough to forestall endless speculation from their friends. Absence would be a clear admission of defeat.

"Well, she doesn't scare me," Serena exclaimed, having clearly decided the same thing. "We're going."

"All right," Noah said. He sounded outwardly calm, but he thought he might be sick.

Now that it was official and they were really going, his heart hammered against his ribs and his stomach threatened to turn itself inside out. Noah directed all his energy to breathing evenly and maintaining an inscrutable expression. He couldn't allow Serena to see how nervous he really was. If he were honest, it shocked him that the prospect of seeing Lexie again had such a visceral effect. It'd been more than three years, and he had to man up. People got hurt every day, but they grieved and moved on, and, if they were smart, learned from past mistakes.

"All right?" Serena cried, her shrill voice cutting across his thoughts. "I knew that was what you wanted all along."

"Serena, you're my wife, and all I want is to make you happy. Lexie is no longer part of my life."

"But she is. She included you in the invitation. Have you two been emailing on the sly?"

"No."

"She emails Remy and Angelina from time to time."

"Yeah, I know. They said."

"So, you talk about her!"

"They mentioned it in passing," Noah explained.

He sounded defensive, but Serena was on the warpath, and he had to prove to her that he had nothing to hide. Nothing at all. Well, maybe something, but she didn't need to know that he still stalked Lexie on social media. He never commented on or liked any of her posts, but some part of him needed to know what she was up to. It was a form of self-torture, he acknowledged that, especially when Lexie giddily mentioned some new guy, but it was easier than not knowing, never seeing. Noah supposed it was wrong to keep tabs on his ex, but plenty of people did it. It was harmless, and it had no bearing on his relationship with Serena.

"She's always on Instagram," Serena was saying angrily now. "Posting her travel photos and inspirational quotes. She just wants to show us all what a glamorous and enlightened life she leads."

"I'm not on Instagram, you know that."

"How do I know you don't have a finsta?" Serena demanded.

"Serena, I do not have a fake Instagram account," Noah snapped, using his annoyance to mask the fact that he did.

Ronnie Keller was the name on his fake account. Ronnie was a boy Noah had been friends with in middle school. The poor kid had died of leukemia when he was thirteen, and Noah deluded himself by reasoning that he used Ronnie's name to keep his memory alive. Bullshit of the highest order, but at least the real Ronnie couldn't suddenly appear and demand to know what the fuck Noah thought he was doing. Noah used Sonic the Hedgehog as his profile picture. It had been Ronnie's favorite character, so it was a kind of tribute. Besides, the hedgehog could never be connected to Noah, so he was safe.

"Here, check my phone," Noah said, and held out his cell to Serena. "Look at my emails. Check my photos. Do whatever you have to do to feel reassured."

He wasn't overly worried that Serena would find his fake profile. He didn't have Instagram on his phone and only looked at it on his work computer. As a marketing manager for a health supplement manufacturer, he was expected to check what the competition was doing, so no one questioned him going on Instagram, X, Facebook, or any other sites where companies advertised their products.

"You probably deleted anything incriminating before you got home," Serena said sulkily.

"There was nothing incriminating to delete. Most of my pictures are of you."

"Really?" Serena asked through fresh tears.

"Yes, really. And a few of Remy's cat."

Serena gave him a watery smile. "I hate that cat. He's evil."

"Yes, he is. But he is cute."

"Yeah," Serena admitted.

She was beginning to thaw, and Noah thought there was hope of making peace before they went to bed. Noah's mother always preached that spouses should never go to bed angry, but when it came to Serena that could mean staying awake for about seventy-two hours before she was finally ready to make up, and waiting a few more days until she let him touch her.

"Come to bed," Noah said. "Please."

It was too early for bed, but if Serena wanted to test him she'd come. She'd want to see if he was focused on her or if his mind was still on Lexie.

"I'll just sit here for a while. You go on."

"I don't want to go to bed without you," Noah tried again.

"I need a moment," Serena said, and Noah took it for the dismissal it was.

She was still angry and upset and would sit in the dark and brood until she either came up with a plan that allowed her to retake control or worked herself up into a lather. Only time would tell which, but neither would bode well for Noah. Richie hadn't been far off the mark when he'd told Noah to take cover. He wished he could.

SIX
SERENA

As soon as Noah finally left her alone, Serena dropped her head and buried her face in her hands. She'd been about to work on her Pinterest baby board when the invitation had popped up. It had only been three days since she found out she was pregnant, and she hadn't breathed a word of it to Noah. She needed time to process the news.

The pregnancy had come as a surprise, but not an unwelcome one. Far from it. She'd been elated to discover she could get pregnant so quickly and easily. Her mother had never been able to have children of her own. There had been every test imaginable—on both her and her adoptive father—and yet, despite no medical explanation, they'd never conceived. Eventually, they'd adopted Serena.

They had loved her as much as any adoptive parents could, but every so often her mother would let something slip. A wistful comment about the baby she never had, the milestones she missed, the experience she felt had been stolen from her. The heartbreak never seemed to fade. And perhaps that was where it started, her own longing to be a mother. She didn't just want a child; she wanted a child of her own. Several, in fact. A house full of little voices, colorful clothes and toys, and joyful laughter. A big, beautiful family that would fill every hollow place in her heart. And she wanted it with Noah.

She'd already begun planning her pregnancy announcement, a heartfelt and emotional video she would post on social media. It would be sure to get more traction than Lexie's photos from an ashram in India, followed by a romantic weekend in Bora Bora. Only Lexie could pull an *Eat Pray Love* routine and make it look like a spiritual epiphany. It infuriated Serena how easily people took the bait, flooding the comments with:

Stunning.

Ooh, I wish I was there.

So glad you're on a healing journey, Lex.

The sunset is gorgeous.

Please post a picture of the new man.

There was no new man. It was all lies. A curated bid for attention. But now Serena would have to wait to share her precious news. She wasn't going to publicly open herself up when her relationship with Noah could be in jeopardy. The baby that until this afternoon was her little miracle was suddenly leverage she could use if Noah began to question his feelings for her. And he would question his feelings, no matter what happened at this cursed reunion.

But if Serena knew anything, it was that Lexie wasn't very likely to show up. After all, she hadn't come home in years, so why would she turn up now? She'd cancel at the last minute and jet off to Bangkok or Sydney, or some other exotic locale, and post lots of scenic shots of perfect sunsets and sandy beaches.

Serena didn't care about Lexie anymore, but something had changed. And if she was going to protect herself and the life she had built, she needed to know what it was and neutralize the threat before it was too late.

SEVEN
ANGELINA

Shutting the door behind her, Angelina tossed her coat over a chair, kicked off her shoes, and deposited her bag on the hall table. She ambled into the kitchen, took out a bottle of Chardonnay, and took a few sips straight out of the bottle before putting it back. It had been that kind of day. What she really wanted was to heat the lasagna her mom had dropped by last week, eat at least half a tray, and chase it up with a pint of Ben and Jerry's, but instead she made a salad, added some leftover grilled chicken, and congratulated herself on her virtuousness. She'd splurge tomorrow, but today she had to be good.

Angelina set her bowl and a bottle of water on the counter and opened her laptop. She liked to scroll through her messages and social media while she ate. After a day spent with patients—first needy and anxious, then radiant with joy as they cradled their newborns—coming home to an empty apartment only made the loneliness more acute. And tonight the maternity ward had been so overcrowded, there were beds set up in the corridors. Happened every full moon. Deleting all the junk emails first, Angelina then turned her attention to the ones she intended to read. She'd noticed the email from SexyLexie69 right away but saved it for last.

It amused her that Lexie had used that name. She could still remember the night she'd hit on it. They had gone to a frat party, then back to Lexie's dorm room. Her roommate, Bella, was home for the weekend, so Angelina had crashed on Bella's bed. It had been the four of them: Angelina, Lexie, Serena, and Mia. They'd smoked a joint—totally against dorm regulations and grounds for expulsion—and giggled madly as they decided to come up with stripper names. Angelina couldn't recall the silly names Serena and Mia had made up, but who could forget Sexy Lexie69? It totally worked too because Lexie's birthday was on June ninth, or at least that was the birthday that been assigned to her when she'd been turned over to whatever agency took charge of abandoned children. Angelina had refused to play, saying she would never be a stripper so to invent a name would be pointless. She'd been a spoilsport even then, she decided as she opened the email.

Very nice, she thought as she clicked on the pictures of the house. She wouldn't mind living in a place like that all year round. Beautiful, spacious, and peaceful, and far enough away from the neighbors to have complete privacy but not so far that she'd feel isolated. The others were bound to be impressed and accept Lexie's invitation. She knew she would. She didn't care if she holed up in a leaky tent during a thunderstorm, as long as she could get out of the city for a while and spend time with people she actually liked. The past few months had been lonely, and sobering. She had thought she and Jake would be engaged by Christmas. Instead, he had moved out and was now shacking up with his firm's summer intern, who was barely nineteen and had been living with her parents until Jake had rented an apartment in Hoboken and moved her in.

Jake's betrayal had come like a thunderbolt out of the blue, and now Angelina knew, or could guess, how Noah must have felt when Lexie broke off their engagement by text, gave up her spot at a prestigious law school, and took off on her three-year adventure without a word of explanation. None of them had seen Lexie in the intervening years, but now she was back, and Angelina looked forward to catching up, but she didn't imagine this would be a fun, relaxing weekend. Tensions were bound to run high, especially if Serena and Noah showed up. Lexie might have broken up with Noah, but Serena was bound to feel threatened and wonder why Lexie had decided to get them all together like this. Serena would never admit to feeling insecure, but she had to be seriously worried.

As Angelina ate her lonely dinner, she thought that for once she wouldn't be the most pathetic person in the room, which she supposed was something positive to cling to. Her breakup with Jake was child's play compared to the drama that was bound to unfold once they were all together again. And she could hardly wait.

EIGHT
NOAH

If he were honest, Noah was glad Serena didn't come to bed. He really wasn't in the mood to play the devoted husband—not when all he could think about was Lexie and the way it used to be with them. With Lexie, everything was different, from the way she reacted to unexpected situations to the way she fought. Lexie was never passive-aggressive. She simply told him how she felt and gave him the space to respond, without the antics Serena normally resorted to. And he was grateful for that, because he was never like Remy or Richie. Those two were born players and never worried about being made fools of, not even when they were still in their teens. They were able to shrug off rejection and move on. Their confidence was their shield against the world, but he was always more introverted and needed to know where he stood with a girl, which was why he had felt so comfortable with Lexie. She didn't play games, and there was no winning or losing an argument. They resolved their differences and moved on. Until that last time—but there had been no argument, at least not as far as he was aware.

Their sex life had been different too. With Lexie, there was no bickering, keeping score, or sulking. With Serena, the sex was all about her. It was a power play. Most of the time, he didn't mind. To be fair, Serena did try to make him happy in ways Lexie never had.

Lexie had been a cotton bra and panties from Target sort of girl, but Serena loved sexy underwear. She shopped at Agent Provocateur, and she never just took off her clothes. With Serena, it was a carefully orchestrated striptease. Her routine never failed to turn him on, but tonight he didn't think he'd be able to get it up even if she put on a hell of a show. He was in the mood, but not for her, and he didn't want her to suspect.

Noah would never hurt Serena that way, not when his dad had tried to nail anything that walked and had slept with most of his mom's friends. All Noah remembered from his childhood was endless fights, tears, and recriminations. He never understood why his mom didn't leave. He guessed she had been scared and ashamed to admit that her marriage was a shambles, but everyone knew. Noah's dad hadn't been known for stealth, nor had he tried to protect his mom from the humiliation his affairs caused her. He hadn't cared enough to do even that much.

Noah didn't want to be like his father. He had made a vow to love Serena for better or for worse, and he intended to honor it, either until one of them died or they reached a point where they both agreed they'd come to the end of the line. The thing was, Lexie's email couldn't have come at a worse time. Serena had been pressuring him for months to start trying for a baby, and he had finally agreed, not because he was ready to start a family—he'd be happy to wait a few years—but because he just didn't want to keep arguing about it and wiping away her tears of disappointment. He figured it would take them a while to get pregnant anyway, and, with the term of the pregnancy added on, it would be another year at least until they had a baby.

Lexie's unexpected return made Noah realize he just wasn't ready. And it wasn't because it was with Serena. He wouldn't want to have a baby with Lexie either. Not now, not yet. He was still trying to establish himself in his career, he had a college loan to pay off, and he just wanted to enjoy his life before every day became about midnight feedings, dirty diapers, and play dates. He loved kids, and he looked forward to being a dad, but he needed a little more time.

The problem was, how could he tell Serena, especially now? She'd think any decision he made had to do with Lexie.

And maybe it did.

NINE

MIA

Mia waited until the guy she'd picked up when she went for a drink after work left, then called Angelina. It was late, but Angelina liked to stay up and catch up on her shows before going to bed. She'd been doing that since Jake moved out, so that she was tired enough to fall asleep once she finally went to bed and didn't stay awake analyzing her failed relationship. Angelina picked up on the second ring.

"You going?" Mia asked without bothering with a greeting.

"Wouldn't miss it."

"Why is Lexie doing this?"

"You mean staging a public reunion between her and Noah?" Angelina asked.

"Just all of it. Where's all this money suddenly coming from? How can she afford to travel the world, then fly in, business class, no doubt, and rent a house that costs nearly a thousand dollars a night for two nights? I mean, come on. Showing off much?"

"Maybe she inherited some money."

"From whom? Lexie was a foster kid."

"She did have relatives. They just didn't want her. Maybe someone's conscience finally started playing up," Angelina suggested.

"To the tune of a million bucks?"

"Maybe not a million. A couple of thousand?"

"Come on, Angie. A couple of thousand might pay for one trip, and Lexie has been traipsing around the globe for the past three years."

"Maybe she gets jobs to pay her way," Angelina suggested.

"And you think waitressing at some café in Bangalore is going to earn her enough money to throw an all-expenses-paid reunion for seven? I don't buy it. But I think everyone is coming."

"I cannot believe Noah and Serena are going. Talk about cruising for a bruising," Angelina said, clearly eager to change the subject.

Angelina didn't like to talk about money and thought it crass to discuss other people's financial situations. Mia could respect that, but, since she'd had to support herself since the day she graduated from high school, money was frequently on her mind, and she couldn't help but put a price tag on things people bought and did. She could barely make ends meet on a teacher's salary, and the prices of just about everything had doubled since the pandemic. She brought her lunch every day and only went out to dinner once on the weekend, and only to places she could afford, unless someone else was paying.

Angelina's family was pretty well off, and her parents frequently bought her expensive gifts and took her on paid family trips. They were really big on Disney, and Angelina went with them nearly every year. She said it really was the happiest place on Earth. Mia wouldn't know. She'd never been. Her family's idea of a vacation was to set up a sprinkler in the back yard and let the kids run around until they wore themselves out.

"Are you sure they're going?" Angelina asked. "Maybe they won't come."

"Yeah, I'm sure. Remy texted about an hour ago. He said they were definitely in," Mia said.

"Did Noah tell him that? Nothing is definite until Serena says so."

"Serena told him. She texted him, then he texted me."

Mia had actually been surprised that Remy had reached out to her. He'd been a bit distant the past two months, but that was Remy. He was moody and temperamental. Always had been. Maybe there was a new woman. He was always secretive about the people he was seeing until they split up, and then he tore them to shreds, but in a way that was so funny, it was impossible to judge him and tell him he was a shit.

"I don't know. This is all really weird, but I'm coming for sure," Angelina said. "Did you see the pictures of that house? There's a private deck, a boat, and a hot tub. I don't care if Serena and Lexie try to kill each other. I just want a few days off."

"Me too," Mia said on a sigh. "I'm seriously thinking about changing careers. I love the kids, but I hate the parents. Their little darlings can do no wrong, and everything is the teachers' fault. How about you put your phone down, Karen, and help your kid with his homework instead of posting endless selfies? Do you really think no one will notice you just shot your face full of fillers? Or take the kids outside so they can get some fresh air and exercise instead of letting them play violent video games that are totally inappropriate for eight-year-olds. I mean, why do people even have kids if they don't want to bother raising them?"

"You should see how happy they look when they pop them out. Everyone is crying and taking pictures and saying it's the best day of their lives and they're going to be the best mom any child has ever had."

"Yeah, until they realize that parenting is actually hard work, and they have to set aside their own needs and be there for their children."

"You ever want to have kids?" Angelina asked.

Mia knew Angelina had been thinking about kids a lot lately and wondering if she'd ever get the chance to be a mom now that Jake was out of the picture. At twenty-seven, Mia thought her anxiety was a bit premature, but that was Angelina. She wanted to have her life neatly planned out and seemed to be referring to some 1950s housewife's manual for a fulfilling existence. Mia didn't suppose she could blame her. Angelina's family life had been tumultuous, and she'd dreamed of parents who were like Mike and Carol Brady from *The Brady Bunch*, minus the divorces and half a dozen kids. Still, she'd had two parents who loved and nurtured her.

Mia's own formative years had been quite different, but she'd never told her friends the truth about her family. All anyone knew was that Mia didn't get on with her parents and never saw her siblings. They didn't know why and weren't about to find out. Some things were best left unsaid.

"Yeah, but not for a few years," Mia said when she realized Angelina was still waiting for an answer. "I'm still too selfish, and it's not like I have a reliable partner."

"I still think you and Remy should give it a try."

"No," Mia said abruptly. "It'd never work."

"You've had a crush on him since freshman year," Angelina reminded her.

"And he will never find out, you hear me?"

"Why are you so afraid to give it a chance?"

Because Remy had the hots for Lexie, and probably still does. And now that she's back, he must be counting the moments until he can make his move. Mia felt a familiar ache in her heart. Why did people never want the ones who loved them and instead chased after the ones who could never appreciate them? Remy and Lexie had always been close, but Lexie saw Remy as a friend, not a boyfriend. Probably because Remy was so fickle, Lexie knew it would never last. It had always been shy, broody Noah for her, until something had suddenly changed.

Mia valued Remy's friendship, but she didn't see him as a boyfriend either. She'd had a crush on him at school, for about five minutes, until she'd realized there was someone else she'd liked. But she'd never told her friends. That was another thing she had decided to keep secret, since she would be opening herself up to a world of humiliation if anyone ever found out. And since she was never going to do anything about her crush, she thought it was best to forget about it and move on.

"For the same reason you never acted on your unrequited love for Richie," Mia finally replied. "Because you know he'll play the field until he meets some dominatrix, and then she'll bring him down to his knees and he'll worship her forever."

"I'd still really like to know what happened in Thailand," Angelina said, deftly avoiding a conversation about Richie.

Only Serena had been there when Lexie had made the decision to break off her engagement to Noah. Lexie and Serena had taken the girls' trip they'd been planning forever, and which would probably have been their last had Lexie and Noah got married. And then Lexie had taken off, and the friendships that had been so strong had fizzled out, the bonds stretched too thin since everyone had gotten their taste of real life.

"I don't know, but according to Serena nothing happened. Lexie just had one of those rude awakenings where she decided she wasn't ready to be a grown-up. I can't say I blame her. Lexie had a tough life. She deserved to have some fun and take a couple of years to find herself. School and work will still be there when she gets tired of living like a nomad."

"But Noah won't be there," Angelina pointed out reasonably.

"Noah's moved on," Mia reminded her. "And so should you."

Mia was tired of rehashing what had happened with Lexie and Noah. They'd given it plenty of airtime when it had happened, and, as far as she knew, nothing had changed. In fact, she suddenly realized she didn't really want to go to this reunion—she didn't like to have things forced on her, and she worried she'd be expected to pay her share after all—but she was too curious to see what would happen to stay away. Besides, she had no plans for Halloween, and, if things between Lexie and Serena got ugly, Halloween would be scary as hell.

"I have to get up early," Mia said. "I'll talk to you tomorrow."

"All right."

They said goodbye and ended the call, but Mia knew they probably wouldn't talk again in person until they saw each other at Witch Lake.

TEN
VINCE

Vince opened the email for the second time while he waited at Starbucks to get his pumpkin spice latte. He wasn't really sure why he had been included. He'd only met the group in their senior year, when he'd started going out with Angelina. They had already been tight, and he had always been on the periphery, tagging along if Angelina wanted to spend time with her friends. He liked the group, for the most part, but they weren't his friends, and he had always known he wouldn't really stay in contact if things with him and Angelina didn't work out.

They had parted ways shortly after graduation. It wasn't a painful or messy breakup. They had just sort of drifted apart, with Angelina going on to a nursing program and Vince taking a job with a prestigious hedge fund. If it wasn't for social media, he wouldn't have kept in touch with any of them. He'd been shocked when Serena had posted that she was engaged to Noah less than a year after Lexie had left him. It seemed too soon, but maybe Noah was just one of those guys who needed to be in a relationship and rather than take his chances on the dating scene had settled for a girl who loved him and wasn't overly worried about being the runner-up.

Vince's grandfather, who'd played the sax in his younger days and had performed at clubs all over Fort Washington and Harlem, had taught Vince everything he knew about women. One thing Terrance Wright had said was that you should never get serious about a girl who was on the rebound. And the second was that you should never marry anyone who isn't your grand passion. Terrance used terms like that, but, although old-fashioned, they still rang true. Terrance had enjoyed his share of affairs, but Vince's grandmother had been his grand passion until the day she died. Terrance had never strayed after they'd met, even though beautiful women had thrown themselves at him after every performance. He simply hadn't been interested because everything he'd wanted had been waiting for him at home.

Vince had thought Lexie and Noah had a grand passion, even though they had been too young to really understand how rare such a thing was. Or maybe they had understood, because they'd gotten engaged right after graduation instead of chalking up their relationship to a college romance and moving on the way most people did. He didn't know what had gone wrong—maybe Lexie had got cold feet, or maybe Noah had cheated on her while she was away and she'd somehow found out. In any case, Vince never would have imagined Noah winding up with Serena. They just seemed so different. Terrance would have said they were like a mash-up of two different songs that might work for people who were tone deaf, but a true musician could always hear that discordant note that undermined the set. Perhaps Noah was tone deaf.

Vince had never felt comfortable around Serena, he recalled as he added sugar to his latte and left the café. There was just something about her that put him on his guard. Perhaps it was her casual racism that had probably bothered him more than it had the others because he'd been the only Black person in the group, or her air of smug superiority. Not that she had anything to feel superior about. Serena had been a good student and had been accepted to several top-notch law schools, but she hadn't done very well and hadn't been able to pass the bar. Last Vince had heard, she was working for some real estate lawyer as a paralegal. If she was disappointed or bitter though, Serena never let it show. She was all about appearances, and her posts looked staged and carefully targeted, much as the wedding had been.

Serena had been a gorgeous bride, glowing with happiness and looking adoringly at her new husband, who'd seemed a bit dazed. The whole affair had been tasteful, extremely photogenic, and clearly very expensive. Vince had almost declined the invitation—he didn't have several hundred dollars to spend on a gift for people he'd likely never see again—but in the end he'd accepted because he'd wanted to see Angelina. A costly mistake in the end, because Angelina had brought a date, so they had only spoken for a few minutes before her new man pulled her away.

Angelina appeared to be single now, since Jake had disappeared from her posts two months ago, so Vince thought he might have a chance. He didn't think that Angelina was his grand passion—he'd come to understand that he was too methodical and rational for such intense and unpredictable emotions. But Angelina was just the same, and he'd never quite been able to get over her. Which wasn't to say that she wasn't capable of passion or devotion. She liked to think things through, but, once she dedicated herself to something or someone, she genuinely cared and was in for the long haul. Vince didn't imagine the split with Jake had been Angelina's decision, and he had no idea where her head was at, but the invitation to the reunion was an unexpected opportunity to see her again that Vince wasn't about to pass up. He had belatedly realized that Angelina was the one who had got away, if people still used that term. Terrance certainly did, and he'd told Vince time and time again to just call the girl. Ask her out, take her to a nice restaurant, and show her that he was serious and wouldn't jerk her around if she gave him another chance.

Vince was too afraid of rejection to call Angelina out of the blue and ask her out, but, if they were brought together for the weekend, he would be perfectly placed to make his move. As long as Angelina came alone and as long as Richie didn't ruin it for him. Richie could be seeing someone—he wasn't one to post about his relationships online, probably because they didn't last long enough to bother posting about—but Vince wouldn't put it past him to hook up with one of the girls at the reunion even if he was. Angelina wasn't the sort to go in for one-night stands, but Richie was good-looking and persuasive, and Angelina did have a type. Most guys she went out with tended to resemble Justin Baldoni, except for Vince. But he thought his uniqueness worked in his favor. Angelina had liked him for him and not because he fit some arcane stereotype of what a hot guy was supposed to look like. Or, more accurately, a hot white guy.

Vince didn't have any trouble attracting women, and the ladies were always charmed by his manners. Terrance had taught him well and had impressed on Vince that class never went out of fashion. Hold the door, help her with her coat, pick up the bill, and always compliment her while looking into her eyes, never at her cleavage. Terrance was a sly old fox and knew what he was talking about. Women's lib was great, and Vince was perfectly aware that a woman could open her own door and pay for her own meal, but he'd also come to see that most women enjoyed a bit of old-world romance and didn't object to being treated like a lady.

He was definitely going, Vince decided as he got off the elevator on his floor. He was through being a coward, and he was going to ask Angelina out, unless Serena had turned her against him. Unfortunately for him, Serena knew too much about what had happened with his ex, Nikki, and wouldn't be afraid to use the information if she wanted to keep Angelina away from him. The drama with Nikki had been the last time Vince had shared anything of a personal nature with Noah. That boy was too whipped to keep anyone's confidence anymore.

ELEVEN
SERENA

Friday
Halloween

The week leading up to the reunion had been tense, but by Friday Noah seemed strangely resigned. Serena had no way of knowing what he was thinking, since he'd done his best to shut her out by agreeing with everything she said and reassuring her that she was the one he wanted whenever he thought she felt insecure, but she could tell that he had come to some sort of decision. She could see it in his eyes. But Serena didn't think the decision was to try to get back with Lexie, so she tried to remain calm and focused on regaining control of the situation in whatever way she could.

She had checked the weather forecast for Halloween weekend several times a day. It was futile to hope that a late-season hurricane would derail their plans and the reunion would get postponed indefinitely, but one could dream. Serena had also carefully read everyone's emails, texted with the girls to feel them out, and met Remy for lunch on Wednesday. If anyone had any dirt on what was going on, it would be Remy. He had a way of ferreting out information, probably because he was such an unapologetic gossip that everyone just told him things, and he was still close with everyone. Remy made an effort to stay in touch, unlike some people, and never let go of a relationship unless he had a valid reason to distance himself. And despite his propensity for drama, he was surprisingly good at keeping secrets and managed to learn everyone else's without ever quite revealing his own.

Serena supposed he'd learned to guard his feelings while living with his strict grandparents, who'd treated him as if he were somehow responsible for his mother's unfortunate life choices, and then navigating the foster care system. That would do a number on anyone, and, whereas it had made Lexie more open and eager to form meaningful relationships, it had made Remy guarded. Or maybe it was because he was a guy, and guys just weren't good at talking about or analyzing their feelings. Serena could tell Noah was bubbling away on the inside, but whenever she tried to talk to him about Lexie he found a way to deflect or suddenly felt an overwhelming need to go for a run or lift some weights. He hadn't worked out this many times in one week since Lexie had dumped him.

Sadly, all her coaxing and prodding had failed to yield results. Remy didn't seem to know any more than Serena did, which was perplexing but also reassuring since the one thing Remy was sure of was that no one seemed to know more than he and Serena did, and they had all learned about the reunion at the same time and via the same source. Serena was still trying to figure out why Vince had been included in the invitation. Was it possible that he was somehow involved in this charade?

Serena couldn't see how he could be, but who knew? Vince was so... She couldn't think of the right word, but a few unflattering adjectives sprang to mind. He'd wormed himself into their group and had somehow managed to remain a part of it even though he wasn't all that close with anyone. Noah had insisted on inviting Vince to the wedding—Lord only knew why, but Serena supposed it was important to have a few black and brown people who weren't part of the catering staff in attendance, so the wedding party didn't look like a bunch of white supremacists in the photos she posted on Insta. Not that she had an issue with minorities. She had proudly voted for Kamala Harris and made sure everyone knew it, and she was really kind to Carmen, who cleaned the office where Serena worked.

Serena liked to judge people as individuals, not as an ethnic group. She'd even had a Jewish friend in high school and had gone to her bat mitzvah. It had been so much fun, and Serena still kept in touch with Rachel and her brother on Facebook, though she never commented on any of their posts about the situation in the Middle East. She couldn't be seen to be taking sides. Noah wasn't as guarded, but he kept his social media circle small and only friended people he actually knew and liked. He used LinkedIn for professional networking but couldn't be bothered with Instagram or X, and never shared any private photos until he'd checked with Serena. Once something was out there, it was there forever, and she didn't want some awful picture to haunt her for the rest of her days. She would have to make sure no one posted any photos of her at the reunion on their social media without her consent.

Serena took one last look around the bedroom, grabbed her phone charger, and stuffed it into her bag, then checked her lipstick. The time had come to face whatever awaited her at Witch Lake, and she was as ready as she'd ever be.

TWELVE
SERENA

As part of her strategy for dealing with any unexpected developments that might arise once they arrived at the house, Serena decided to leave work at two o'clock on Friday and convinced Noah to leave the office at three. She wanted to get out to the house early enough to see everyone arrive and also take the best room. As the only couple, they surely deserved to occupy the master bedroom. And, of course, she had to finish packing. They were only going for two nights, but it was crucial to bring the right outfits and make-up. She didn't want to show off or stand out too much, but it was important to look good. Men used to wear armor into battle, and her looks and her sense of style were Serena's shield. She'd use them to hide her vulnerability from the others and would come out of this weekend victorious. After all, no one knew the truth of what happened or how she really felt. She'd just tough it out and deal with any unexpected revelations by playing it cool.

Once she and Noah were finally on their way, Serena felt less sure of herself and suddenly wished they had declined the invitation. This was ridiculous. She had nothing to prove and shouldn't have to put herself through this when she was already feeling fragile and emotional due to her pregnancy. But it was too late to come up with an excuse that wouldn't make her look like a coward, so she shut her eyes and silently repeated her mantra.

I'm calm, serene, and content, Serena chanted. *I'm calm, serene, and content.*

The mantra helped somewhat, and Serena opened her eyes to look around. Even though it was Halloween, the traffic wasn't too bad, but the streets were already crowded with groups of small children trick-or-treating with their parents. The kids were adorable in their costumes, especially the toddlers, and for a moment Serena was lost in a fantasy in which she and Noah enjoyed their first Halloween with their baby. Her dream was rudely interrupted by a pack of teenagers that passed close to the car just as they were about to turn onto the Henry Hudson Parkway. The kids were loud and aggressive, and jeered at passersby as they pushed past them on the sidewalk. Serena wasn't ready to imagine her baby as an obnoxious teenager, so she peered at the GPS, wondering what time they would arrive at Witch Lake. It showed that they'd get to their destination just after five o'clock, which was what she had planned. This little affirmation made her feel a bit more in control, and she settled in for the drive.

Once they left the city behind and Noah took the exit for the Taconic Parkway, he opened the window, which annoyed Serena to no end since the breeze ruffled her carefully curled hair.

"Will you close that?" she shrieked.

"But the air is so fresh," Noah said, and sucked in a deep breath before shutting the window. "And look at that foliage. Incredible. I always forget how beautiful Upstate is in the fall."

"Yeah, it's nice," Serena allowed.

It really was glorious, and she probably would have enjoyed getting out of the city for the weekend if she didn't have to spend the next two days pretending to have a good time. She did her best to appreciate the scenery, but the peaceful moment was short-lived. Noah put on his favorite playlist and started singing along to Green Day. He loved Green Day, especially the *American Idiot* album. She would have preferred Adele or even Taylor Swift, but she bit back the comment she was about to make and let Noah enjoy himself. In the song, Billie Joe Armstrong was begging for Novocain, and Serena could relate. She wouldn't mind getting sedated herself.

If not for this damn reunion, Serena would have really loved this drive and would have used the scenic backdrop for her pregnancy announcement, but she was keeping the baby news to herself and had not looked at her baby board on Pinterest even once. Maybe she could convince Noah to leave early on Sunday and go apple picking. She could make apple pie or apple cinnamon muffins and use them in her baby announcement, which would make her appear wholesome and maternal. And it would help her to control the narrative if anything damaging from the reunion were posted online.

Serena's nerves began to really play up by the time she spotted the exit sign for Kingston. Witch Lake wasn't too far away from Lake Onteora. It wasn't nearly as big or well known, but Serena had checked the real estate listings, and the houses that fronted the lake went from a modest five hundred thousand to a mil and a quarter. The cheaper houses were older, some of them probably built in the 1970s, but a waterfront property was always desirable, and a house could be modernized. Their Airbnb was one of the newer properties, and according to the website had four bedrooms, two bathrooms upstairs and a half-bath downstairs, and a large, modern kitchen. The furniture was country bumpkin chic, but Serena supposed that was what people signed up for when spending their vacation in upstate New York.

Witch Lake didn't offer any water sports, but the reviews of the area mentioned that there was fishing, hiking trails, and some historical sites. Noah didn't fish, but maybe they could go out on the lake in the morning. The pictures would look amazing on Insta, especially if she wore the burnt-orange top and her new green jacket, which would work great with the backdrop of lake, sky, foliage, and those very expensive homes. And then in the afternoon, maybe they could skip out on the togetherness and go for a scenic walk or visit the State House or the Old Dutch Church. The less time they spent with the others, the better.

According to the GPS, they were about ten minutes from the house, and Serena's heart thumped painfully in her chest. She really was nervous. No, not nervous; nervousness was reserved for job interviews and lunch with Noah's needling mother and leering father. She was terrified, and she wished Noah would reassure her, but he was staring straight ahead, his posture so rigid, Serena could only assume he was as uncomfortable as she was and mentally preparing himself for the awkwardness that was bound to ensue once they were all together.

Noah turned off the music, and the unexpected silence was jarring. The air between them crackled with tension, and Serena suddenly felt very cold. Noah didn't look at her, but he sucked in a sharp breath and gripped the wheel tightly, and Serena knew that the situation was about to change once again. She doubted it would be in her favor.

"Ree, there's something I need to tell you," Noah said quietly. His gaze was still fixed on the road, and his knuckles had turned white. "I know this isn't the right time, and we can talk about it once we get home, but I need to say this before we see the others."

Oh, God. What now? Had Noah decided he didn't love her and wanted out? Serena's pulse raced, and panic squeezed her lungs until she couldn't breathe.

"Whatever it is, I'm sure we can work it out," she choked out as a way of diminishing the complication.

"I know we can. And it's really not a big deal, even though it might seem like it at first."

"What is it, Noah?" Serena exclaimed.

She couldn't take the suspense any longer. She was anxious enough already, and she thought her heart might burst out of her chest if she had to wait to find out what she was up against a moment longer.

"Look, I know we agreed to start trying for a baby, but I'd like to wait. Just a few months. That's all I ask. And this has nothing to do with Lexie," he hurried to explain. "I just need to work through some things."

"What things?" Serena managed to ask, even though she really didn't care. *No*, she wanted to scream at him. They weren't waiting. If people waited until they worked through their issues to start a family, the world would come to an end.

"You know I've always had a difficult relationship with my dad. I just don't want to make the same mistakes with my own child."

"And you just thought of this now?"

"No, I've been thinking about it for some time. But I figured you might tell everyone we were trying, and I wanted to make sure you didn't."

"Tell everyone?" Serena repeated.

She gaped at Noah in stunned disbelief. Did he know her at all? She wasn't the sort of person to share her most private thoughts and moments with anyone, not until she was ready, and only when she was certain her revelations would have the desired effect. She hadn't told anyone she was seeing Noah until he'd said he loved her, and she didn't announce their engagement until he'd presented her with the perfect ring, and they'd set a date. Why would she tell their juvenile, insensitive friends that they were trying for a baby, just so they could make snarky comments and keep asking if she was pregnant?

"I just don't want anyone to know," Noah reiterated, digging his grave just a little bit deeper. "Not yet."

Serena felt like a baby elephant had just settled on her chest, but forced herself to breathe deeply and think rationally. Noah was right about one thing—this wasn't the time or the place to have this conversation. They would be at the house in a few minutes, and she had to look and feel her best and keep her emotions under stringent control. That was the only way she could deal with what was to come. If she felt worried or insecure, the others would catch on right away. They were like dogs, able to sniff fear.

"Fine. We'll talk at home," she said sweetly. "Don't worry; I wouldn't dream of mentioning it to anyone."

"You do understand, right?" Noah asked, his tone pleading.

"Of course. No baby. Am I allowed to talk to you about Lexie, or is that off limits too?"

"Why? What about her?" Noah asked.

He looked like a deer caught in the headlights, and Serena was torn between bitter laughter and the tears that threatened to spill from her carefully made-up eyes. Noah had tried to play it cool, but he couldn't disguise his nervousness, not when he expected to come face-to-face with Lexie any minute now. He was as panicked as Serena was, though for slightly different reasons.

"Nothing," Serena muttered just as Noah turned onto a narrow road that was hardly more than a dirt track. It seemed they had arrived, and the conversation was over, but far from finished.

Two cars were parked on the gravel patch to the right of the house, and Serena's stomach lurched violently as Noah pulled in and shut off the engine. The Kia belonged to Mia, but the Nissan looked like a rental since it had South Carolina plates and rental cars usually had out-of-state plates. So the car could belong to Lexie.

Serena took a deep breath, pulled her shoulders back, and lifted her head. She had no idea what this weekend would bring, but she would not be intimidated, nor would she give anything away. Beauty was her shield, but silence wasn't her only weapon.

THIRTEEN

REMY

Remy, in the car he'd rented for the weekend, was the first to arrive, well before five o'clock. For once, he didn't have a photo session booked for the afternoon, and had decided to leave before the police started to set up the street closures ahead of the Halloween parade that went past his building every year.

The key was in a lockbox to which Lexie had provided a code, and there were several packages on the step, all addressed to Lexie. Remy moved them inside and took a peek. There was an assortment of booze, a box of fruits and vegetables, and a large Styrofoam container packed with dry ice and filled with all sorts of goodies. Expensive goodies.

After he put the groceries away, Remy opened a bottle of red and, once it had a chance to breathe, poured himself a glass. While he waited, he set out the charcuterie board Lexie had ordered on the kitchen counter. He loved a good charcuterie, and this one didn't disappoint. It even had candied pecans and dried cranberries, both of which he adored. Remy sampled a piece of cheddar, popped a few nuts and berries into his mouth, then stepped out onto the deck and settled in an Adirondack chair. The view of the lake was spectacular, the air was crisp and smelled of woodsmoke, and the sun would soon begin to set. Remy would not have enjoyed spending the weekend at the lake house all by himself, but, since his friends were about to arrive, he savored the brief interval of peace.

Mia pulled up just before five. She used the deck stairs to come up and gave Remy a hug and a kiss on the cheek.

"You okay?" she asked.

"Yeah, I'm good. Why?"

"No reason."

Remy knew exactly what Mia was referring to but didn't want to engage. He'd been a bit less available to Mia and Angelina the past two months, but he had his reasons and didn't care to get into them. And after today, he hoped it would no longer matter and things would go back to normal, or as normal as they could be with Lexie around.

"Do you think Lexie is going to stay?" Mia asked once she'd set her things down in one of the bedrooms, poured herself a glass of wine, and joined Remy on the deck.

"I don't know. I haven't spoken to her. I called and texted, but she never got back to me."

"She didn't get back to me either. Seems odd that she hasn't reached out to any of us now that she's back in the country," Mia said.

"I think she wants to see us all at the same time. Maybe she's going to make some big announcement," Remy speculated.

"Like what?"

"Maybe she's getting married."

"Or maybe she's pregnant and wants her baby to be born in New York, where she has friends and a support network," Mia suggested. "But things are different now. Everyone has their own life, and people have changed since the pandemic. It seems like everyone got just a little more selfish and self-serving, don't you think?"

"I'll be there for her," Remy said firmly. "I haven't changed."

"No," Mia said, even though she clearly didn't agree and probably would have liked to list all the ways Remy had changed.

When Remy said nothing, Mia excused herself and went inside to pick at the charcuterie board. Remy heaved himself out of the deep chair, descended the steps, and walked to the end of the narrow dock. It would be dark in less than an hour, but just then the sky was lavender and pink, the lake slate blue with vibrant slashes of burnished orange and red at the edges, where the stunning fall foliage was reflected in the water. There were only six houses on Witch Lake, and the other five were almost entirely obscured by the leafy trees, only their lifeless docks visible in the gloaming.

It was still early, so the occupants might make themselves known later on, but at the moment it felt like Remy and Mia were the only people in the world, the lake and its surrounds exactly as they must have looked hundreds of years ago when Native Americans—Remy thought it was the Mohicans or the Lenape—had lived on this land, before the first Dutch pioneers had begun to build their settlements and introduced a European way of life to the new colony.

A shiver ran down Remy's spine, and he turned his back on the lake. He was a city boy through and through and loved his life in Greenwich Village. Those people were his tribe, and the city streets were his stomping ground. He felt intimidated by all this quiet nature. Most people assumed it was peaceful and harmless, but they were wrong. Nature was primitive, cruel, and unpredictable.

Remy had no idea where this conviction had come from or why he was suddenly afraid, but all he knew was that, although he could tolerate this place for two nights, he couldn't wait to get the hell home.

FOURTEEN

MIA

"She's not here yet," Mia said as soon as Serena mounted the steps and joined her on the deck.

Serena looked effortlessly glamorous in a tan cashmere sweater, skinny jeans, and brown suede boots. Her hair looked professionally done for the occasion, and her make-up was perfect, but Mia detected a hum of anxiety beneath her calm exterior. It thrummed like a distant motor, and Mia felt its nearly imperceptible vibration as Serena dropped into a chair after returning Mia's hug. Her gaze shot straight to Mia's nearly empty wineglass.

"Getting a head start?" she asked.

The judgy comment irritated Mia, but she chose not to rise to the bait. She liked to have a couple of drinks after work. So what? Everyone had their vices, and red wine wasn't high on the list of destructive habits as far as she was concerned. She could do much worse.

"You can too," Mia said, keeping her tone light.

"Is there any sparkling water?"

"No, but there's still water in the fridge."

Serena made no move to get up, so Mia remained where she was. This wasn't her party, and she didn't have to play the hostess and offer people drinks. If Serena wanted something, she could just get it herself. Instead, Mia turned her attention to Noah, who'd just arrived with two matching overnight bags. He set them down, bent down to kiss Mia, and called out a greeting to Remy, who gave a brief wave. Noah looked casual in a hooded sweatshirt and jeans. His dark hair was longer than when Mia had seen him at the wedding, and his hazel eyes radiated uncertainty.

"Not here yet," Mia said again, for Noah's benefit.

He nodded, then went inside, and returned a few moments later with a beer. Noah went to speak to Remy, so Mia returned her attention to Serena. She tried to appear cool, but the fear in her eyes was unmistakable, and her gaze slid toward the dirt track with increasing frequency, clearly watching for incoming cars. This wasn't just anxiety. This was pure terror. Were things shaky between her and Noah? Mia wondered as she took a sip of her wine and watched Serena from beneath lowered lashes.

Noah was a standup guy. He wouldn't have married Serena if he didn't love her. Mia couldn't blame him if he felt resentful for the way Lexie had ended things though, and expected their first meeting in years to be awkward. But ultimately it was all water under the bridge, or it should be after all this time. There were much bigger problems than a broken engagement.

As if reading her thoughts, Serena spoke. "I honestly can't believe Lexie had the nerve to do this. It's like some medieval challenge," she said through gritted teeth.

"What do you mean?" Mia asked. Serena used to gobble up historical romances in her teenage years, and sometimes came out with strange references no one really understood.

"You know, like throwing down the gauntlet," Serena explained.

"Is that what you think Lexie is doing? Challenging you? A fight to the death?" Mia asked with a chuckle.

"Seems like it."

"Maybe that's not it at all," Mia said.

She suppressed a sigh. She wanted this weekend to be fun, an unexpected getaway she'd been excited to attend, but Serena was clearly bracing for a confrontation and would probably initiate one as soon as Lexie showed up.

"So, what is it, ha?" Serena asked belligerently.

"Maybe Lexie thinks it'll be fun to hang out together. She knows you and Noah are married, she could conceivably be happy for you. She was the one who walked away, remember?"

"Yes, but Noah never got closure, and Lexie hasn't spoken to me since Thailand. It's not like I haven't tried."

"Maybe Noah doesn't need closure anymore," Mia said.

And maybe Lexie has her reasons for not speaking to you, Mia added inwardly. Something had happened on that trip, but neither Serena nor Lexie had ever addressed the rift and had carried on like they'd had a great time.

Everyone was allowed to reevaluate the direction their life was going in and change course, but taking off like that had been completely out of character for Lexie, who'd craved security and stability after being bounced around from one foster family to another for eighteen years. It hadn't occurred to Mia until that moment, but she suddenly realized that there was one thing that would change everything for Lexie and cause her to reexamine what she thought she wanted. Perhaps Noah and Serena hadn't started seeing each other *after* Lexie had left but had hooked up while Lexie and Noah were still together. Mia wasn't going to say anything, but now that the idea had come to her she knew she'd be looking out for clues that might support her theory.

"You know, Lexie might be coming with someone," Mia said instead. "Did that ever occur to you?"

"Why do you say that? What do you know?" Serena practically pounced on her.

"Nothing. I'm just saying. Maybe things got serious with one of the guys she met on her travels, and he's come back to the States with her."

"Do they have ashrams and silent retreats for couples?" Serena asked acidly.

"Probably. I wouldn't know. Not really my thing."

"Mine either."

"And anyway, you were there for Noah when Lexie broke his heart. You stood by him, supported him." *Swooped in when he was lonely and vulnerable and carved out a place for yourself*, Mia added silently. "You've been the perfect wife," she said aloud, and raised her glass to Serena. "So, cheers to you."

"You're right, Noah is lucky to have me."

"He is," Mia agreed.

She was growing tired of talking about Noah and Lexie and wanted to move on. "The fridge is stocked. There's shrimp, salmon, and tomahawk steaks. Remy is in heaven. There's even cake."

"What kind of cake?"

"Chocolate mousse and strawberry cheesecake. And there's lots of booze. Sure you won't have a glass of wine? You seem a bit tense." Which was the understatement of the year.

"I'm not drinking this weekend," Serena announced.

"Something you want to tell us?" Mia teased.

"I'm on antibiotics. I always have to take them before a dental procedure, so I can't mix."

"Well, there's Diet Coke."

"I no longer drink diet soda."

"Anything else you no longer do?"

"Yeah, drugs. I'm clean as a whistle these days."

"Really? When was the last time you indulged?"

"With Lexie, in Phuket. We met these guys from Australia, and we partied on the beach. We stayed there all night," Serena said, and smiled at the memory. Mia realized that was the first time she had smiled since she had arrived.

"Did you guys hook up with them?" Mia asked. "Was that before Lexie broke up with Noah?"

"My lips are sealed," Serena said with a sly grin.

"Didn't Lexie go to Australia after Thailand? Was it to be with the guy she met?"

Serena's gaze slid away, toward the lake, but the answer was clear even before she spoke. "Sometimes the attraction is so strong, you just have to give in to it and see what happens."

"I wonder what happened to him. What was his name?" Mia asked.

"Jason. No, Jared. I don't think he was looking for anything serious, though. Anyway, he was a cokehead. I would never date a guy who lives for a fix."

"Me neither, but it's tough out there," Mia admitted. "The guys I meet are either total douches, men who are divorced and will always prioritize their kids, or computer geeks who don't know how to talk to women."

"You'd think they'd use ChatGPT to write a script," Serena joked. They both chuckled, and Serena's gaze floated toward Noah and Remy, who were talking on the dock. "Remy seems to be seeing a different girl every month."

"He always did say that he liked to try all the flavors."

"That was ice cream," Serena reminded her.

"Ice cream. Women. It's all about pleasure and keeping an open mind. I don't think he'll ever date a model, though. Not after the way his mother..."

"I guess. He looks good though," Serena said. "Content."

"Noah looks good too. Settled," Mia observed.

"To me, that usually means the guy has a beer belly and is starting to lose his hair."

"That's not what I meant, and you know it," Mia protested.

Noah was hot. If Serena wasn't her friend and Noah wasn't married, she'd see how far she could take things, but Mia didn't believe in hurting other women. That wasn't her style. She might feel Richie out, though, when he arrived. He was still single, and, unless Angelina finally went for it, maybe they could at least have a good time this weekend. Mia didn't think Richie was up for more. Too good-looking, and too immature. But it did bother her that he'd hooked up with Serena. It had happened their senior year, during a party off campus that had got out of hand and turned into a free-for-all. Serena had never told anyone and wouldn't be drawn on the subject, but Mia had seen her stumble drunkenly out of the bathroom, then seen Richie follow her outside a few seconds later, her pink panties sticking out of his pocket. They'd totally done it. The only question was, had they ever done it again?

Whether they had or not really hadn't mattered then, but it did now. Noah and Richie were friends. Had been since before they'd both started at Quinnipiac. They'd played football in high school and had been teammates. It would put an end to their friendship for sure if Noah ever found out, and possibly create problems in a marriage that already seemed to be going through a rocky patch.

"You guys have been married for a while now, are you thinking about having kids?" Mia asked.

"Noah is desperate to start a family, but I'm not ready." Serena sighed dramatically. "It's just so nice when it's the two of us. Having that freedom..." She gave Mia a meaningful look, probably meant to convey that they went at it like bunnies and had fucked all over their swanky apartment. Mia would think twice about eating anything that had been on their kitchen counter.

"Well, you have time. You're not even thirty."

"Exactly. Thirty is a good age to start a family," Serena agreed.

Thirty loomed large, and Mia suddenly felt a desperate longing for something of her own. She was tired of being alone and recently had even caught herself missing her family. But there was no going back, not now, not ever. Lexie had been like a sister to her all through college, but then Lexie left without a word of explanation. She had probably made new friends and had people who mattered to her a lot more than her college pals. Mia had missed Lexie, and she was looking forward to seeing her, but she doubted they would pick up where they'd left off. That ship had sailed, as had so many others.

Mia was glad of the distraction when headlights sliced through the near-darkness and a black Jeep slowly approached the house.

"I wasn't expecting that," she said when the deck lights that worked on a sensor briefly illuminated the front seat of the oncoming car before it turned into the parking area. Richie was driving, and Angelina was in the passenger seat.

"Me neither, but good for her," said Remy, who'd just joined them. "Angelina would be good for Richie."

"Is Vince coming?" Serena asked. "I didn't see his reply."

"He'll be here. That's probably him now," Remy said. Another car was coming up the track, the driver clearly male.

"Strange that Lexie would be the last to arrive to her own party," Serena mused.

Noah had remained resolutely silent as he stood behind Serena's chair, and his expression seemed pained as he watched Richie and Angelina get out of the car and smile at each other in a way that was more than friendly but less than loved up.

"Maybe she wants to make an entrance," Mia said. She knew she was goading Serena, but she couldn't help herself. Talking to Serena reminded her just what a righteous bitch she could be, and Mia thought it was time someone took her down a peg or two.

"Hey, kids," Richie called out as he joined them on the deck. "Richie's in da house. Let's get this party started."

"You know, a party can actually start without you," Mia teased as she accepted a hug from him.

"Yes, it can, but will it be awesome?" Richie asked with a shit-eating grin.

He kissed Serena on the cheek and gave each of the guys a manly one-arm hug. Angelina wasn't as restrained and hugged and kissed everyone enthusiastically.

"So, what are the sleeping arrangements?" she asked, her gaze drifting toward the car that had just pulled in.

"They are whatever you want them to be," Remy said. "You can bunk with whomever you like. Richie, you game?"

"To bunk with my girl Angelina?" Richie asked. He lifted one dark brow, as if he'd never considered the possibility. "Sure, unless Mia wants to join in. I had such fantasies about you two in college," he added, and his slow grin painted quite the picture.

"And fantasies they shall remain," Mia said. "Angie, want to share?"

"Definitely," Angelina said. Mia thought she'd love to share with Richie but was too embarrassed to admit to it in front of everyone. "I should put these in the fridge."

"I brought cannoli," Richie explained. "Nonna insisted on making a batch when she heard we were all getting together. She loves you guys."

"Mm, a taste of heaven," Angelina moaned just as a tight-lipped Noah disappeared into the house. "Don't let me have more than one."

"You can have as many as you want," Richie said. "Nonna made two dozen. Half of them chocolate, since she knows how much you love chocolate."

"Evil woman," Serena quipped. "Is she trying to make us fat?"

"No one is forcing you to eat them," Richie snapped, and his dark eyes flashed with annoyance.

Angelina took the Tupperware container from him and followed Noah inside. Mia saw the light from the open fridge a few minutes later, then got distracted by the buzzing of her phone. Angelina's phone pinged just as she emerged from the kitchen sans the cannoli container and with a glass of white wine. Remy's phone buzzed too.

Pulling out her cell, Mia checked the text that had just popped up.

"It's from Lexie," she told everyone. "She says she's stuck in traffic and to start dinner without her. She'll get here when she gets here."

"I got the same text," Angelina said. "I didn't realize she still had the same number."

"I guess it's working again now that she's in the States," Remy said as he looked down at his own phone. "She'd have to pay for an international plan for the phone to work overseas."

"You would think she'd splurge on an international data plan if she can afford this pad," Richie said, looking up at the house. "Sweet. When's dinner? I'm starving."

"We should probably start cooking," Serena said after she'd checked the time. "Remy, I assume you're grilling?"

"Of course. I wouldn't trust any of you losers with those steaks. They're worth their weight in gold. Take them out to breathe and I'll get the grill going. Ladies, if you would make some sides?"

"Richie, make yourself useful for once and help with the cooking," Mia said.

"I only know how to cook pasta," Richie said sulkily.

"Seriously?" Remy teased, hands on hips. "Is that your only talent?"

"Oh, I have other talents, just not in the kitchen," Richie replied, and smiled suggestively at Mia, then Angelina. "They don't call me the Sicilian Stallion for nothing."

"And who calls you that?" Remy demanded. "Nonna Immaculata?"

"You leave my nonna out of it, bro," Richie said. "And if you don't know why the ladies call me that, then I guess no one's ever commented on the size of your baguette, Frenchie."

Remy looked horrified by the metaphor, but Richie had already moved on. "Vince," he exclaimed as Vince came up the steps and smiled around awkwardly.

"Hello," Vince said, and his gaze immediately went to Angelina, who smiled in welcome.

"Good to see you, buddy. Is that Tito's I see?" Richie immediately appropriated the bottle of vodka Vince was carrying. "A man after my own heart. Let's get this opened. Who wants a drink?"

"I'll have a glass of white wine," Angelina said.

"And I'll take a refill on the red," Mia chimed in.

"A beer, if there's any left," Vince replied when he spotted the bottle in Noah's hand.

"I'm not drinking," Serena said gloomily. "Antibiotics."

"Your loss," Richie replied, and went inside to open the bottle he'd taken from Vince, while Vince predictably sidled up to

Angelina, who spoke to him for less than a minute before she followed Richie inside.

This was going to be interesting, Mia decided as she watched Angelina through the patio door. She looked tense, and Mia wondered what she was thinking. Perhaps she was annoyed with Lexie for inviting Vince without consulting her, or maybe she was just upset that Lexie was running late. Mia knew how much Angelina had looked forward to seeing Lexie and hoped they'd reconnect now that Lexie was back.

But as far as Mia was concerned, nothing good ever came from going back.

FIFTEEN

NOAH

Noah soaked up the quiet of the empty house. Most rooms were dark since no one had bothered to turn on the lights, but he could navigate by the deck lights. He wished he could go to bed and stay there until morning. His head was pounding. Maybe he could find some painkillers in one of the bathrooms. He was sure Serena had brought a bottle of Advil or Tylenol, but he didn't want to ask. She would immediately assume that his head hurt because he was tense about seeing Lexie. That, coupled with her cold fury about putting their baby plans on hold, was bound to make for an excruciating night.

It was the worst thing he could have done, telling her like that just before they'd arrived, but he didn't want her making an announcement just to stick it to Lexie. To him, making the decision to start a family was intensely private, and he didn't need everyone making jokes about his lazy swimmers or Serena's boobs finally getting bigger once she got pregnant. She had always been sensitive about the size of her breasts and envied Angelina, whose double Ds he'd noticed during junior year when Angelina had dressed as a Hooters waitress for Halloween. Mia was well stacked too, but there was something about her that had always put him off. She was a bit butch, and he resented the way she had just taunted

Serena downstairs. Women could be so catty, even when they were supposedly friends.

Noah had overheard part of the conversation and he'd felt sorry for Serena. She could be snide and judgmental, and he knew his friends wondered why he'd turned to her after Lexie had left him, but they didn't know Serena the way he did. Under the surface, she was so insecure, and the only way she could deal with everyone's judgment was to develop a hard shell that kept her safe. She had once told him that she was like an M&M, hard on the outside, but soft and sweet on the inside, and that had probably been the moment he'd truly seen her. She'd opened herself up to him and had shown him her vulnerability when he had been likely to reject her. That had taken guts. And Noah knew Serena would never be unfaithful. She had fought too hard and valued what they had too much to ever jeopardize their relationship. She was in it for the long haul, and Noah had to be mindful of her feelings.

At times he wondered whether he was too mindful. He'd been close with Angelina at school, and they had spent many a night talking on the phone after everyone had fallen asleep. Angelina was perceptive and genuine, but he'd had to distance himself from her once he'd started seeing Serena. Serena had been bound to read something into their friendship. Noah supposed it was a small price to pay to keep her happy. He still had Richie and Remy, and, even though he couldn't go to their Friday night hangs anymore, he hoped they'd be friends for the rest of their lives.

Serena wasn't close to Richie, but she'd kept in touch with Remy, mostly because Remy worked in the fashion industry and had insider knowledge. He'd helped Serena decorate their apartment and sometimes gave her fashion tips and texted her about sample sales. Noah didn't mind. Remy had never been interested in Serena in that way. She wasn't his type. Or Richie's. Richie liked women who looked like Barbie dolls and were just as empty-headed, but would probably end up with some super-smart, dark-haired Italian chick who'd keep him on a short leash and own at least one housecoat and a rolling pin. The image made Noah smile, but that small action sent a bolt of pain into his skull.

The medicine cabinet in the half-bath on the first floor was empty. Noah supposed the owners weren't going to leave drugs lying around, even garden-variety painkillers, so he made his way upstairs. The second floor was lost in darkness, the light from the deck not reaching the hallway, but Noah didn't feel like turning on the light. The darkness was soothing.

He pushed open the door to the bathroom, his eyes adjusting to the gentle glow from the moon and stars nightlight. There was nothing in the cabinet, but a girly toiletry bag sat on the vanity. Noah unzipped it and looked inside, and was thrilled to find several single-use packets of Advil. He ripped one open, popped the pills in his mouth, and dry-swallowed them. When he went to zip the pouch, he spotted an orange prescription container. He knew he shouldn't look, but he couldn't help himself, and if he knew whose Advil he'd taken he could thank them and apologize for rifling through their toiletries.

The medication was eszopiclone, and the prescription was made out to Mia. Noah had no idea what it was for, so he pulled out his phone and googled the name. Generic Lunesta. So, sleeping pills, then. Well, at least it wasn't something serious. Noah didn't have a prescription, but he kept a bottle of Unisom in his bedside table for emergencies.

He was about to return the prescription to the pouch, then changed his mind. He opened the bottle, took out one pill and wrapped it in a tissue, then stuffed it into his pocket. Mia would never know, and the medication would help him get to sleep if he got too anxious about the upcoming confrontation and wasn't able to talk himself down.

Where was Lexie, anyway? Noah wondered as he left the bathroom and reluctantly headed downstairs. Surely she should have been there by now.

SIXTEEN
ANGELINA

Angelina missed Lexie. After Lexie left, she tried calling and emailing. She just wanted to talk to her, to share what was going on in her life and to hear about Lexie's experiences firsthand. But Lexie never picked up and rarely replied to her emails. And when she did, they were short and noncommittal.

Miss you too. I'm having such an amazing time. We'll do something just you and me when I get back. Love you.

But she never came back, and eventually the emails stopped. If Lexie could find time to post on Instagram, surely she could find time to call or write a longer email. Angelina got it. Lexie had moved on. Angelina's mom had always said that would happen. Most of her school friends had drifted away once real life set in and they suddenly didn't have much in common. It was normal, expected even—but she never expected it of Lexie. Lexie wasn't like anyone else she had ever known; she'd never worried about what others might think. She was warm and genuine, and the most real person Angelina had ever met. Lexie could juggle dozens of friends without ever making anyone feel ignored or judged.

Lexie had been the only person at school who knew the truth

about Angelina's dad. Angelina told her friends that her father died when she was thirteen, but she never said that he'd overdosed, and that she had been the one to find him when she came home from school. Angelina had never really blamed him. He'd been in torment, but, like many people who needed help, he thought he could figure things out on his own and learn to manage the PTSD that came courtesy of three back-to-back tours in Afghanistan.

Angelina wasn't ashamed of what her dad had done, but she didn't want to be that girl whose father had killed himself. She didn't want the insincere pity or the judgment. She only wanted to fit in and enjoy her college experience. But Lexie had been so open about her own tragic past that one day Angelina just let it all pour out. She told Lexie how volatile life had become once her dad got back, how her parents had argued, and her mother had cried and begged him to see one of the therapists recommended by the Veterans Affairs office. She shared how terrified she had been coming home each day, not knowing what sort of mood she'd find him in. He might have completely ignored her, flown off the handle for no apparent reason, or experienced prolonged, terrifying panic attacks after a car had backfired or the sound of gunfire and explosions from the neighbor's kid playing *Call of Duty* filtered through the thin walls of their apartment.

Lexie hadn't offered pretend sympathy or banal clichés. She had said Angelina was strong and brave to have overcome trauma like this and told her about the sense of isolation and the sorrow that still plagued her after all these years. Lexie had admitted that she suffered from a crippling fear of abandonment. It was one thing to grieve a parent who was gone, but to know that her parents were out there, alive and well, and possibly loving other children, was unbearable. Lexie hid it well, but she harbored a deep resentment toward the people who'd left her in a cardboard box at a local firehouse. She'd been told by an insensitive social worker that she'd resembled a discarded Christmas angel.

Lexie had said she wanted to have a houseful of children and give them the love she'd never had. And she wanted those children with Noah. She thought he'd make a wonderful dad, and they talked about their future family all the time, impatient to start their life together once they got married and had a home of their own. Lexie had even asked Angelina if she would like to be godmother to one of her babies when the time came. And Angelina had agreed, overcome by Lexie's affection and uncomplicated acceptance.

Was it any wonder she thought she and Lexie would remain friends for the rest of their lives? But Lexie had left. Or maybe that wasn't it at all, and coming back had never been a choice. Angelina had to admit she was nervous about tonight, but she also hoped they would get some answers—maybe a long-overdue apology—and that, for some of them, there would finally be closure.

SEVENTEEN
ANGELINA

Angelina opened the fridge and began to take out the items they'd need to prepare dinner. Remy hovered at her shoulder until she handed him the steaks, and he set about seasoning the meat, all the while demanding that someone locate the meat thermometer. Mia was in charge of potatoes, and Richie was mixing a drink he called the Brooklyn Buzz, which as far as Angelina could see was three parts Tito's, one part cranberry juice. Vince stood by the door, unsure what to do until she suggested he set the table. And then he went about collecting the items he needed with his usual precision, counting the number of plates and utensils under his breath. Angelina reached for a knife and started to cut the potatoes. Mia was taking forever with each one and, at this rate, they'd never eat.

And then, Serena finally deigned to come inside, and paused by the kitchen island, looking unsure. "What can I do?" she asked. "You all know I'm not much of a cook."

Serena could cook, but she clearly didn't want to get her hands dirty.

"Can you make a Caesar salad?" Angelina asked.

"Sure. Is there ready-made dressing?"

"I'll make the dressing," Richie offered. "Are there any anchovies? What about Worcestershire sauce?"

"You'll have to make do without either," Angelina replied, remembering the contents of the fridge.

Richie scoffed. "Then it won't be real Caesar dressing."

"It's just salad, dude," Serena said, and accepted the package of romaine lettuce from Angelina while Richie hunted for the ingredients.

Serena approached the sink to wash the lettuce, then stopped and looked at Angelina, her gaze sliding to the neckline of Angelina's top.

"That's a stunning necklace," she said. "Looks expensive. What are those gemstones?"

"It was a gift," Angelina replied softly. She had worn her favorite new necklace with the dragonfly pendant. It was handcrafted and priced at nearly two hundred dollars, and Angelina had fallen in love with it the moment she'd seen it, and knew she had to have it. The wings were fashioned of paper-thin blue fire opal, and the head was a tear-sized aquamarine. She'd returned to the Grand Bazaar flea market several times, strolling casually past the jewelry stall, until her decision had been made.

"A gift?" Serena asked, smiling in that knowing way Angelina hated. "From whom? Some unsuspecting merchant?"

Serena turned away then, and fixed her attention on washing the lettuce, but the shot she'd fired had struck its mark. Angelina didn't want to give Serena the satisfaction of letting her see that she'd rattled her, but she really needed a moment to regroup.

"I forgot my phone outside," she muttered, and strode toward the patio door.

Relieved to be alone, she leaned on the deck railing and peered into the darkness. The lake shimmered in the light spilling from the house, and the trees moved gently in the soft breeze, the leaves rustling in whispered conversation. It was as if they were sharing confidences, the way Angelina, Lexie, Mia, and Serena had done so long ago, when there had still been trust between them. Secrets —everyone had them, and some were more damaging than others. Serena knew Angelina's secret and had made sure to remind her of that fact, in that high-handed, condescending manner she sometimes adopted. Had Richie heard what she had said? Would he think less of her if he knew the truth?

Angelina didn't know why she felt compelled to take things. It wasn't that she couldn't afford to purchase a two-hundred-dollar necklace. It was the thrill of the steal, the fear of being caught and getting arrested for shoplifting, then the joy of possessing an item she really wanted, and the smugness of getting away with something again and again. She had been busted twice but had managed to talk the pieces' owners out of calling the police, and had ended up buying the things she had taken in the name of goodwill. It wasn't worth it to get a criminal record for taking a fifty-dollar silver ring or a hundred-dollar bracelet, but she didn't love the items she'd paid for as much as the ones she'd taken. They seemed flat and boring, and when she wore them she felt uninspired.

So, Angelina had stolen again, but she also acknowledged that one day her luck would run out, and the fallout could result in the loss of her job and her reputation. Once something was posted online, there was no suppressing it, and if a potential employer or even a nosy boyfriend looked her up they would know what she had done. Would Serena tell anyone? She was certainly capable of being a bitch, but what would be her endgame? Had she been trying to deflect attention from herself, attempting to discredit Angelina, or simply making an off-the-cuff remark? There was no way to know but, if Serena alluded to the necklace again, Angelina would have to take her aside for a carefully worded warning.

EIGHTEEN
SERENA

There was something to be said for the comfort of old friends. Funny how quickly everyone fell into the old patterns. They were changed from their college days but also almost exactly the same, only a few years older. The guys had matured and no longer resembled the gangly, insecure boys they'd been at eighteen. Richie looked good. Serena had always had a soft spot for him, but he was one of those guys who peaked in his twenties, maybe early thirties. Then he'd settle down and become one of those fat, boring suburbanites who talked about mortgage rates with their wife's friends' husbands and coached their kids' baseball team, if they could be bothered to get up off the couch. Remy was being Remy, and Noah was brooding and doing his best to avoid being drawn into a conversation.

Serena hadn't seen Angelina and Mia in a long while. Angelina was her usual self. She was the mother of the group, and everyone was happy to let her take the lead, at least in the kitchen. Although Serena did think the way Angelina had brandished the knife when she'd asked her to make a salad was a bit aggressive. Angelina probably hadn't even realized it, she took herself so seriously, but Serena wouldn't be micromanaged. She wasn't going to be made to cook, not here.

Angelina had clearly been spending a lot of time in the kitchen lately, Serena observed. She had gained weight since the pandemic, and those mom jeans were not doing her any favors. She had the potential to be attractive, but she always downplayed her looks. That wouldn't help if she wanted to get with Richie—which she clearly did. If Angelina wanted him to see her as a sexy woman and not just as a friend, she should wear a tight, low-cut top and show some cleavage. Richie was always a boob man, and he did like brunettes. Vince couldn't take his eyes off her though, and Serena thought that Angelina should go for the guy who actually wanted her. But it was just like Angelina to self-sabotage.

Mia's transformation was a surprise. She had finally highlighted that mousy brown hair and learned how to put on make-up. With her space buns, cat eyeliner, cropped pink sweater, and low-rise cargo pants, she looked like an anime girl. All that was missing was a Hello Kitty backpack. She was clearly spending way too much time with eight-year-olds, but, Serena had to admit, Mia did look kind of hot. It was jarring, actually. She caught both Richie and Remy watching Mia out of the corners of their eyes, studying her as if they were seeing her for the first time. It was like Mia had finally emerged from her cocoon and become a butterfly. Serena had never seen Mia as competition—until today. But she doubted they would all get together again anytime soon. Serena had a feeling that after tonight, nothing would ever be the same again, for any of them.

NINETEEN
RICHIE

Richie had learned at a young age that some people were repulsed by pain and grief, while others fed off it like vultures. Richie's happy life fell apart when he was twelve. It happened so quickly, he barely had time to process it. One day he had a family, and then he didn't. His dad was always working—he and his brother were partners in a plumbing business—so he only saw him for a few hours after work. But his mom was at home, and, although it was totally uncool to admit it, she was Richie's world. She was a typical Italian mother, exactly like her own—outspoken, over-the-top emotional, and extremely affectionate. Richie could come to her with any problem, and she would always make him feel better. He'd go to her in tears and, before he knew it, they'd be laughing while she whipped up a batch of zeppole or made veal parm, his favorite when he was a kid. There were always people at the house, and his mom made a big deal of every holiday, even Valentine's Day, when she always prepared something special and put on the red stilettos. Richie was sent to bed early with a pink-frosted cupcake and told to put in earplugs.

And then his mom died. Just like that. They said it was a brain aneurysm, and she wouldn't have suffered or even known what was happening, but Richie didn't believe them. He was heartbroken and desperate for support, but his dad disappeared into himself and didn't emerge until he met Gina, whom his brother had hired to answer the office phones and keep track of appointments. Gina moved in exactly a year after Richie's mom passed, and brought her two kids. She slept in his mom's bed, used her best dishes—the ones Mom had taken out only on special occasions—and sold Mom's jewelry.

Richie knew it was wrong, but he started to act out. He frequently got into trouble at school, and picked fights with the neighborhood kids when he came home, causing confrontations that usually resulted in parents getting involved. Richie was in pain, and he wanted people to see it and help him, but no one really cared. His friends started to avoid him, and his dad took Gina's daughters' side when they called him a bully. His dad really lost his shit when Richie got into a fight with a kid who called him a Guinea. Richie dragged him into the boys' bathroom, pushed him head-first into the toilet, and held him down. He nearly drowned him. After that, Richie was sent to live with his grandparents until he learned how to behave.

When Gina gave birth to Frankie six months later and Ritchie wasn't invited to the christening, he tried to hang himself. His nonna found him in his room. Richie was halfway gone, but as soon as he came around she slapped the living shit out of him, then held him and cried and said he owed it to his mom to live and be happy. She would have wanted that for him. Nonna got Richie to see a grief counselor, and Poppy signed him up to a boxing gym owned by his friend's grandson, who gave him a hefty discount. Richie was told to let out his aggression.

Eventually, Richie was allowed to visit his dad's new family, and he came to realize that everyone seemed to like him when he clowned around, so he learned to hide his feelings behind humor and stupid antics that made people laugh. He still did that. It disarmed people, but that didn't mean Richie didn't feel things deeply or get angry when someone crossed a line. And Serena had crossed a line yesterday. She never contacted him directly or even acknowledged that they had hooked up, until yesterday when out of the blue she'd called and left a bitchy message, in which she'd threatened to amputate his balls with a pair of rusty shears if he ever told Noah about that night or made any mention of it at the reunion. He wasn't going to. Why would he?

Richie didn't give a shit about Serena, but Noah was his friend, and he wouldn't humiliate him that way. But that phone call had really pissed him off, which was why he was kind of glad Lexie was back. It would be fun to watch Serena squirm, 'cause it was obvious to anyone who cared to look that the girl was in fear for her life.

TWENTY
SERENA

As the evening wore on and Lexie failed to show, Serena began to feel calmer. Surrounded by old friends whose snarky banter felt as comfortable and natural as the air she breathed, she felt bolstered and brave. She had been silly to get so worked up. Noah was fine, hanging out with his friends and talking about work, sports, and politics. The girls were chatting and catching up, and Richie hadn't let on that she'd called him yesterday. She may have been a bit abrupt in her message, but she'd needed to get her point across. Richie was just jackass enough to make some loaded comment and get Noah wondering. God, how she wished she could erase that embarrassing episode from memory.

She had been drunk, Richie had been there, kissing her and telling her she was beautiful, and before she'd known it they'd been in the bathroom, Serena bent over the toilet, Richie behind her. Just thinking about it made her cringe, not because she hadn't enjoyed it but because it was Richie, and she'd had to see him all the time and had to ignore that knowing smile as his gaze would inevitably slide toward the bathroom, one brow lifted in invitation. Bastard!

She was never doing that again. She had loved Noah, and she'd known that if she was patient eventually he'd notice her. First loves rarely lasted, and, when Noah and Lexie inevitably broke up, she'd be there, waiting. And she'd been right. Noah had turned to her once Lexie had gone, and Serena had thrown herself into making him happy. And happy he would stay, she silently vowed. Unless Richie decided to go and ruin it for her. Granted, he had never said anything before, but Richie had been kind of weird to her the last few times she'd seen him, and she couldn't take the chance of him talking, not now.

It was nearly nine o'clock by the time they finally sat down to dinner. Angelina found mercury glass votive candle holders and set the candles on the table. The only source of light, the candles glowed through the speckled glass and cast everyone in a golden glow, their features softened and their eyes reflecting the light. Everyone seemed happy and relaxed, probably due to the amount of alcohol they had consumed, and they eagerly heaped food onto their plates. There were the steaks Remy had prepared, shrimp sautéed in olive oil and garlic, Caesar salad, and crispy roasted potatoes. It was like Friendsgiving, minus the turkey and all the trimmings. In fact, Serena had almost forgotten it was Halloween.

The house was like a tiny island where the outside world wasn't allowed to intrude. There were no creepy decorations or glowing jack-o'-lanterns, no trick-or-treaters ringing the bell for hours on end, and no obnoxious teenagers dressed as zombies and monsters and acting dumb as they egged each other on. No one had mentioned Lexie in at least an hour, and Serena hoped they'd manage to get through dinner before she was reminded once again why they were all there in the first place.

"Hey, let go of the potatoes," Remy exclaimed when Richie reached for the bowl and transferred a dozen chucks onto his plate. "You're not supposed to be having those."

"I don't care," Richie said belligerently. "I'm having carbs tonight. And tomorrow. And probably the day after. I can't take it anymore."

"Let the poor guy have some potatoes, Remy," Mia said on a laugh.

"You'll thank me in the morning," Remy said as he took half the potatoes off Richie's plate and transferred them to his own.

"You'll pay for that," Richie growled.

"Really? What are you going to do?"

Richie glared at him but didn't reply. He stuffed a potato into his mouth, then closed his eyes and moaned in ecstasy. "Better than sex," he announced once he'd swallowed.

"You must be having seriously mediocre sex," Remy said.

Everyone laughed, but Richie's gaze slid to Serena, and a cruel little smile tugged at his lips as he cut his eyes in the direction of the hall bathroom. Except this time the silent suggestion wasn't playful. Richie's dark eyes glinted with menace and Serena quickly looked away, suddenly afraid of what he might do. Thankfully, no one had noticed, and Noah, who'd been applying himself to his steak, had suddenly turned toward the window. He'd gone perfectly still as if he'd heard something, but then he seemed to relax, and turned his attention back to his plate. Serena glanced out the window that opened onto the deck. the deck lights had turned off automatically, and the night beyond was very dark, just a pale sliver of moon hanging above the pitch-black waters of the lake and the woods beyond. The houses on the opposite shore were just dark shapes against the trees, and the silence was like nothing one ever experienced in New York City. It felt dense and menacing, as if nature were holding its breath while it waited for something to happen.

"I wonder why it's called Witch Lake," Serena said, speaking almost to herself.

"Oh, I know this one. I looked it up," Angelina said, visibly very pleased with herself for knowing the answer. She looked around the table, relishing her moment in the spotlight. Angelina lowered her voice, as if she were telling a spooky story around a campfire, and began. "In the sixteen hundreds, the Dutch settled this area and called it New Netherland. New York was called New Amsterdam. Did you know that?"

It was clearly meant to be a rhetorical question, but Richie nodded and said, "We learned about it in school. Did you play hooky that day, Angie?"

"I must have," Angelina admitted with a rueful smile. "Anyhow, Kingston was called Wiltwick in those days. I like Kingston much better. Sounds regal."

"As it was intended to," Mia said under her breath. "So, what does it have to do with the lake?"

"The story goes that a young girl caught the eye of the colony lothario," Angelina said.

"I can't believe you just used that word," Remy cut in.

"Will you shut up and let me finish?"

"By all means. I believe you were at lothario," Remy replied.

"The girl, Anouk DeVries, was seduced by the mayor," Angelina continued. "But his wife, who couldn't stand the humiliation in front of the other settlers because she couldn't hold her husband's attention, accused Anouk of witchcraft."

"As one did in those days, because naturally the husband was innocent and had to have been bewitched in order to pursue a girl half his age," Mia said with disgust.

Angelina glared at her, and Mia went quiet.

"Anyway, the minister and the rest of the men backed the accusation, fearful that their own indiscretions might be tried at some point and ensuring that a woman got the blame instead of one of their own."

"So what, did they murder her?" Vince asked, his voice shaking with outrage.

Everyone went quiet while they waited for Angelina to reply, and in the silence there was the sudden creaking of wood, as if someone had just mounted the steps and was walking across the deck. Remy sprang to his feet and went to the window. He turned his head from side to side, then craned his neck to see the part of the deck closest to the parking area.

"Is it Lexie?" Mia called out to him.

Remy turned away from the window and shrugged. "I don't see anyone."

"Are you sure?" Angelina asked.

"Unless they're intentionally keeping out of sight, I don't think anyone is out there," Remy said and returned to his seat.

"So what the hell was that?" Serena demanded. She was spooked.

"Probably just the wind," Angelina replied. "Or the house settling. Why would Lexie creep around on the deck and not come inside?"

"So what happened to Anouk?" Mia interjected. "Did the elders sentence her to death?"

"As good as," Angelina replied sadly, her gaze no longer on the darkened window. "Anouk was cast out. Alone, and no doubt terrified, she wandered until she came upon the lake and built a shelter."

The deck creaked again, but this time no one got up to investigate.

"That's a sad story," Remy said quietly. "It was nearly impossible to survive outside a community in those days, especially for a woman."

"It gets sadder still," Angelina announced dramatically. "Anouk's sister snuck out to see her and brought her food and other items she would need to get through the winter, since Anouk had been forced to leave home with nothing but the clothes on her back. In the spring, when Anouk's sister came to find her after not visiting for several months, she found Anouk hanging from a tree, a withered baby still attached by the umbilical cord dangling between her legs."

"You're making this up," Serena exclaimed. She was deeply disturbed by the story, especially the part about the baby, who might have been born alive and would have died a long and agonizing death. "How could anyone even know that? It was in the sixteen hundreds. They didn't exactly keep a written account of every death, especially when it came to women."

"Well, they recorded this one, and probably used it as a cautionary tale for the other young girls," Angelina said.

"And named the lake after the poor girl they'd condemned to death," Mia grumbled. "There's nothing worse than selfish, dishonest men who pose as religious leaders and abuse the women in their care."

"And their babies," Serena said softly.

"And I guess the mayor went on to live happily ever after, respected by his peers and adored by his wife," Remy concluded. "Human beings can justify anything to themselves when it serves their purposes."

"They really can," Angelina said. "From a single murder to genocide, there are always those who feel they're justified in taking a life."

"And now that we're all really depressed, we need to do something to liven things up," Richie suggested. "Hey, how about we make a fire and smoke some weed? And we need music. I'll be taking requests, but first up my girl Cardi B. I love me some Cardi," he said with feeling.

"I bet you're a big fan," Serena said to Vince, who looked at her in surprise but didn't respond.

"That's actually a great idea," Mia said. "That story really bummed me out."

"What about the cheesecake?" Remy asked. He sounded like a little kid who'd just been told he had to go to bed without dessert.

"We can have dessert later," Angelina said as she pushed away from the table. "I'm not going to bed until I have a cannolo."

"Noah, you all right, man? You're awfully quiet," Richie said.

"Just thinking about cannoli," Noah muttered.

"Should we clean up?" Vince asked as he looked around the table. "At least put the leftovers away."

"Don't worry about it, Vinnie," Richie said dismissively. "We can do it later, before we go to bed."

Angelina looked like she was about to argue, then gave up. It was clear she wanted to follow Richie outside and grab the chair next to his. She'd probably complain that she was cold and try to climb into his lap, Serena thought spitefully.

"Hey, anyone hear from Lexie again? It's ten o'clock," Mia said. "I'm getting worried."

"So text her," Angelina said. "She did say she was stuck in traffic."

"For this long?"

"It's Halloween. People are going to parties and bars. She'll get here," Richie said. He took out his phone and chose Cardi B's "WAP," which blared from the Bluetooth speaker he'd set up.

"Oh, yeah," Richie said as he got up and started to dance around. He sang along to the words. "Wet ass pu—"

"I'm not listening to this crap. It's gross," Mia cut across him, and headed outside.

"You're such a douche, Richie," Serena said with contempt.

Richie fixed her with a narrowed gaze. "Am I? And you're a total bitch." His voice was low and threatening, and Serena took an involuntary step back.

Normally, Richie turned everything into a joke, but she realized she'd gone too far and would have to keep her distance from him for the rest of the weekend. She'd given in to her fear and anger and had unwittingly made an enemy of Richie in the process. She shouldn't have left that nasty voicemail. If he hadn't said anything to Noah until now, he wasn't going to suddenly blurt it out. And now he had power over her because he realized how easily he could destabilize her life. Serena wondered if she should apologize, then dismissed the idea. She was sure Richie had heard worse from other women. He'd get over it, and they'd agree to a truce.

Everyone trooped outside, and Richie was ordered to put on Sabrina Carpenter, whose sweet voice pleaded with her boyfriend not to embarrass her and let his devil out tonight. Richie crooned along, and Mia joined in.

"It's like we're right back in school," Angelina said, and Serena wasn't sure if Angelina was feeling nostalgic or if she meant that Richie's antics made her cringe.

"Want help with that?" Vince asked as Angelina began to pile wood into the firepit. "You have to stack it like a teepee. It'll catch faster if there's airflow."

"Didn't know you were an expert," Serena observed. "Not really your people's thing, camping, is it?"

She and Noah had gone camping with his cousins a few times, and she hadn't seen a single Black family at the campground. Most of the campers had been white, and kind of trashy, the sort of people she chose to avoid in everyday life. Serena didn't like camping at all, but Noah had fond memories of camping trips with his parents and thought Serena would learn to love the great outdoors. Looking out over the calm black waters of Witch Lake, she thought she could enjoy nature if she stayed at a gorgeous home that was equipped with all the comforts, like this, but at some gross campground in the Adirondacks? Not so much. Her reverie was interrupted by Vince, who once he'd finished stacking the wood had unfolded himself to his full height.

"My people?" he asked. "You mean hedge fund managers?"

Angelina shot Serena a nasty look, and Serena went quiet. The cracks people had made in college were no longer acceptable, and one wrong comment could ruin her life. She could lose her job and her social media followers if she was branded a racist. She didn't think Vince was the sort of person to make a public accusation though. He settled his scores in private, and not with his fists. He was too smart for that.

And if she were honest, Serena had no idea why she was baiting him. Maybe it was because he wasn't really part of the group and made for an easy target for her anger, or maybe because she really was a horrible person. She didn't want to be the sort of mother her child would be ashamed of. She would have to work on herself and be more cognizant of the things she said and how they sounded to others. And she would start right now.

"Sorry, Vince. I'm just on edge. I didn't mean it," she choked out.

"It's fine," Vince replied, but Serena could see that it wasn't. She'd offended him, and now she'd have to tiptoe around Vince for the rest of the weekend. That made two people she now had to worry about—three once their host finally showed up.

Serena walked to the edge of the deck, leaned on the railing, and peered into the darkness beyond. With the deck lights off, the lake resembled a huge puddle of gasoline. The oily water rippled at the center, as if there was something hovering just beneath the surface, and Serena suddenly thought that maybe taking out the rowboat wasn't such a good idea. Who knew what lived in that lake or what sort of harmful bacteria polluted the water. She was just about to turn away, when she thought she'd spotted a light in a second-floor window of the house diagonally across the lake. Serena expected other lights to come on now that someone had finally come home, but the glow was extinguished, the house plunged into darkness.

After a while, Serena wasn't even sure if the light had been inside the house. The luminescence could have been a reflection of the moon, or the glint of distant headlights from the opposite shore. She was just feeling jittery, unnerved by the loss of control and intimidated by the creepy eeriness of this isolated spot. She was glad once the fire got going and Remy passed around a mirror with lines of coke neatly arranged on the surface. He was nothing if not thorough. Angelina didn't have any coke but accepted one of Richie's spliffs. Serena was tempted to smoke some weed—she didn't think it'd hurt the baby—but decided to stick to her resolution and remain vigilant and clear-eyed.

"I think it's time for shots," Remy said, and brought out shot glasses and a bottle of tequila. With a flick of her hand, Serena declined.

The sight of her high, drunk friends was even more disturbing when she was stone sober,

and Serena wished she could join in, if only so she could relax and stop thinking about what this thing with Lexie really meant and what would happen once the real reason for this reunion was finally revealed. She fixed her attention on Mia, who kept glancing fearfully at the attic window. Serena looked up but didn't see anything other than darkened panes of glass. Mia turned and peered toward the parking area, as if she expected Lexie to materialize out of the darkness. She probably couldn't wait to see Lexie again.

Mia and Lexie had been close, but Serena had always suspected there was more to it for Mia. Mia liked men—God knew she'd gone through enough guys in college—but Serena thought she might also have had a crush on Lexie. Lexie had never alluded to it, but she'd distanced herself from both Mia and Angelina toward the end of their senior year and had been adamant that neither of them should come to Thailand.

Had something happened between them? Had Mia misread the situation and made a move that was rebuffed? Or had Lexie been into it and the realization had thrown everything she'd known about herself into turmoil? The possibility had never occurred to Serena before, but things weren't so black and white anymore when it came to people's sexuality. People were more open to experimenting, and many heterosexuals had engaged in a same-sex experience at least once. It would be interesting to see how Mia acted this weekend and if she would be interested in hooking up with either Remy or Richie.

Mia disappeared inside and returned with a second bottle of tequila. More shots were poured, another baggie of white powder appeared as if by magic, and the fire started to peter out since no one was paying it any attention. Serena was cold, tired, and jittery, and wished she could go upstairs. Tomorrow was another day, and maybe she'd find an excuse to go home. She was sure Noah would agree to leave. He was joining in, but there was tension in his shoulders and a defensive set to his jaw. He periodically glanced toward the parking area, no doubt searching for oncoming headlights and bracing for the moment Lexie would finally make an appearance.

Not wanting to be the first to go to bed, Serena went inside to grab her warmer jacket. If she had to keep up the pretense of having a good time, she may as well be warm.

TWENTY-ONE
NOAH

The booze and the coke had taken the edge off a little, but Noah still couldn't relax. His stomach was in knots, and the steak he'd eaten at dinner just sat there like a brick, making him queasy as it fermented in the wine that sloshed and fizzed in his belly. The headache had receded somewhat, but he still felt pressure behind his eyes, and the throbbing in his temples was becoming more insistent. This place didn't help either. The darkness beyond the deck felt like a solid, ominous mass, the houses that fronted the lake as featureless and lifeless as the plastic Monopoly houses he liked to play with as a kid. The unnatural quiet was making him twitchy.

On any other day, Noah might have enjoyed the peace and would have appreciated the soothing backdrop of nature, but today it seemed all wrong. He wanted to be back in New York, where the lights blazed all night long, the traffic never came to a stop, and there were always other people around to take the focus off him and remind him how small and insignificant he was in a city of millions. There were times when the faceless multitudes made him lonely, but tonight he felt lonely among his friends, and he realized how far apart they'd grown these past few years and how little they actually cared for one another.

All Noah wanted was to go to bed, wake up in the morning,

and leave before anyone else was up. Lexie hadn't shown, and, although he was worried about her, he was also relieved that the confrontation he'd dreaded had been pushed off by one more day. But not the argument with Serena. She would tear into him as soon as they were alone, he could see it in her eyes. Serena had been bracing herself for this reunion all night and was clearly on edge. She hadn't partaken in the partying and had sat there like an ice queen, her nose wrinkled with disgust and her gaze shifting from one person to the next with an air of self-righteous judgment. She was determined to make this as difficult as possible for them both until he proved his loyalty and undying love, neither of which he was feeling at the moment. Not for the first time that evening, he found himself wishing he hadn't rushed into marriage and was still free to choose his own life. But he'd made his bed and would have to lie in it until he either got comfortable or decided to set the bed on fire.

Desperate for some water, Noah went inside and found a clean glass in a kitchen cabinet. He filled the glass from the tap, gulped down the contents, then refilled it and drank the water slower this time. The charcuterie board was still on the kitchen island, the row of Ritz crackers untouched. Everyone was too weight conscious to waste calories on the buttery treats. Noah grabbed a handful of crackers and ate them slowly, one by one, hoping they would help with the indigestion.

He turned around when Richie slid open the patio door and walked into the kitchen. He moved slower than usual, and his heavy-lidded eyes were glazed with intoxication. Richie shut the door behind him, then stopped, as if he couldn't recall what he'd come for, then his gaze settled on the crackers in Noah's hand.

"You okay?" Richie asked, the words a bit slurred.

Noah shrugged. "Just can't seem to relax."

Richie pulled a baggie from his jacket pocket and dangled it in front of Noah. "I have some ketamine. It will help you to relax. But don't tell anyone. I could get in real trouble for this."

"No thanks."

"Suit yourself. I should offer it to Vince. He can't seem to relax either," Richie said with a sly grin, and Noah was sure he was referring to the ugly things Serena had said to Vince earlier. Richie cocked his head to the side and sighed dramatically. "No offense, man, but your girl is a bitch."

"None taken," Noah muttered.

He should be offended. Serena was his wife, and it was his duty to defend her, but he simply couldn't find the will to get into it with Richie, especially when he knew his friend to be right. Serena was nervous, and her nastiness was a defense mechanism in a situation that was making her extremely uncomfortable, but Noah couldn't blame the others for being annoyed by it. God knew he was. He couldn't stomach another cracker, and tossed the rest onto the board as his stomach roiled in protest.

Richie shrugged. "I guess you're used to it, but the rest of us don't have to take her shit."

"So don't," Noah replied, and walked away. He heard Richie scoff behind him but didn't bother to turn around.

"One of these days, someone is going to give her a dose of her own medicine," Richie said quietly.

"Well, it better not be you," Noah said before he stepped out onto the deck.

The remainder of the night was a blur, and Noah was relieved when people started to nod off. The deck was littered with empty bottles, plastic cups, and plates smeared with cannoli cream and bits of chocolate. The fire had been reduced to a pile of smoldering ash that began to blow in their faces once the wind picked up. Angelina said something about putting the leftovers away, but no one paid her any attention, and even Vince, who usually tried to make himself useful, didn't offer to help but continued to suck on his vape.

Mia was the first to drift inside, and everyone followed, eager to get to bed. No one mentioned Lexie as they muttered goodnights and shut the doors to their bedrooms.

TWENTY-TWO

ANGELINA

Saturday
November 1

Angelina was the first one to come downstairs. The house was quiet since everyone was still sleeping off the effects of last night. They had finally gone to bed around two, everyone except Serena barely coherent due to the mixture of alcohol, drugs, and fatigue. Mia had actually held on to the wall as she teetered toward the bedroom she shared with Angelina. Angelina could barely recall anything that had happened after midnight, but she did remember that it had grown cold and everyone had gone inside to grab warm jackets, which were now strewn all over the place, the colorful puffers reminiscent of deflated balloons.

The kitchen was a mess. The garbage was overflowing. There were dirty dishes on the island and in the sink, and empty bottles on the counter, and the greasy pots and pans had been left on the stove. The dining room was littered with the remains of their dinner, and the entire first floor reeked of congealed fat, garlic, rancid salad dressing, and spilled alcohol. Angelina's stomach lurched in protest, and her head ached dully as more precise memories of last night began to surface. The third cannolo had been a mistake, but it had been so good she couldn't resist. And she hadn't drunk this much in years.

Sighing heavily, she threw open the window in the dining room, then eyed the filthy dishes and decided she would start to clean once she'd had coffee and eaten something that would absorb the sour bile in her stomach. Half a loaf of French bread was still sitting on the cutting board, and Angelina was suddenly reminded of the crack Richie had made about Remy's baguette. She chuckled and shook her head. It was hard to believe Richie was allowed in a courtroom and Remy was a well-respected photographer whose photos appeared in both domestic and European magazines. They'd come a long way, those two, but when they got together it was as if they were eighteen again. Raunchy comments, dumb jokes, and inevitable references to penis size.

Angelina was glad Noah and Vince hadn't got in on the act. Noah had been understandably tense, and Vince wasn't the sort to get down in the gutter and had kept the low-brow statements to a minimum. Vince treated everyone with respect, even if they didn't deserve it. Angelina didn't think she should fight his battles. Her jumping in would only embarrass him, so she had kept her mouth shut, but Vince really should have said something to Serena when she'd made those offensive comments. Serena had eventually deigned to apologize, but the apology hadn't been for Vince—it had been for herself. She didn't want to be thought of as a bad person or to be called out for her inappropriate behavior. She'd find it too embarrassing. What did she have against Vince, anyway? It wasn't as if he'd shown up uninvited. Their hostess was paying for the reunion and had invited him, so he had every right to be there. It was time Serena grew up and stopped thinking the world revolved around her and her feelings.

Angelina turned on the Keurig and rooted around in the cabinets until she found a box of K-Cups, and was happy to note that it was a bold Hawaiian blend. She made a mug of coffee, then tore off a piece of bread and covered it with a fat chunk of Brie. She pulled on her jacket and boots, grabbed her breakfast, and headed outside, where she settled in the chair farthest from the stinking firepit. As she settled the plate on her knee, she glanced toward the parking area. No new vehicles. She'd ask Mia and Remy when they got up if they'd heard from Lexie since that last text, but for now she was going to put Lexie from her mind.

The morning was too perfect to spoil with endless worrying. The air was cool and fresh, fluffy clouds raced overhead, and the flame-colored trees blazed like a forest fire around the lake. As she ate, Angelina's head cleared, and her stomach began to settle. At home and at the hospital, she always used low-fat milk, but there was only half-and-half in the fridge, and she savored the decadent richness of her coffee. She supposed she should take out the trash and start loading the dishwasher, but housework could wait. This was such a nice moment. She felt the tranquility settle around her shoulders like a velvet mantle. When would she get another chance to enjoy the beauty of nature and soak up the peace and quiet? Soon everyone would come down, looking hungover and bleary-eyed, and her peace would be shattered.

Maybe there was a trail that went around the lake and she could go for a walk, or she could take out the boat. Rowing was good exercise, and Angelina longed to be out on the water, away from the sour smell of the empty bottles, the acrid stink of ash, and the reek of congealed fat that wafted through the open window. After setting her empty dishes on the deck, she went down the steps and walked toward the dock. She wished she'd brought her sunglasses. The morning sun was very bright, but she didn't feel like going back inside to get them in case someone else was already up and wanted to chat. She really wasn't in the mood for small talk.

Angelina reached the end of the dock and squinted down at the boat. Water lapped gently at the wooden posts and the sides of the boat, which was painted pale blue. The oars lay across two rows of benches, and two orange life vests were stowed beneath the bench in the prow. The shimmering surface of the lake was dotted with colorful leaves, and there was something floating in the water that clearly didn't belong there. At first glance, it looked like an emerald-green puffer jacket, but then, once her eyes adjusted to the piercing light, she could make out a pale oval surrounded by what looked like rippling fronds of seaweed.

And then she was screaming and sprinting down the dock and along the shore toward the spot closest to the body. She knew exactly who the jacket belonged to, just as she knew that the person wearing it was dead.

TWENTY-THREE

MIA

Mia had just brewed a cup of coffee when she heard the awful, gut-wrenching scream. She splashed hot coffee on her hand as she lurched toward the window, hoping that Angelina or Serena had just seen a spider or a mouse and that nothing was seriously wrong. Or was that Lexie screaming? Mia had fallen asleep before her head hit the pillow, so she had no idea if Lexie had finally made an appearance, but she had seen something last night that had given her pause. Of course, by that point she had been completely shit-faced and might have imagined the whole thing, but when she'd looked up at one point she'd thought she'd seen a face at the attic window. Was it possible that Lexie had been there all along, and had just been waiting for the right time to come down?

That would be an odd thing to do, but the whole evening had been odd, Mia reflected as she dried her hand on a kitchen towel and peered out the window. What was up with Serena and Richie? Serena had never been Richie's biggest fan—she probably resented him for not asking her out after they'd hooked up—but there had been real animosity between them last night. And Serena had been baiting Vince. And now that Mia thought about it, Serena and Noah had barely said a word to each other all evening and had sat at opposite sides of the table at dinner and across from each other on the deck.

Mia stepped outside and spotted Angelina, who was standing by herself on the shore, her gaze fixed on something in the water. Angelina had her arms wrapped around her middle, and even from a distance Mia could tell that she was trembling. Mia sprinted down the steps and across the grassy bank. Her bare feet were cold and damp from the dew, and a stiff breeze tore at her flimsy pajamas.

"Angie, what is it? Are you okay?"

Angelina mutely shook her head. Mia followed the direction of her gaze, and that was when she saw it. It was a person, floating on their back. If they hadn't been fully dressed, Mia might have thought someone had joined the Polar Bear Club and decided to go for an invigorating morning swim, but it was clear that the person in the lake had not gone in on purpose. Mia squinted, but without her distance glasses on she couldn't make out the facial features. What she could tell from the stillness of the body, though, was that the person was probably unconscious and possibly even dead.

"Oh, Jesus," she cried. "Who is that?" When Angelina didn't reply, Mia tried again. "Have you called an ambulance?"

Angelina shook her head. "It's too late, Mia," she whispered. "It's too late."

"What the hell is going on?" Richie exclaimed as he joined them.

He wore black-and-gray lounge pants and a black T-shirt, and his feet were bare. When he saw what they were looking at he sucked in his breath and without another word plunged into the lake.

"What's happening?" Vince called out as he and Remy appeared on the deck. When they spotted Richie in the water, they came running and stopped next to the women.

All four of them watched with bated breath as Richie swam out to the body, grabbed the person by the arm, and headed back to shore. He emerged from the water, pulled the body onto the bank, and laid it on its back. Richie was dripping and shivering, and his teeth chattered from the cold, but no one paid him any attention. All eyes were on Serena, who was white and still, her lips blue, the hair she had been so proud of plastered to her skull and reeking of silt. Richie dropped to his knees and took hold of her wrist. He tried to find a pulse, then, when he failed, he unzipped her jacket, bent down, and pressed his ear to her chest.

"She's gone," he pronounced grimly.

"Oh, my God," Angelina wailed. "This can't be happening."

"Where's Noah?" Mia exclaimed.

Everyone looked around, but Noah was nowhere to be seen. That was strange, since Angelina's screams had woken everyone else. Vince pulled off his hoodie and draped it over Richie's quaking shoulders.

"Thanks," Richie muttered, but all his attention was on Serena.

When he next spoke, the vain, cocky man-child of last night had been replaced with a criminal attorney. "No one touch the body. Leave it where it is until the police get here. Remy, get Noah. Mia, get some clothes on. Your lips are turning blue. And take Angelina with you. She's clearly in shock. Vince, call the police." He pulled an iPhone from the pocket of Vince's hoodie and handed it to Vince, who took it without comment.

"Where are you going?" Vince asked when Richie turned toward the house.

"To get some dry clothes on and dispose of anything that can get us arrested." He looked at the silent group. "Well, come on."

"What do you think happened?" Mia cried to Richie's retreating back.

"Hell if I know, but before we start speculating we need to take care of business," he shot back.

Remy trotted after Richie, and Vince dialed 911. Mia noticed that his hand shook as he put the phone to his ear. She couldn't bear to look at Serena, and angrily wiped at the tears she couldn't seem to stop dripping onto her pajama top.

Angelina was white and dry-eyed, her eyes staring and her

mouth moving as she repeated, "I don't understand. What was she doing out there?"

"Come on, Angie. Let's get you inside."

Mia put her arm around Angelina and guided her toward the house. Angelina was trembling, even though she was the only one fully dressed. Richie was right; she was in shock. Otherwise, she would have examined the body. Mia knew Richie had taken a first-aid class, and since he worked with special needs kids he needed to know the basics in case of emergency, but Angelina was a nurse. Maybe she could have spotted something Richie had missed. But dead was dead, so it probably didn't matter. Mia was glad Richie had taken charge. She was good at following orders, but she didn't want the responsibility, and Richie was an officer of the court. He would know what needed to be done.

As soon as they came inside, Angelina sank into a kitchen chair and buried her face in her hands. Mia was shaking with cold and desperately wanted to put on something warm and take a moment to process what had happened. But she couldn't leave Angelina, so she made her a mug of coffee, added some sugar and cream, and set it before her. Then she made another coffee and brought it out to Richie, who'd changed into jeans and a sweatshirt and was rooting around the deck. He was on his hands and knees, checking for drug-related paraphernalia.

Richie was still shivering, his hair was damp, and his jaw was covered in dark stubble. He resembled an addict looking for a fix, Mia thought, and instantly felt ashamed of herself. No one would bat an eyelash at the weed, but if he was caught with illegal drugs he might face disciplinary action or maybe even get disbarred. He had every right to be worried, and needed to make sure the police found no traces of cocaine or ketamine. Mia handed him the steaming mug, and he took it and nodded his thanks before taking several hurried sips and setting the mug on the deck.

Vince was still standing next to the body, phone in hand. His lips were moving, so perhaps he was explaining the situation to the police. Mia hoped someone would come soon. It seemed wrong to leave Serena's body out there in the cold, her hair sopping wet and her clothes smelling of lake water. She would have hated that. She had always taken such pride in her appearance.

A sob tore from Mia's chest, and she ran back inside, unable to stand the sight any longer. Angelina stood and opened her arms, and Mia threw herself into her friend's embrace. They held each other as they cried, the magnitude of what had happened finally sinking in with terrifying finality.

TWENTY-FOUR

REMY

Remy stood before the door to Serena and Noah's bedroom, unable to go in. He wished someone else had been sent to get Noah. How did you tell your friend his 26-year-old wife was dead? How did you comfort him when you could hardly make sense of it yourself? What had happened last night? Had Serena gone for a walk and fallen in? She was a good swimmer, and she had been sober last night, the only one of them not to take part in anything that might impair her judgment or prevent her from trying to save herself. Would anyone have heard her if she'd called for help? Probably not, since they had all been dead to the world.

But when had she left? Remy had seen everyone stumble to their rooms last night and presumably go to bed. And why would Serena go outside by herself in the middle of the night? It had been windy and cold, and, once the lights were off in the house, the darkness would have been nearly impenetrable. Had she gone out this morning then? Serena always said she was an early riser—maybe she had woken up early and gone for a walk. But that made even less sense. How could she fall into the lake in broad daylight? Had she suddenly passed out? Or had she gone in on purpose?

The question struck Remy like a bolt out of the blue. He hadn't considered suicide, not until that moment, but he supposed it was possible. Had Serena been so devastated by Lexie's sudden return that she'd taken her own life rather than face the possibility that she might lose Noah? Remy thought Serena had been more emotionally fragile than she'd let on, but suicide? And before anything had even happened? Except that maybe it had, and they'd all slept right through it. What if Lexie had shown up last night? If she had, she wasn't here now. So, where the hell was she?

Remy was still standing in front of the door when Richie pounded up the stairs. "What the hell, Remy?" he demanded. "Why didn't you wake him?"

"I—I couldn't bring myself to tell him," Remy said.

"Do I have to do everything myself?" Richie bitched under his breath as he shoved open the door.

Noah was sprawled across the queen-size bed, his face ashen in the light streaming through the window. At first, Remy thought he was dead too, and grabbed the door jamb to steady himself, but then he realized that, although his breathing was shallow, Noah's chest was rising and falling, and he was simply in deep sleep.

"Noah," Richie called. "Noah, wake up, bro."

Noah didn't respond.

"Noah." Richie sat on the edge of the bed and took Noah by the upper arm. "Noah," he tried again. Noah didn't stir.

Getting frustrated, Richie slapped Noah lightly across the face. Then again, a little harder. Then harder still. Noah's eyes flew open and he stared at his friends, his cloudy gaze befuddled with sleep.

"What the fuck, Richie?" he moaned.

"Noah, you need to wake up. Now."

"Leave me alone," Noah growled, and his eyelids began to flutter closed.

"Noah," Richie roared, startling him awake.

"Noah, something's happened," Remy said gently.

Noah struggled to wake up, but when he finally pried his eyes open his gaze was clearer. "What's wrong?" he groaned. "I took a sleeping pill last night. I'm really groggy."

"Noah, it's Serena," Richie said. His tone was softer now, his eyes warm with compassion.

"What about her?" Noah sat up and rubbed his eyes, then glanced from Richie to Remy and back again. "Where is she?"

"Angelina found Serena this morning. She's gone, Noah," Richie said.

"Gone where?"

"She's dead," Remy said, and his voice quavered with emotion. "Serena is dead."

Noah seemed frozen with shock, and then he exploded out of bed and ran toward the door and down the stairs, Remy and Richie behind him.

"Wait," Richie called. "Noah, don't touch the body."

Remy grabbed Richie by the arm and yanked him backward. "Why do you keep saying that, man?"

"Because I don't think it was an accident, Remy. Serena was murdered."

TWENTY-FIVE
RICHIE

Richie hadn't wanted to say it out loud, not until the police got there and he could share his suspicions, but Noah was sprinting toward Serena and would no doubt throw himself at the body. Richie ran after him and tackled him from behind before Noah could go down on his knees next to the corpse.

"Noah, no," he yelled over Noah's roar of protest. "You can't touch her."

"What the hell are you talking about, Richie?" Noah bellowed. "She must have fallen and hit her head. She could still be alive."

"She's gone, man. She's gone," Richie cried. "We need to wait for the police."

"The police?"

"Yes. Vince called the police. You called them, right, Vince?" Richie asked.

Vince was standing off to the side, a dazed look on his face as he watched Noah and Richie wrestle.

"There was a pile-up on 9W. Everyone is there. The dispatcher said they'll send someone as soon as they can."

"We can't leave her here," Noah wailed. "I'm not leaving her here."

"All right, all right," Richie said in what he hoped was a soothing tone. "How about we cover her up?"

"We need to bring her inside," Noah insisted.

"We can't do that."

"Maybe we can just lay her on the bed or something," Remy said.

"We can't do that. Remy, please, get Noah inside."

"I'm not going anywhere," Noah ground out. He planted himself on the grass right next to Serena's body. "I'm going to wait right here. I'm not leaving her alone."

"All right. I'll stay right here with you. How is that? Remy, can you bring our jackets? It's cold out here."

"Sure," Remy said, and headed toward the house.

"Do you need anything else?" Vince asked.

Richie shook his head, and Vince left them alone. Once Vince and Remy were gone, Noah went into some sort of trance. His lips were moving, and Richie thought that maybe he was praying, either for Serena's soul or for his own. This didn't look good. It didn't look good at all. Richie had noticed the bruises around Serena's neck as soon as he'd unzipped her jacket. Angelina must have noticed them too. She was a trained professional, but she had been in shock and had tried to avoid looking at the body, so there was a chance she hadn't. But surely they could all see this wasn't an accident and it was important to preserve the scene.

Richie shivered as a blast of cold wind ruffled his wet hair. He was so cold, and the ground was spongy and damp beneath his jeans. Noah seemed oblivious to the discomfort and stared straight ahead, unable now to look at his dead wife. But Richie looked at her, not as a friend but as someone who'd analyzed the minutes for dozens of murder trials while in law school. Serena had been floating face-up, which was unusual. Drowning victims usually floated face-down due to the weight of the head and the limbs. Richie thought the air in her thick puffer jacket might have acted as a life preserver and prevented the body from flipping over, which meant that someone had either pushed her and she'd fallen backward, or she had been backing away from someone and had gone over the side of the dock. But if she had been facing up the whole time, she wouldn't have drowned.

He supposed the body could have turned over on its own once Serena was dead. He wasn't a pathologist and only knew what he'd learned by reading, but Serena couldn't have sustained those bruises on her neck from falling against the dock or striking the rowboat on the way down. The bruises encircled her throat, as if someone had tried to strangle her. And if she had committed suicide, which he highly doubted, she would hardly have tried to strangle herself. Unless she'd tried to hang herself first. The possibility made him feel slightly ill, but he pushed the painful childhood memory away and focused on the present. He looked around, searching for rope or a branch that was thick enough to hold a body, but didn't see anything in the near vicinity.

Besides, why would Serena kill herself? Sure, she had been understandably nervous about seeing Lexie, but she'd had nothing to truly worry about. Lexie had been the one to leave, to blow them all off as she went in search of a new life and new friends. It had always struck Richie as odd that she'd do that. Lexie had been so focused on going to law school and had been the one to drill Richie when they'd studied for their LSATs together. She had been determined and brilliant, and had been very definite about her choice of family law. But perhaps she'd had some sort of spiritual awakening while abroad. People sometimes did. Maybe getting the best settlements for her clients and working out custody agreements hadn't seemed important anymore and she'd realized that wasn't the way she wanted to spend her life.

Richie could understand that. He'd had no illusions when he'd chosen criminal law. Statistically, a large percentage of the accused were guilty, which was why lawyers never asked their clients if they had committed the crime. Knowing the truth would make it morally reprehensible to represent the pervert who'd molested a child or the husband who'd murdered his wife, stuffed her remains into a suitcase, and thrown it into the East River. Richie had graduated top of his class and had entertained several offers from private law firms, but he had refused. Maybe once he was older and considerably more disillusioned, he'd take on the fat cats who needed someone to invent reasonable doubt and were willing to pay top dollar for a barracuda who'd do anything to win, but Richie was just starting out. He was young and idealistic, and he needed to see justice done, at least some of the time.

As he sat next to a silent Noah, Richie wondered if Lexie had found God during her travels. She had never been a churchgoer, but maybe she had hit on something out there that had helped her make sense of it all. Richie could never see going to an ashram himself. His spiritual awakening had been the first time his dad had taken him to a baseball game when he was six. He had dreamed and prayed every night that he would become a famous ball player. God had chosen to ignore his pleas, just as he had ignored most of his prayers over the past twenty years. God had not resurrected Richie's mom or prevented his dad from marrying Gina.

God had seen him through, though, by making sure he got to live with his grandparents. Nonna and Poppy had loved him unconditionally and had made sure he had grown into a decent human being. And God had given him Frankie. It had broken his father's and Gina's hearts that Frankie was autistic, but the kid had such a pure, guileless heart, Richie found that he never had to pretend with him. He could be entirely himself and know that he'd still be loved. Frankie worshipped him, and Richie loved him with all his heart, and that would never change, even if Richie got married and had children of his own. And he would take care of Frankie if anything ever happened to his parents. It wouldn't be a burden but his privilege.

Noah began to tremble, so Richie put his arm around him and held him until Remy finally returned with their coats and Noah's sneakers. Noah was catatonic, so Richie pushed his feet into the shoes and draped the jacket over his shoulders. Richie would have killed for dry sweatpants and another cup of coffee, but he could hardly focus on his own needs when his friend was dealing with the death of his wife.

"Remy, stay with Noah for a while," he said, and got to his feet.

"Where are you going?" Remy asked.

"I'm going to call the police again and make sure no one leaves."

"Why?" Remy asked, staring at him as if he'd just said he was going out for donuts.

"Because someone in this house knows what happened to Serena, and it's important the police get everyone's statement," Richie said, very quietly, but he shouldn't have bothered. Noah didn't appear to have heard him. His gaze was as dead as his wife's.

TWENTY-SIX
VINCE

Vince made a cup of coffee, then poured himself a bowl of Raisin Bran from a box he found in the kitchen and went to eat in the living room. He needed time to think, and the dining room reeked of alcohol and food that had been left to sit out overnight. It was gross, and he would have gladly started on the cleanup, but he worried that someone might question his motives and think he was trying to dispose of incriminating evidence.

He had gone to bed at the same time as everyone else, around two o'clock in the morning, and had a room to himself. He had been relieved not to have to share, but in light of the morning's events his solitude had suddenly become problematic. He was a Black man in a house full of white people—well, except for Angelina, whose dad was of mixed race—and he was a visitor in a town that was probably pretty colorless. He knew the statistics, and the cops, who were probably as snow white as the cocaine they had enjoyed last night, would surely focus on him as a person of interest. He'd complained to Angelina only yesterday that Serena was a world-class bitch and he'd be happy never to see her again. He'd almost blurted out that the only reason he'd come to the reunion was to see Angelina, but it hadn't seemed like the right time.

Vince never had understood why Noah had settled for Serena

after he'd had someone like Lexie. Serena had been stunning, he couldn't deny that, but it was a remote sort of beauty, the kind that reflected the coldness within her. She had cared about Noah, that was plain to see, but there was something off about her relationships with the others. Vince thought the only reason Lexie had befriended her was because they had been assigned to the same room their freshman year and Lexie tended to attract the walking wounded. Most of her friends came from broken homes and were emotionally fragile, or brittle, as was the case with Serena.

Back when they'd been dating, Angelina had mentioned that Serena had been sexually abused as a child. Vince thought it might have been by her uncle, but he wasn't sure and had never asked. It was none of his business, but Angelina liked to talk, and he was happy to listen and took it as a sign of acceptance. Vince had never told anyone in the group that his father had walked out when he was two and then his mom had died of ovarian cancer three years later, but Angelina might have, and Lexie had welcomed him into her club like he was a card-carrying member. But Lexie wasn't here now, and the only person he felt close to in this band of misfits was Angelina.

Would she tell the police what he'd said about Serena? People talked smack about each other all the time; it didn't mean they were going to murder them. And it had to be murder. Vince had seen the bruises around Serena's neck, and Richie had instantly assumed that the police would look for forensic evidence. Weed was legal now, but they could still be charged with possession, especially if the local police decided to accuse someone with intent to supply. And who would be the most likely suspect in this group? It didn't take long to come up with an answer.

Vince wished he could leave and pretend last night had never happened, but the police would probably order them all to remain until they could either make an arrest or, should they fail to find any evidence of wrongdoing, let them go. The cops would probably read volumes into Lexie's desertion in Thailand and then her sudden desire to reconnect, but, privately, Vince didn't think

Lexie's decision had anything to do with any sort of betrayal. He thought the about-face resulted from the pandemic. He saw it in his business all the time. People weren't planning for the future as much as they used to, and indulged in what the media liked to refer to as doomsday spending, their rationale being that they may as well enjoy their money while they were still alive.

Lexie hadn't had any money, as far as anyone knew, but she might have decided to give herself a break and put off adulting for a few years. She could defer her acceptance to law school, and what was the rush to get married? She'd been twenty-two when she and Noah became engaged. These days, that was the emotional equivalent of twelve. Privately, Vince thought people had no business getting married before thirty, when they finally had a sense of themselves and understood what they needed in a life partner.

His thoughts were interrupted by what sounded like a police siren in the distance, and he googled the population of the nearest town. Just over two thousand people, so it wasn't likely to have a large police department. They would have had to call it in to Kingston. Or Albany. Vince wished he could talk to Angelina, but she had gone up to her room with Mia. Remy and Noah were still by the lake, presumably waiting for the police to arrive, and Richie was on the dock, talking on his cell. The siren faded into the distance, and Vince let out a long breath, then took his dishes to the kitchen and put them in the sink. It was a beautiful day outside, so he stepped out onto the deck, desperate for a breath of fresh air. Squinting at the row of cars, he noted that no one had come or gone since he had gone up to bed last night.

What had happened to Lexie?

TWENTY-SEVEN

NOAH

Noah felt a sense of relief when Richie walked off. He appreciated the support, but he needed to examine his feelings honestly, and he couldn't do that with Richie watching him like a hawk. Thankfully, Remy also finally got cold and went inside, leaving Noah on his own.

Noah's first reaction to the news had been shock, followed by disbelief, and then fear. His first, crazy thought was that Serena had done this to punish him, but she wasn't the sort of person to do something this dramatic and not hang around to enjoy the aftermath. Serena's death was either the result of a tragic accident or something much darker, and that terrified him far more.

Noah had been miserable the night before, conscious of everyone watching and speculating on how he might react to seeing Lexie after all this time. He was relieved when she didn't show, but his outward calm had been the result of a dangerous combination of booze and drugs. By the time he stumbled up to bed he could barely stand, but he'd been worried he wouldn't be able to sleep, so he took Mia's sleeping pill. Noah had craved oblivion, not an argument with Serena, who was sure to lash out as soon as they were alone. He'd dropped a bomb on her when he said he wanted to hold off on the baby and hadn't given her a chance to respond. He was certain that, beneath her cool exterior, she was seething and ready to boil over the moment they were alone, which was why he made sure to come upstairs while she was talking to Remy. He'd needed a few minutes' head start.

Sleep had come like death: quick, dark, and deep. Noah couldn't recall getting drowsy or dreaming. And he couldn't remember feeling Serena's body next to his in bed. Had she even come to bed? She'd been wearing her coat when Angelina found her, so she must have gone outside after everyone had gone to bed. Why? Had she seen someone or heard something? Had she hoped for a confrontation with Lexie? Had she gotten it? Did anyone see or hear anything, and were they waiting to tell the police?

He looked over at her body. Serena looked white and still. Her eye make-up was smeared, and her hair was starting to frizz as it dried out. She hated her hair frizzy or too curly and always used a flat iron to make it straight, then curled it with a curling iron. Serena's make-up had always been perfect, even when they weren't going anywhere and were just hanging out at home. Now she'd never do her make-up again. Noah just couldn't believe she was gone. His brain refused to accept it, and he kept thinking she was going to open her eyes and rip into him for leaving her cold and wet on the bank.

Richie had said not to touch the body, but Noah couldn't help it. He needed to be sure, so he reached out and touched Serena's face. His hand recoiled when his fingers met cold, damp skin that somehow no longer felt human. Noah yanked it away, unable to bear the touch but also glad no one was there to see his revulsion. He grieved the loss of a life and felt apprehensive about the changes Serena's death would bring, but somewhere deep inside, a tiny seed of relief had taken root, and a bubble of hope had floated to the top.

After Lexie left, Noah had been crushed—broken. Lexie had been his first love, and he hadn't known how to put up walls to protect his heart. He'd been full-on, ready for anything as long as Lexie came with him. When Noah turned to his family and friends for support, everyone had said the same thing. You're better off. You're too young for such a serious commitment. Better you let her go now, before you've built a life together. Sow your wild oats, Noah. Play the field. There's plenty of fish in the sea.

But Noah hadn't wanted to sow his oats or catch other fish. He had wanted Lexie. He had needed her and had felt as if something vital had been stolen from him and would never be returned. Serena had been the only one who understood his grief. She had been there for him and had filled in the cracks Lexie left, the way a Japanese artist mends a broken plate and fills the fissures with gold, turning it from a useless piece of junk into a work of art. Serena had anticipated Noah's every feeling and every need, and, when she kissed him one night, he kissed her back—not because he loved her, but because he couldn't bear to hurt her, and because he was lonely and sad and could pretend she was Lexie if he shut his eyes. She hadn't smelled the same or kissed the same or felt like Lexie beneath Noah's hands, but she had made him feel like a man again and given him her love even though she knew he still loved her friend.

Noah had allowed himself to be seduced by the promise of security and unconditional love, but, even as he stood under a flower-bedecked canopy with Serena by his side and made his vows, a part of his heart had still longed for Lexie. And as the minister pronounced them man and wife, Noah had wondered if he'd just made a terrible mistake. As the months passed, his doubts had intensified. Serena was no longer as understanding or as giving. She wanted to control everything, and sometimes he felt as if he were being erased, his thoughts and feelings irrelevant to a woman who had clearly had a very precise plan all along and was willing to put in the work to get what she wanted. And the latest thing she wanted was a child.

And now Serena was dead, and Noah was suddenly free. He could sow his wild oats, play the field, and fish in the sea. The prospect didn't seem as daunting or painful. And perhaps he'd catch Lexie, and this time, she would remain on the hook.

TWENTY-EIGHT
ANGELINA

Angelina looked up when Richie walked into her and Mia's room. She was sitting on her bed, leaning against the wall for support. Mia had stayed with her for a while, then gone for a walk to clear her head. Angelina thought Mia just needed to be alone, and she was glad to be on her own as well. She needed time to process this in her own way.

Richie sank onto Mia's bed. He looked like he'd aged a decade since last night, and his eyes were filled with deep sadness.

"Are you all right?" he asked.

Angelina nodded. "What do we tell the police?"

"We stick to the truth," Richie said. "We tell them everything, *except* the part about the recreational drugs. I got rid of everything, and if they find traces on the deck they won't be able to prove it's from us. These houses are rented to new guests every week."

He was really worried, Angelina thought in a detached sort of way. Should she be worried as well? No one would care if a photographer or a hedge fund manager did a line of coke, but she was a nurse, and Mia was a teacher. For them, a drug charge could prove career-ending.

"Did you see or hear anything that might explain what happened?" Richie asked.

Angelina swallowed hard. She'd been going over it in her head, debating whether she should say something, but she knew she would. She couldn't keep this to herself any longer.

"I heard something last night," she blurted out. Richie's focus instantly sharpened, his dark gaze watchful and alert. "I woke up. I don't know what time it was, but I wasn't feeling well and wanted a drink of water. I heard someone arguing outside."

"Who was it?"

"It was a man and a woman. Mia was asleep, and Lexie never showed, so the woman had to be Serena. I think she must have been arguing with Noah."

"What makes you say that?" asked Remy, who'd just appeared in the doorway.

"Did you not notice the tension between them last night?" Angelina asked, looking from Remy to Richie.

Remy nodded. "Now that you mention it, yes. They barely looked at each other."

"Maybe they had a fight on the way up," Richie said. "They were probably both anxious about seeing Lexie."

"That's what I thought," Angelina admitted. "But when I saw Serena this morning... And Noah looked so..."

"So what?" Richie asked.

"Guilty," Angelina said. "Do I tell the police?"

"Did he look guilty to you?" Richie asked Remy.

Remy shrugged. "He looked stunned, but maybe he had no recollection of what happened. He was pretty out of it last night. We all were."

Richie turned back to Angelina. "Did you hear what was said?"

"No. I wasn't really listening. I drank some water and pulled the blanket over my head."

Richie sighed heavily. "Whenever a woman dies in suspicious circumstances, the police always look at the partner, because statistically they're the most likely suspect."

"Wait, what are you saying, that Noah murdered Serena?" Mia exclaimed. She'd just come up the stairs and slipped past Remy to get inside. She sat down, her shoulder brushing against Angelina's, but all her attention was on Richie.

Richie instantly backtracked. "I'm not accusing Noah. I was just saying."

"How did Serena actually die?" Mia asked.

"I'm not qualified to answer that. The coroner will order an autopsy," Richie said.

"Who would have reason to murder Serena?" Angelina asked.

No one replied.

"I think I heard a car last night," Remy said. "It was around two thirty."

"Did you hear it leave?" Richie asked.

"I fell asleep. Did you hear anything?"

"I slept like the dead," Richie said apologetically. "Didn't hear anything until Angelina started screaming this morning."

"Has anyone heard from Lexie?" Mia asked, looking around the group.

"I tried calling her last night, but it went straight to voicemail," Remy said.

Richie nodded. "I tried calling her too. Same."

"I texted her this morning, before I came down," Angelina said. "The text showed delivered, but she didn't reply."

"Let's try her again," Mia said. She pulled out her phone, selected Lexie's number, and put the call on speaker. The call went to voicemail. "Where is she?" Mia cried. "And what the hell is she playing at?"

"Her phone must be off," Richie said.

Angelina looked from one anxious face to another. "I didn't want to say anything before, but this whole thing feels really off. Lexie suddenly comes home without telling anyone, books this place without speaking to any of us first, and then doesn't show. It doesn't make any sense. And all this." Angelina gestured at their surroundings. "This had to cost a few grand. Where would Lexie get this kind of money from? And even if she did have money to burn, she was never one to show off. This is so unlike her."

"People change," Richie said. "None of us have seen Lexie in years."

"Look, all I'm saying is that we don't know what really happened between the three of them," Angelina said. "We know Lexie sent Noah a text and broke off their engagement, but we don't know why, or if Lexie and Serena got into a fight while they were away. Something happened on that trip."

"Has anyone ever considered that Lexie might have had a damn good reason for breaking things off with Noah?" Mia asked. "What would make you break off your engagement and walk away from your best friend like that?"

The question was directed at Richie, but it encompassed them all.

"If said best friend had slept with my fiancé," Richie promptly replied.

"And then married him," Remy added.

"Exactly," Mia said, her expression grim. "We all assumed Lexie broke Noah's heart, but what if it was the other way around and Serena was the other woman all along?"

"And once Lexie came back, the truth would come out," Remy said.

"But why would any of this matter now?" Angelina cried. "If Noah and Serena were hooking up, clearly they both knew about it. And if Lexie knew, she made her choice and walked away. What would be the point of bringing it all up now? And why would Serena and Noah agree to come if they knew they were walking into a confrontation?"

"Maybe Lexie wanted revenge on the two people who'd hurt her," Mia said.

"So she arrived under cover of darkness and murdered Serena?" Remy snapped.

"Things might have escalated," Mia said. She looked uncomfortable as she glanced around the room. "I thought I saw someone in the attic window last night."

"Are you suggesting Lexie was here all along?" Richie asked, his eyes widening in surprise.

"She could have been," Mia said. "No one checked the attic."

"There were no other cars here when I arrived," Remy pointed out.

"She could have parked somewhere else and walked. Or had someone drop her off," Mia replied. "Look, I love Lexie, and I'm not trying to frame her or anything, but we have to consider all the possibilities here, or one of us could be falsely accused of murder."

"Do you know what it takes to kill someone?" Richie asked. "It's not that easy, especially when the person is staring you in the face."

"Why? Have you tried it?" Remy asked, clearly going for humor and failing miserably.

"No, I haven't."

"I don't think Lexie is capable of that," Angelina said.

"But Noah is?" Mia asked.

"Statistically, how often do women strangle other women, Richie?" Angelina retorted.

"Not very often," Richie admitted. He turned to the window and looked toward the bank, where Noah sat perfectly still, his head in his hands, his shoulders slumped. "I think I need to advise Noah before the police get here."

"Advise him to do what?" Mia asked.

"Not to say anything dumb," Richie replied.

"If he 'no comments' the interview, the police will think he's guilty," Remy argued.

"Maybe he is," Richie said. "Who else among us would have reason to kill Serena?"

"What about Vince?" Remy asked.

"Vince?" Angelina exclaimed.

"Serena was always taking pot shots at him, putting him down. Maybe he'd had enough," Remy replied.

"No way," Angelina retorted.

Richie sighed. "Let's be honest. The only reason any of us

became friends with Serena was because of Lexie. And we stayed friends because of Noah. I would have never kept in touch with her if it hadn't been for him."

"Me neither," Angelina said. "Serena had this way of looking down at people, making them feel small."

"I never liked her," Mia said. "But that doesn't mean I wished her dead."

"She really wasn't that bad," Remy protested. "She could be a bit high and mighty, but she was just insecure. And you're the one who screwed her," he reminded Richie.

"Yeah. Once. And I regretted it. And so did she. She called me on Thursday and told me not to tell Noah."

"Why would you?" Angelina asked. "Not like it happened last week."

"I don't know. I guess she thought with Lexie here everyone would suddenly start confessing their sins."

"And that would make someone decide to commit murder?" Mia asked.

"Unless you're a hitman, you don't walk into a situation ready to kill," Richie said. "Hence the bruises on her neck. Strangulation is a crime of passion. It's up close and personal."

"Whoever went for Serena didn't come prepared," Remy reasoned. "They must have killed her in a moment of madness and panicked, so they threw the body in the lake, hoping we'd think it was an accident."

"The coroner wouldn't think it was an accident," Mia said.

"No," Richie agreed. "But even if it can be conclusively proven that Serena was murdered, there might not be any forensic evidence left on the body after several hours spent in the lake."

"Your DNA will be on the body," Mia said. "You pulled Serena to shore and then touched her repeatedly."

"Are you saying I killed her, then jumped into a freezing lake just so that I could explain away my DNA?" Richie demanded angrily.

"I'm just playing devil's advocate," Mia replied.

"Well, don't," Richie snapped. "Or I might have to kill you next."

They were all startled when an approaching siren pierced the quiet of the autumn afternoon. One by one, they returned downstairs and piled into the kitchen. Mia's gaze went to the dirty dishes, as if she were worried that the state of the house would reflect badly on them, and Remy looked twitchy as he silently stood next to Richie. Leaving them in the kitchen, Angelina went to see where Vince had gone. She found him in the living room, sitting on the couch with his head in his hands. He looked up, and she saw terror in his eyes. Angelina wished she could offer Vince the support he clearly needed but suddenly realized that at this point, she couldn't trust any of them. Not even Mia.

TWENTY-NINE

MIA

Mia hadn't said anything that morning, and she wasn't going to mention it now, but Serena had gone at her the night before. It had been just after eleven, when Mia came upstairs to get her jacket. Serena had been in her bedroom, the green jacket she was later found wearing hanging open as she stared at herself in the mirror. The hallway had been dark, so Serena hadn't seen Mia right away, but Mia had seen Serena clearly, and the look on her face stopped her in her tracks. It had been furtive and—maybe she was reading into it now that Serena was dead—fearful. Serena had placed her hands on her belly, then pulled the jacket back and turned sideways in front of the mirror. Maybe she had been concerned about gaining a few pounds, but Mia thought it had been more than that. Serena had seemed genuinely worried.

And it was that expression that brought back something Mia had completely forgotten. It had been a few months before graduation. End of February, and a Friday. Mia had gone to the Planned Parenthood in Hamden for her annual exam and to get a prescription for birth control pills. Serena hadn't had classes on Friday and had told them she was going home for the weekend on Thursday night, but then Mia saw her at Planned Parenthood as she was leaving. She had been white as a sheet and walking very slowly, as if she were in pain. Mia had been about to go up to her and ask if she was okay or needed a lift back to school, but then Serena's mom had pulled up. She had gotten out and helped Serena into the car, and, as Serena turned to buckle up, she had seen Mia. She had that same look then—secretive and fearful—and when Mia raised her hand and waved, Serena had turned away, and hadn't looked back as her mother drove off.

Mia never asked Serena about it. It was clearly private, but she had strongly suspected she had had an abortion. Serena hadn't been dating anyone, and as far as she knew hadn't hooked up with anyone for months. But if it had been some minor procedure, Serena wouldn't have felt the need to keep it secret and lie about going home on Thursday night. Clearly, she had called her mother and asked her to come with her, and then stayed at home until she was ready to come back to school on Monday.

And then, a few months later, Lexie had broken off her engagement and taken off for Australia. Had the baby been Noah's? Was that why Lexie never came back and Noah felt he had to marry Serena? Did he feel guilty or obligated? Or had Mia invented the whole thing because she needed to make sense of what had happened?

But why would Serena be worried about getting pregnant now? She was happily married, or so she told them at every opportunity, and Noah had always liked kids and said he wanted to be a dad. It didn't make sense, unless there was something else at play that Mia didn't know about.

Mia must have made a sound, because Serena had whirled around and gone off on her. "Are you spying on me?" she had exclaimed, her tone so accusing, anyone would think Mia had a history of stalking people.

"No, I—" Mia had begun, but Serena had cut her off.

"So why are you sneaking around? You startled me."

"Sorry, I didn't mean to. I just came up to get my coat," Mia had hurried to explain. "Are you pregnant?"

She knew she shouldn't have asked as soon as the words left

her mouth. Serena clearly wasn't in a sharing mood, and her eyes had flashed with anger.

"If you tell anybody, I swear, I'll make you regret it."

"You don't need to threaten me," Mia had said. "And there's really nothing you can do that would make me regret anything."

She shouldn't have said that either. It was the equivalent of waving a red flag in front of a bull. Serena's eyes had narrowed, and at that moment she had looked surprisingly ugly and older than her twenty-six years.

"Are you sure?" Serena had asked, her voice low and menacing. "I can think of a few things, your extracurricular activities for one."

"What are you talking about?" Mia had asked, playing dumb and hoping Serena was referring to something else.

She'd thought only one person in the house knew what she had been doing, but, given the gleeful derision in Serena's gaze and the nasty smile playing about her mouth, Mia now had to assume it was two.

"I know how you earn your money," Serena had said, watching her for any sign of weakness.

"And?" Mia had challenged her.

"Does your principal know you're on OnlyFans, or your coworkers, or the Teachers' Union? Imagine what the parents of your students would say if they found out their little darlings are being taught by a stripper."

Mia's heart had sunk. "I had no choice," she had choked out.

"There's always a choice, Mia," Serena had said. "And now I have a choice as well. Do I tell, or do I keep what I know to myself?"

"I won't say anything," Mia had pleaded.

"See that you don't," Serena had said, and swept past her without another word.

Mia was sure no one had overheard, since she hadn't seen anyone in the hallway or on the stairs when she had gone across to get her jacket, but she was suddenly very nervous. She had joined OnlyFans last year, and it had been an act of gut-wrenching desperation. She had been barely making ends meet, and there had been no one she could ask for help. Elementary school teachers didn't get paid all that much, and with her student loans, the skyrocketing cost of living since the pandemic, and the fact that she had no partner or roommate to share the burden, she had been drowning. If Mia hadn't found a way to make some extra money, she would probably have had to find a roommate and share her one-bedroom apartment and give up her car, which had been her path to freedom on the weekends.

Mia had thought long and hard. She wasn't the sort of person to make bargains with her conscience or do things she would be ashamed of for the rest of her life, but it had been either that or get a second job that paid not much more than minimum wage, which really wouldn't have helped her situation in any significant way. So, she had gotten an OnlyFans account. There were providers who posted sexually explicit content, but what she offered was tastefully presented eroticism. It was a form of entertainment that had been socially acceptable since burlesque clubs first opened their doors, and the shows they offered weren't just for horny men who wanted to get off in private, but for couples who took pleasure in visually alluring titillation. Knowing that she had female fans kept Mia going. It was them she imagined when she went through her routine, and it was their pleasure she thought of. It turned Mia on and brought out the side of her the viewers responded to.

And strange as it might sound, what Mia did made her feel safe. No one had any cause to associate the sexy siren they saw on their screens with unassuming, efficient Mia Olsen. And even though she bared a part of herself on screen, none of the individuals who watched her content could touch her. She was completely out of reach, unlike a woman who worked at a nightclub, or even a tutor, who had to deal not only with the child they were tutoring but most frustratingly with the parents, who wanted to pay as little as possible but still expected miracles from a child who was struggling.

It had taken weeks to come up with what Mia thought was an

acceptable routine, and then months to attract a few dozen subscribers, but then, once she had gained a little experience and felt more confident, her viewership had steadily increased. But only because of Remy. She had been reluctant to confide in anyone but, if any person knew what would sell, it was Remy. She had never shared the content with him, since she would be absolutely mortified if he watched the videos, but she might have unwittingly revealed her onscreen name. Remy had advised her to do a monthly pay-per-view special, in which she offered previously unseen, slightly more intimate content, intended only for her most devoted fans. It had worked. The viewers who had enjoyed a bit of a tease were now ready for more, and they were willing to pay.

Within a year of joining OnlyFans, Mia had been able to pay off her credit card debt, catch up on her student loan payments, and put some money in the bank, a little nest egg that made her feel less vulnerable at last. But her hard-won independence depended on her keeping her teaching job, which offered not only security and eventual tenure but also excellent health insurance, 401(k), pension, and good hours. Unlike her friends with corporate jobs, she got out at 3:00 p.m. and had multiple holidays, breaks, and summers off. Her life was finally on track, for the first time since the pandemic.

By the time Mia had returned downstairs to the others, she thought the incident with Serena had been resolved. But no sooner had she taken her seat than Serena launched into a story about a former client of the law practice where she worked—Amy, who had created an OnlyFans account after her divorce to supplement her income. Amy had been doing quite well until someone informed the principal of the parochial school where she taught what she was up to, and she was fired on the spot. Once Amy's ex-husband found out she was unemployed and learned the reason for her dismissal, he filed a motion to reassess the conditions of the divorce settlement. Amy lost custody of her kids, and the judge ruled that she was no longer eligible to receive alimony.

Mia's gaze had momentarily settled on Remy, who had been

listening intently, and she had been certain that he'd grasped precisely what Serena was up to. It wasn't difficult to make the connection when Serena's eyes had glittered with malice as she recounted Amy's troubles. She'd smiled slyly at Mia, as if to remind her that she now had the power to destroy her life. And she did. Posting risqué content on OnlyFans wasn't illegal, but Mia had no doubt she would lose everything she'd worked for since leaving home if her sideline came to the attention of her principal or the Parent Teacher Association. And she wasn't about to allow Serena to hold her hostage for the rest of her days. Mia hadn't had a chance to confront Serena after her nasty little performance out on the deck, but if the police found out that Serena had threatened her, they'd think Mia had a motive to kill her, so she had to ensure that the one person who knew the truth remained silent.

Because if the police got wind of her OnlyFans account, they'd also discover that Mia went by SexyLexie69.

THIRTY

RICHIE

"Let me do the talking," Richie said as a police cruiser pulled up, the vehicle blocking all the cars in the parking area. If the rest of them were going to make a break for it, they would have already done so, so the positioning seemed like an unnecessary act of police intimidation.

SHERIFF was stenciled on the side of the car, and Richie braced himself for a difficult meeting. These small-town cops usually had a chip on their shoulder when dealing with someone from the city, and felt they had something to prove—and maybe they did. How could they compete with the knowledge and experience of New York City police officers? These guys were used to dealing with feuding neighbors, parking violations, and the occasional car theft or break-in. Had they even had a murder here in the new century? If they had, it had probably been something straightforward that hadn't required too much investigating or manpower.

Two officers got out of the car. The driver was a woman of about forty with frizzy dark hair pulled into a bun and a make-up-free face. She was what Richie's nonna would call an apple, someone who carried all their weight in their torso and had disproportionately narrow hips and thin legs. The unflattering uniform didn't help, but there was something kind in the officer's face, and Richie thought she looked maternal and empathetic.

Her passenger, who was clearly the sheriff, was the full melon. Everything about him was round, from his buzzed head to a belly that strained against the buttons of his shirt. He had wide hips, short legs, and a combative stance that didn't bode well for the upcoming interview. He was sure to distrust young, up-and-coming urban dwellers.

"Good afternoon," Richie said politely as he stepped onto the deck and descended the steps. He held out his hand to the sheriff. "Richard Vaccaro, assistant DA, Manhattan District Attorney's Office."

Angelina and Mia followed him outside and stood near the steps. Remy and Vince hung back, remaining close to the sliding door.

"Sheriff Alan DeVries and Officer Nunes," the sheriff replied.

It was clear he didn't want to shake Richie's hand, but it would have been rude, not to mention antagonistic, to snub him, so he gave a brief and very aggressive shake, then yanked his hand away.

"DeVries?" Mia asked behind Richie.

"That's right. Have we met before, young lady?"

"No, it's just that we were talking about the story behind the name of the lake..." Mia's voice trailed off.

"My family has lived in these parts for centuries," the sheriff replied dismissively. "So, what happened here?" His gaze went to the lake, where Noah still sat cross-legged next to Serena's body.

Richie decided to give DeVries as little as possible and keep his suspicions to himself. For one, the sheriff would probably not welcome his insights, and for another, Richie was curious to see how much the man would deduce for himself.

"We came up last night for a long-overdue reunion," Richie said. "We had dinner, enjoyed a few drinks around the firepit, and went to bed. Angelina was the first one up this morning." Richie gestured to Angelina, who gave a shy wave. "She was going to go for a walk when she spotted something in the water. On closer inspection, she realized it was the body of our friend, Serena Paulson."

"Who's he?" DeVries asked, and jutted his chin toward Noah.

"Her husband, Noah. Noah Paulson," Richie amended.

DeVries turned to Officer Nunes. "Start taking down their contact details. I need to look at the body."

The sheriff's gaze was narrowed and hard as it swept over them, but Officer Nunes smiled sympathetically as she came up the steps. "Shall we go inside?" she asked politely, and gestured toward the sliding door.

Richie went first, and she followed him in, the others trooping in behind her. Officer Nunes wrinkled her nose in disgust when she saw the stacks of dirty dishes and must have got a whiff of the rotting food coming from the dining room. Despite the open window, the house stank of rancid meat, and the smell of alcohol lingered in the air.

"We were going to clean up, but then Richie told us not to touch anything," Angelina explained, and smiled ruefully.

Officer Nunes' gaze sharpened, and she shot Richie a questioning look. Angelina seemed to realize that she shouldn't have said anything, and looked at Richie apologetically.

"You don't think it was an accident," the policewoman said.

"I thought it prudent to leave things as they were," Richie replied. He wasn't about to spout that he thought Serena had been murdered and put any more attention on himself.

"Smells like coffee in here," Officer Nunes said as she walked into the kitchen.

"Would you like some?" Angelina asked, obviously glad to have something to do.

"I wouldn't mind. It's been a hell of a morning. And now this. Milk and two sugars, please."

Angelina made the coffee, while the rest of them crowded around the island, not sure what to do. Officer Nunes took a sip of coffee, sighed with contentment, then turned to the group. "If you wouldn't mind waiting in the other room. I'll speak to you one at a time."

"Do you want our statements?" Mia asked.

"Not yet. For now, just your name, address, cell number, and email. Once Sherriff DeVries comes back, we'll have a clearer idea of what's required. Ladies first?"

Mia remained in the kitchen, and Richie followed Vince, Remy, and Angelina to the living room, where they settled in to wait their turn. Richie couldn't sit still, so he walked over to the window and looked on as Sheriff DeVries squatted next to Serena. He couldn't think of Serena as a corpse, even though he'd referred to her as a body. That would surely come later, but for now, she was still a person, a woman he'd had some strong feelings about only yesterday. Had anyone noticed that he'd been snarky towards her? Would they mention it to the sheriff?

There were a few things Richie had noticed last night, like the fact that Mia wouldn't look at Serena after she'd come down with her jacket, or that Serena had barely looked in Noah's direction all night. And there was the moment when Serena had stepped out onto the deck, wearing that distinctive green jacket, and she'd looked really angry. Remy had asked if she'd like something to drink and she'd nearly bitten his head off. And then there was the way she'd treated Vince.

Vince hadn't risen to the bait, but Richie knew just how he must have felt. There had been a kid in high school who'd kept calling Richie names. Kevin had been smart enough to make sure no one else ever heard or he'd get suspended for bullying, but he'd say stuff under his breath so only Richie could hear. *Guido, goombah, Dante*, and he didn't mean the poet. He was referring to Dante from *The Sopranos*. Having learned his lesson about fighting, Richie had pretended not to hear, but he'd been raging on the inside, and if he could have got away with it he would have shown Kevin just what a *capo* would do to someone like him. Was Vince capable of violence? He was a likable guy, but everyone had a breaking point. Vince was currently trying to blend into his surroundings, but Richie knew from experience that he'd be the first person DeVries would look at, and he felt sympathy for the guy. Why had he even come?

It had to be because of Angelina, but Angelina wasn't interested in Vince. Of late she'd been sliding into Richie's DMs and texting him with increasing frequency. Then she'd asked him for a ride to the reunion, and had openly flirted with him all the way up. Angelina had cooled it once they'd arrived, but she'd been there for the taking, whenever and however he wanted. And even now she was watching him, gauging his every reaction. With her soulful brown eyes and long dark hair, Angelina was pretty, and he did prefer curvy girls, but he had no interest in dating her, and it wouldn't be right to hook up when he knew she wanted more. Angie was a friend, and Richie respected that and wouldn't cross the line. He should never have fucked Serena. He wondered if it was going to come out now that she was dead, or if DeVries would find out that Serena, who hadn't called him in years, had suddenly called him two days before she was murdered.

Richie watched as DeVries leaned over Serena. He couldn't bend too far, his belly was in the way, but since he wasn't very tall he probably got a good look anyway. His lips were moving, so he had to be speaking to Noah. After a few moments, Noah pushed to his feet and headed back toward the house. He looked like an old man and stared at the ground as he walked. He had to be chilled to the bone after sitting out there for so long, but getting warm would have to wait, especially since DeVries had pulled out his cellphone as soon as Noah had walked away and was talking into it urgently.

"What did he ask you?" Richie demanded as soon as Noah walked into the room. He kept his voice low so Nunes, who was speaking to Remy now, wouldn't hear him.

"He just asked what happened."

Noah was shivering, his skin had a gray cast, and his eyes looked glazed. Shock, Richie thought as he studied his friend's stony face. He'd seen it so many times, both at home and in the courtroom. Noah was still processing what had happened, and then the grief would come and level him like a steamroller.

"What did you tell him?" Richie asked.

"The truth."

"Did he ask any leading questions?" Richie tried again.

"Like what?" Noah was totally out of it, his eyes unfocused as he sank onto the couch and wrapped his arms around himself.

Vince grabbed a chenille throw from the love seat and tucked it around Noah, who muttered his thanks without looking at the other man.

"Like if you and Serena were happy, or if maybe you had a fight last night," Richie probed.

"No."

"Did he say anything about the cause of death?"

"No. He was pretty tight-lipped."

"Okay. Let's see where he takes it from here," Richie said.

"Where do you think he's going to take it?" Angelina asked.

"That all depends on how cocky he is."

"What do you mean?" Angelina pressed.

"I mean, if he thinks he knows it all, he'll jump to conclusions and then try to fit the facts into his theory."

"And if he doesn't?" Vince asked carefully.

"If he doesn't, then he will do things by the book."

"Suddenly, I'm not sure which is worse," Vince said under his breath.

"Unless you have legitimate reason to worry, you'll be fine," Richie replied.

Vince gave him a look that nearly made Richie cringe with shame at his arrogance. Vince had every reason to worry, and they both knew it.

"I got you, man," Richie said.

Vince nodded and looked away, probably embarrassed by his vulnerability and resentful of having to depend on Richie to defend his civil rights if it came to it.

DeVries came inside about ten minutes later. He looked grim

and asked everyone to gather in the living room, even though Nunes hadn't finished taking down their details. They all sat down, but DeVries remained standing, his back to the window. His nearly colorless gaze swept over each person in turn and paused on Vince just a beat longer than on anyone else. He wasn't hostile, but neither was he friendly or sympathetic.

"The coroner will arrive shortly to collect the body. I have requested a postmortem."

"Don't you need to ask Noah for permission?" Mia asked.

"Not in the case of suspicious death," DeVries replied. "I have also called for a crime scene investigation unit. They will get here when they get here since they'll be coming from Kingston, or more likely Albany. In the meantime, I will ask you all to remain inside. Officer Nunes and I will take your statements."

"Can we leave after you do that?" Remy asked.

"We will not keep you any longer than necessary," DeVries promised.

Richie had to admit that he was impressed by the man's demeanor. The sheriff was calm and professional without giving in to annoyance or unsubstantiated suspicion. That was a good sign that he would be thorough and unbiased, but things could go to hell very quickly if someone became belligerent or started to make unreasonable demands.

DeVries turned to Angelina. "Since you discovered the body, I'd like to start with you, if you don't mind."

"Of course," Angelina said, her gaze flitting toward Vince for just a second. His attention was fixed on DeVries, but there was no challenge in his eyes, only resignation.

Richie would do whatever he could to help his friends, but at this point he wasn't sticking his neck out for anyone. At least not yet. Unless someone had come onto the property last night, one of the people in this room had murdered Serena, and, until he figured out who it was, he was looking out for number one.

THIRTY-ONE

REMY

The questions seemed to go on forever, interrupted only by the arrival of the coroner. Sheriff DeVries went to speak to the man in person, and they stood over Serena's body for a few minutes before the coroner returned to his van. Everyone watched in solemn silence as the body was bagged and deposited on a folding gurney, which went into the back of the van. Remy blinked away tears, embarrassed to be seen crying, but he wasn't the only one. Everyone was sniffling and blowing their noses, except for Noah, who stared straight ahead, his gaze unseeing.

Remy stepped out onto the deck, turned a chair to face the lake, and sat down. The sun was warm on his shoulders, and the lake shimmered in the afternoon sun. Today would have been perfect, a day filled with laughter, silly banter, and the usual jokey snark. They might have gone into town or for a walk. There were probably some great antique shops in the area, and these little towns always had quaint diners and places that sold homemade ice cream. That night they might have ordered pizza and watched a movie, or sat outside and looked at the stars. Instead, they woke up to tragedy.

It had been a shock to learn Serena was dead, but this morning there was still room for them to hope that her death had been a tragic accident. Now that her body was on the way to the morgue and would undergo an autopsy, shit had just got real, especially since they had been told they couldn't leave. They hadn't been officially detained, but they were all suspects, and the thought was quite frankly terrifying. Who would point the finger at whom, and how far would someone go to divert suspicion from themselves?

How far would he have to go? Remy had been discreet, so much so that he'd kept his distance from Mia and Angelina these past few months. Guys were usually clueless when it came to the subtle undercurrents within the group, but girls could smell subterfuge a mile away and might have caught on that he was keeping something to himself. Remy never meant to get involved in Serena's plan, but she'd asked him to do her a favor, and he had agreed. He never imagined his well-intentioned help would backfire so spectacularly. And now, if the truth came out, he'd be implicated in Serena's murder, so all he could do was pray that she had deleted the incriminating file from her computer. He certainly had.

But the police would have no reason to look closely at him. It was always the husband, wasn't it? And who else would have reason to hurt Serena? Maybe that was why Noah was catatonic. He couldn't believe what he'd done and probably hoped this was just a bad dream and he'd wake up and find Serena in the kitchen, complaining that no one had bothered to buy almond milk or that the steak had been too rare.

When Officer Nunes came out to get him, Remy sighed heavily and stood up. It seemed it was his turn to make a statement, but how honest did he want to be? And how much of the truth had bearing on the case?

Just as Remy was about to step inside, the CSI team rolled up, the individuals who got out of the van looking like aliens in their white coveralls. They wordlessly separated, each going in a different direction, metal cases in hand. It seemed the real investigation into Serena's death had officially begun.

THIRTY-TWO
ANGELINA

Sheriff DeVries and Officer Nunes questioned everyone at length and jotted down contact information for Lexie, whose phone was still turned off. She hadn't replied to any emails or texts, and, from what Angelina could gather, the others were beginning to think that maybe Lexie really did have something to do with Serena's death, and this had all been some elaborate setup meant to get Serena to this isolated location.

A timeline of events, starting with their arrival at the Airbnb, had been established, but no one could be sure what had happened after they'd all gone to bed in the early hours of Saturday morning. The sheriff spent a long time with Noah, who seemed to be on autopilot. Through the closed door, Angelina heard him speaking in a quiet monotone that was punctuated by periods of raw emotion.

Mia's tip that she'd seen a face in the attic window sent the CSI techs to the attic, but all they found was a mannequin wearing a black dress, along with a dressmaker's dummy and several storage boxes filled with cuts of fabric and crafting supplies. The owner of the house clearly liked to sew and had turned the attic into a craft room, complete with a sewing machine, a long table covered with dress patterns, and tiny plastic drawers filled with buttons, sequins, zippers, and grommets.

The techs took everyone's fingerprints for the purposes of elimination, which was perhaps the most sobering moment of all. They were now on the police database, their names forever linked to a murder investigation. Richie explained that this was routine and wouldn't show up if a potential employer ran a background check, but no one seemed to feel particularly reassured, especially since they weren't allowed to leave and hadn't been given an estimate of when they might be able to return home. They were trapped in this house until further notice, and one of them could be taken into custody.

Desperate for something to occupy her once the techs were done with the first floor, Angelina cleaned the kitchen, loaded the dishwasher, and took out the trash. She then went to work on the dining room, which resulted in another bag of trash and a second load of dishes. It would have been nice if someone had offered to help, but the rest of them just huddled on the deck, talking quietly and coming up with endless theories about what must have happened. Even Vince kept his distance.

Angelina didn't care to speculate with them. She found it all extremely stressful and asked Sheriff DeVries if she might get her earbuds from her bedroom so she could listen to music while she cleaned. He had no objection. But once she'd finished, she felt isolated and alone inside the house and went outside to join her friends on the deck. They'd run out of theories by then and were just sitting around in near silence, their gazes fixed on anything but each other.

It was after six o'clock by the time the police and CSI techs finally left. Once the last of the daylight faded, a dense, choking darkness settled over the clearing. The moon and the stars were completely obscured by thick, low clouds, and the lake gleamed, slick as congealed blood, the black water surrounded by the hulking shapes of the trees that swallowed the neighboring houses in looming shadows. Despite the dropping temperature, no one wanted to go back inside. The house was silent and dark, except for the track lights Angelina had left on in the kitchen. The doors and windows were covered in black fingerprint powder, and the rooms had been searched for anything that might prove incriminating. An unpleasant smell lingered in areas where the techs had sprayed luminol, clearly searching for traces of blood, even though Serena did not appear to have bled.

No one felt like lighting the firepit, and eventually it got too cold to remain outside. Despite the stress of the day, or maybe because of it, everyone was starving, but no one wanted to cook or even look through the stuff in the fridge. They ordered pizza and ate from paper plates, and drank only non-alcoholic beverages, even though there was plenty of wine and beer left. Noah set his plate down on the coffee table after a few bites and headed upstairs. No one tried to stop him. He needed space, and, after a day of answering questions, he probably longed to be alone so he could examine his feelings and give vent to his grief.

Once Noah had gone, Remy put on *Naked and Afraid*, and they watched in silence, everyone pretending to be absorbed in the plight of the contestants. It was better than analyzing how emotionally exposed and terrified they all were, and how much they feared what tomorrow would bring. They were meant to be going home on Sunday afternoon, but now they would have to remain, effectively under house arrest until they were all released or one of them was arrested.

By ten o'clock, Angelina could no longer stand the tension. She was absolutely exhausted and wanted only to be alone, or as alone as she could be in a shared bedroom. She wished she could ask Richie for a hug. It wasn't a sexual thing. She just needed solace, and he was the only person whose comforting embrace could help her feel safe in this terrible new reality. But Richie hadn't offered, and Angelina wasn't about to make a fool of herself in front of everyone and beg for comfort. She said goodnight and trudged upstairs. Mia was right behind her, and Angelina locked the door as soon as they were safely inside.

"I want to go home," she moaned.

"Me too, Ange. This was hands down the worst day of my life, and I just want to be in my own space." *Alone* hung in the air between them.

"Are we safe?"

"I don't know, but the house is only booked through tomorrow, so they'll have to let us leave, won't they? They have our contact information and statements. What more can we do here?"

"I'm sure they'll let us go," Angelina said, but she realized she was trying to convince herself rather than Mia. "They can't hold us for days. Can they?"

"I hope they manage to contact Lexie and find out what's really going on," Mia said angrily. "I mean, what the hell, Ange? Where is she? Why isn't she answering her phone? Why did she organize this whole thing and then not even bother to show? It doesn't make any sense."

"I don't think she ever meant to come," Angelina said quietly.

"So, what was the point of this whole setup?"

"I have no idea, but it all feels so wrong." Angelina lowered her voice to a whisper. "Do you think Noah did it?"

"I don't know," Mia said on a sigh. "DeVries spoke to him for a long time. Is he even allowed to do that, without a lawyer present, I mean?"

"Richie would have objected if they were somehow violating Noah's rights. It was a voluntary interview."

"Noah refused to let Richie sit in," Mia said.

"That could be the best or the worst decision of his life," Angelina replied. She didn't know Richie had offered to represent Noah, but could an attorney who was also a suspect represent another suspect? Probably not. That had to be illegal. "Lawyering up before any accusations are made would make Noah look guilty," she speculated.

"But not lawyering up can cost him everything. If DeVries thinks Noah is guilty, he'll find a way to make the evidence fit."

"They only do that on TV. If the CSIs didn't find any physical evidence, they can't accuse Noah of murder."

"You think?" Mia asked, clearly not convinced. "DeVries is basically in charge. It's not like in the big city, where they have to answer to their superiors and the police commissioner."

"He must answer to someone," Angelina protested.

Mia sighed again. "I have no idea how any of this works, but he did call in the forensic unit, so I guess maybe he does."

"What about the rest of the group?" Angelina asked. "Do you think any of them might have had a motive?"

"Look, we've known these guys since freshman year—well, everyone except Vince—and have you ever known any of them to hurt a woman?"

"No, but that was before the #MeToo movement. Maybe they did and no one was brave enough to speak up."

"I don't believe it," Mia said with a stubborn shake of her head. "You can tell when someone is capable of violence. I've seen Richie lose his shit and punch a wall, and I've seen Remy get really pissed when that girl in our accounting class called him Pepé Le Pew. He was embarrassed and posted some nasty comments on her socials, but he never threatened her physically."

"And Vince?" Angelina asked carefully.

"I can't see Vince killing Serena because she said some stupid shit."

"There's stupid and there's racist. And Serena was definitely racist."

"Then why did you remain friends with her?" Mia asked.

"Because if I cut out every person who ever said something hurtful not realizing my grandmother was Black, I'd have no white friends left."

"Do I say hurtful things?" Mia asked, and Angelina could tell that she was really worried. "Am I racist?"

"No, you're not, and I love you," Angelina said. "And I love the rest of them, especially Richie."

"Yeah, we all know. Maybe one day you'll finally get to ride the Sicilian Stallion," she said with what was probably meant to be a teasing smile but looked more like a grimace of pain.

"Richie doesn't see me that way. I'm his pal Angie. The end."

"Vince does. He watches you with this lovesick look in his eyes. Do you think you could ever be with him again?"

"I can't think about that right now, not after everything that's happened. I'm too exhausted. Let's go to bed."

"I wish we had some CBD gummies, but Richie got rid of everything, even those. I swear, he was like The Cleaner, getting rid of all the evidence like a pro."

"He is a pro, Mia. If anyone knows how to avoid culpability, it's Richie. He literally has a degree in it."

"Did he have motive to hurt Serena?" Mia asked, her eyes searching Angelina's face for an answer.

"They hooked up in college. Maybe something happened between them since then."

"Something was definitely going on between them last night," Mia said, her gaze sliding to the door as if she were afraid someone would overhear.

"Like what?"

"I don't know, but Serena was seething when we sat down to dinner, and I think it was directed at Richie."

"He was fine on the drive up. His usual self. And I didn't see them argue."

"Serena called Richie a douche."

"I'm sure he's been called worse."

"Yeah," Mia agreed. "I didn't say anything to DeVries. I stuck with the facts."

"So did I," Angelina said. "I don't want to point the finger at anyone, especially when I don't know anything."

"Do you think we'll all still be friends after this?" Mia asked wistfully.

Angelina shrugged tiredly. "I think that depends on what happens tomorrow."

THIRTY-THREE
VINCE

Sunday
November 2

On Sunday, everyone got up early and gravitated toward the kitchen. As if by mutual agreement, they wore somber colors, and no one had bothered with their appearance. Angelina and Mia wore no make-up and their hair in messy buns, and the guys hadn't shaved or even bothered to brush their hair. Everyone looked tired and unkempt, and they peered around uncertainly, as if unsure if they should try to engage in conversation or maintain a respectful silence around Noah.

Although still visibly shaken, Angelina assumed the role of house mother and made pots of coffee and a stack of toast, and put out cheese, butter, yogurt, cereal, and fruit. Noah nursed a cup of black coffee, while the others helped themselves to the food. They ate in near silence, their faces swiveling toward the window every time they thought they heard a car.

Vince was surprised when Mia announced, "I'm leaving."

"Sheriff DeVries told us we couldn't." Angelina was clearly startled, the toast she was about to bite into suspended halfway to her mouth.

"He has no right to hold us prisoner. Does he, Richie?" Mia demanded.

"No, but it's probably best to wait. He'll be by this morning," Richie replied through a mouthful of yogurt.

"How can you be so sure?" Remy asked.

"He's on the level," Richie said. "I admit, I misjudged him."

Vince was reserving judgment. DeVries and Nunes had seemed all right and had treated him no differently than the others, but he was still a prisoner in this house, with these people.

"He'll let us go today," Richie said.

"How do you know?" Mia asked.

"Serena was murdered outside, so I doubt the techs were able to find anything useful in the house," Richie replied. "Unless the pathologist can isolate her assailant's DNA in the course of the autopsy, DeVries will have no cause to hold us."

"And if they are able to identify someone else's DNA?" Vince asked.

"Then they will take samples from us and arrest whoever is a match."

Everyone looked suitably spooked at the prospect of having their DNA tested.

"Can they do that?" Angelina asked. "I thought they could only take a DNA sample if someone is under arrest."

"They can ask for a voluntary sample," Richie said. "If someone refuses, they can arrest them if they feel there's sufficient cause."

"I just want to go home," Angelina said miserably.

"Can I give you a ride home?" Vince asked. It was out of his way, but he really didn't mind making a detour, not if it gave him an opportunity to spend time alone with Angelina and offer what he hoped was comfort.

"She came with me," Richie reminded him, and Vince sensed a challenge.

"I didn't realize you two were a thing," he replied deferentially. "If I misread the situation, then I apologize."

That shut Richie up pretty quickly, and Angelina looked away in embarrassment. She'd probably hoped that Richie would stake his claim, but, even if he had considered getting together with Angelina, he wasn't about to make a public announcement. That would make him feel obligated, and Richie wasn't up for that.

"Aren't you going back to Stamford, Vince?" Angelina asked, clearly still looking for an excuse to go back with Richie.

"Yeah, but I don't mind going out of my way. I had nothing planned for the rest of the day." Vince realized he was beginning to sound desperate, but couldn't seem to help himself.

"By the time they let us go, there might not be a rest of the day," Mia said sulkily.

"Look, just sit tight, all right?" Richie said. "I'm sure they're doing their best."

"What can they possibly know?" Mia asked. She was starting to sound hysterical, and Noah turned to stare at her, his gaze clearing for just a moment before it slid to the lake, which was visible through the window.

"Probably more than you imagine," Richie said as he reached for a strawberry.

"How?" Mia demanded.

"The science is so advanced, they can sometimes crack a case using evidence derived from one skin cell or a partial fingerprint," Richie said.

"Does anyone want more coffee?" Angelina asked. Her eyes seemed to ask, *Must we keep talking about this?*

She jumped up and grabbed the box of K-Cups, which was quickly emptying. Angelina needed to keep busy to feel less anxious, so Vince said, "I'll take a cup, if you're offering. Is there any more toast?"

"I'll make some. Do you want scrambled eggs?" Angelina asked.

"No, thank you. Just toast."

That was all he could eat when he was nervous. The bread soaked up the bile that flooded his gut before it could travel upward, burning its way up the esophagus. He probably shouldn't have more coffee since it might upset his stomach and make him more jittery, but, if it helped Angelina to feel better, then he'd take it and say thank you. But as he accepted a refill, he wondered just how deeply DeVries was going to dig into their pasts.

"Would you like to take a walk after breakfast?" Vince asked Angelina once she'd handed him a piece of toast and sat down.

"Vinnie, my boy, this really is not the time to be making a move," Remy chided, his mocking tone making Vince want to punch him in the throat. He was so smug and sure of himself, even now, when they were in uncharted waters and needed all the support they could get. Vince felt heat rising in his face, but he wasn't going to back down from an argument. He had nothing to lose since he'd probably never see Angelina again after this.

"I don't recall asking you for advice, Remy, *my boy*. Maybe you should focus on your own life."

Richie sniggered into his coffee, and Angelina looked at Vince with something akin to respect. That made it all worth it.

Remy held up his hands in a gesture of surrender. "Just saying, man."

"Well, don't," Vince replied, pressing his advantage.

"Sure. I'd love to, Vince," Angelina said, shooting him a look of gratitude. "I could really use some air."

Vince and Angelina finished their breakfast, stacked the dishes in the sink, and grabbed their coats. It was cold outside and windier than yesterday. The falling leaves danced on the breeze and settled gently on the surface of Witch Lake, making it look like a speckled tablecloth. The air was fresh and crisp, and smelled slightly of woodsmoke. Maybe there was someone close by, even if they couldn't see signs of life. Vince glanced at the houses around the lake but saw no plumes of smoke rising from their chimneys. They looked as uninhabited as they had when he and the other guests had first arrived.

"Thanks," Angelina said as they walked along the shore. "I really needed to get out of there."

"Me too. This has been brutal."

"Do you mind if we don't talk about it?" Angelina asked.

"Sure. What would you like to talk about?"

"I don't know," Angelina said, and began to cry, her shoulders quaking with the force of her emotions. She turned her tear-streaked face up to Vince, and he saw naked terror in her eyes. "I'm really scared, Vince."

"Do you think you're in danger?" Vince asked.

"I think we all are."

Vince hadn't thought so until that moment. All he'd worried about was being wrongly suspected of being involved in Serena's death, but now that Angelina had said it he realized she could be right. One of the people they were sequestered with was a killer. Who knew how they would react if they felt cornered?

THIRTY-FOUR

RICHIE

After several hours of aimlessly drifting from room to room and trying to find something to occupy them, everyone's nerves were on edge, and by noon they came together in the kitchen once more. The girls were talking quietly, and Vince and Remy were on their phones. Noah stared out the window but must have heard the car approaching before anyone else did—he sat up straighter, looking terrified. His eyes found Richie's and silently pleaded for support.

"They're probably just coming to tell us we can leave," Angelina said with feigned optimism.

"They could have called," Remy said sourly.

"Maybe they have something to tell us," Angelina countered.

Sheriff DeVries and Officer Nunes entered the kitchen via the patio door. They looked grim, and Richie noticed that Nunes' hand hovered near her gun. Was she expecting an outburst of violence?

"Good morning, officers," Richie said as pleasantly as he could. "Any news?"

"Good morning, and yes, there's news," Sheriff DeVries replied, equally cordial. "But I'm not at liberty to share our findings at this time." He turned to Noah, and his expression turned considerably less friendly.

"Mr. Paulson, you're hereby under arrest for the murder of

your wife, Serena Paulson. You have the right to remain silent. Any statement you make may be used for or against you in a court of law. You have the right to an attorney. If you cannot afford a lawyer, a public defender will be assigned to you. Do you understand these rights?"

"What?" Noah asked, his mouth falling open and his gaze swinging wildly between Nunes and DeVries. He looked utterly shell-shocked.

"You're under arrest," DeVries repeated. "Do you understand?"

"I didn't kill Serena," Noah cried.

"You will have an opportunity to state your case," DeVries responded calmly. "Now, hold out your hands."

Noah balked. "You don't need to cuff me, I'll come quietly," he said.

"Hold out your hands, Mr. Paulson."

Noah held out his hands to DeVries but turned to face Richie, his gaze pleading. Richie had about five seconds to decide if he was willing to represent Noah or if he should step aside. There were ethical concerns but also private doubts. He couldn't think of anyone else who would have reason to murder Serena. Noah was the only one who had something to gain by her death. Both her trust fund, which had been left to her by her wealthy grandparents, and his freedom—unless he was found guilty and sent to prison. Even with good behavior, it would be years until he was eligible for parole.

"Richie," Remy appealed to him quietly.

That jolted Richie out of his thoughts. Of course he had to help Noah. Noah was his friend, and he was innocent until proven guilty. Representing Noah wouldn't tarnish Richie's reputation even if he lost the case. He would give it his best if it came to a trial, but for now he had to question every statement and do his utmost to invalidate whatever evidence the police had against Noah. Unless they had irrefutable proof, in which case maybe he could help Noah work out a plea agreement.

"I'll meet you at the station," Richie told DeVries. "I am Noah Paulson's legal counsel."

"Is that acceptable to you, Mr. Paulson?" DeVries asked. Clearly it was a formality, but procedure had to be followed.

"Yes."

The word was more an exhalation than an actual sound, but it was enough. Noah looked like he could breathe again and allowed Sheriff DeVries to walk him out the door and toward the cruiser. DeVries put his hand on Noah's crown and pushed him downward so he wouldn't hit his head while entering the car. Richie had seen that done so many times but never to anyone he actually knew. It was surreal to see Noah cuffed and in the back seat of a police car, his head bowed in either resignation or shame. He grabbed his jacket, phone, and keys, and strode toward his Jeep. The others spilled out onto the deck, watching silently as he backed out and followed the police car down the track.

As Richie drove, pretty houses with neat front lawns all decorated for Halloween slid past his windows. Life-size skeletons, witches, and carved pumpkins looked harmless in the bright light of day, the toothy smiles of jack-o'-lanterns playful and the skeletons and gravestones dotting manicured lawns nothing but cheap plastic ornaments.

Had Noah killed Serena in a fit of anger? DeVries had to have some pretty solid evidence to have arrested Noah. No one wanted to be accused of prejudice against the suspect or find themselves the target of a social media hate campaign that could result in a public lynching. Did Nunes wear a body cam, and was there a dashcam on the cruiser? Was any of what DeVries was doing properly documented should it come to trial?

As he drove down the main street that looked like a Norman Rockwell painting depicting small-town American life, Richie wished he'd resisted the impulse to do the noble thing and allowed DeVries to call in a public defender. He felt in his bones that he'd just made a terrible mistake.

THIRTY-FIVE

RICHIE

The police station was a squat, utilitarian red brick building that had parking on three sides and a narrow lawn on the other end with a round green metal table surrounded by a curving bench. When he parked and walked in, Richie was greeted by an excited-looking and very young officer, who asked for his ID, then waved him right through since he was expected. Richie could see the entire office through the glass that comprised the top half of the dividing wall.

There were several desks, the computer screens displaying the police logo as a screensaver. A short counter built into the side wall was equipped with a coffee maker, nondairy creamers and sugar in plastic containers, and a plate of bagels with cream cheese and muffins that looked like they'd been sitting out since early that morning. What Richie didn't see was other officers, and he thought the station probably employed fewer than a dozen people, and that by the looks of it most cops were out on patrol.

The duty officer directed Richie to an interview room just off the main hallway. The windowless space was painted slate blue and furnished with a table and four chairs. There was recording equipment, a security camera mounted near the ceiling and pointed toward the table, and a trash can near the door. DeVries and Noah were already inside. Noah's hands were no longer cuffed, but his gaze was just as haunted as it had been when DeVries had taken him into custody.

DeVries sat across from Noah, his belly pressing against the table and a look of deep satisfaction on his face. This was probably the most exciting thing to happen to him in years, and if he managed to solve a murder in two days he would be forever hailed as a local hero. Officer Nunes was coming down the hall, the door to the ladies' room swinging shut behind her.

"I'd like a word with my client," Richie said from where he'd stopped in the doorway. "In private. And not in here."

He didn't want to confer with Noah in a room full of recording equipment. DeVries had no right to record their conversation, and if something was caught on tape it wouldn't be admissible in court, but it might point DeVries in the right direction when questioning Noah, or lead to a second search of the property.

"Of course," DeVries said, and pushed heavily to his feet. He approached the door and pointed to a room just down the hall. "You can talk in there."

"Noah, come on," Richie said when Noah failed to move.

Noah stood slowly and shuffled across the room as if his ankles were shackled and he was afraid to rattle the heavy chains. They entered the room, and Richie shut the door behind them. There was a small white table and two white plastic chairs. He didn't see any cameras.

"Sit," Richie ordered.

"Richie, I didn't do it—" Noah began, but Richie cut across him.

"I didn't ask you if you did. Now, listen to me. We don't have much time."

"They must have evidence if they arrested me," Noah said. His hands were trembling on the table, and Richie wished he'd pull himself together. Appearances mattered, and Noah looked terrified. Innocent people had nothing to fear, other than a miscarriage of justice, which Richie intended to prevent. But Noah needed to do his part.

"I doubt they have anything concrete," Richie said as he sat down across from Noah. "This is a fishing expedition, so don't get caught. Tell them how devastated you are and how much you loved Serena. She was the perfect wife. If they ask leading questions, don't answer."

"What sort of leading questions?"

"They will try to imply that you had a difficult marriage. You fought all the time, or you didn't trust each other. They need to build a foundation."

"The marriage was fine. We were good," Noah said defensively.

"Then act like it. I need you to walk in there and look like an innocent man. All couples fight. People have moments of jealousy, insecurity, and doubt. It's normal, and human. Unless they have rock-solid evidence that points to you killing Serena, they can't hold you. Now, are you ready?"

"I guess."

"That's not good enough."

"Yes. I'm ready," Noah replied in a stronger voice.

"Let's do it, then."

They walked back to the interview room, where DeVries had resumed his seat and was now speaking to an attractive Asian woman who sat beside him. She had jet-black hair cut in a blunt bob and very dark eyes that were expertly lined. The woman wore a navy blue pantsuit with a lavender silk blouse and mulberry-colored lipstick that offset her olive skin perfectly and matched her nails. But it wasn't her fashion sense that stopped Richie in his tracks. It was the badge that was attached to the waistband of her pants and clearly visible from the doorway.

"You called in the Feds?" Richie asked, and knew he sounded like a little kid whose mother had tattled on him to his father, and he was about to get grounded for the rest of his life.

"I had no choice, Mr. Vaccaro. This case is not as straightforward as it first appeared."

"How so?" Richie asked as he took a seat.

He didn't think the case was straightforward at all, but DeVries had to have discovered something that had far-reaching implications if he thought the situation warranted the involvement of the FBI. Noah, whose mouth had gone slack with shock, did not have the look of an innocent man, and his hunched shoulders and panicked gaze were not helping his case. DeVries did not answer Richie's question. He turned on the recording device and Officer Nunes shut the door to the interview room as she left.

"Sunday, November second, 2025, 1:13 p.m. In the room are Sheriff Alan DeVries, Agent Asha Singh, Noah Paulson, and his legal representative, Richard Vaccaro. In the case of the murder of Serena Paulson on November first of the same year. Agent Singh, if you would start us off," DeVries said.

Agent Singh studied Noah for a moment as if she were trying to determine if he was capable of murder, then began. Her voice was low and melodious, but underneath the velvety tone was cold, hard steel. In this room, she was the one to watch out for, Richie decided as he turned his attention to the Fed.

"According to the postmortem, Serena Paulson died in the early hours on Saturday. She was strangled, then either fell or was pushed from the dock. The water in her lungs indicates that Serena was still alive when she went in the lake."

"How do you know she didn't jump off the dock?" Richie asked.

"Serena was struck on the back of her head. We found skin cells and traces of blood that match her DNA on the stern of the rowboat, suggesting that she went into the water backward. The official cause of death is drowning." Agent Singh fixed Noah with her dark gaze. "The victim was in good physical health at the time of death, and approximately seven weeks pregnant."

"What?" Noah cried, nearly exploding out of his chair in his agitation. Richie clapped a hand on Noah's shoulder and gently pushed him back down.

"You weren't aware your wife was pregnant, Mr. Paulson?" Agent Singh asked. She looked sympathetic, but Richie thought it was a cleverly set trap. Why wouldn't a woman tell her husband she was pregnant unless she feared his reaction?

"No. I didn't." Noah's voice quavered with emotion, or maybe terror. He clearly understood the implications and tried to preempt the agent's next question. "I'm sure she was planning to surprise me with a romantic announcement. Serena loved those pregnancy reveal reels on Instagram."

"Yes, those are very sweet," Agent Singh agreed. "Did she often post reels?"

"She did sometimes," Noah replied.

Richie was sure DeVries and Singh had already checked out Serena's social media accounts and knew precisely what sort of content she'd posted and liked.

Agent Singh opened a file that was way too thick for a murder that had happened only yesterday. She took out an evidence bag that contained an iPhone in a sparkly rose gold case.

"Do you recognize this phone, Mr. Paulson?"

"Yes. It's Serena's," Noah said. And it was. Richie had seen her use it.

"The phone was inside Serena's pocket. The pocket was zipped, and the coat was waterproof, so luckily it wasn't damaged. Serena had set your anniversary as her password, so it didn't take long for our techs to access the information."

"Is there anything on the phone that points to who killed her?" Noah asked eagerly. He seemed to be holding his breath, but Richie knew it wouldn't be that simple, or Noah wouldn't have been arrested and taken into custody.

"The last text she received was from Lexie Hall, sent at 2:17 a.m. Lexie asked Serena to meet her outside, on the dock."

"Lexie? So, then she must have killed her," Noah exclaimed.

"Remy thought he'd heard a car. Why haven't you picked her up? Is she here?" he asked, his head snapping toward the door.

"She is not here," Sheriff DeVries said. He looked at Noah with something akin to pity.

Agent Singh gave Noah a look that seemed to say *all in good time*, then took a sip of water and continued. "Serena had several social media apps on her phone, and she maintained an active presence on all of them. There were accounts in her own name but also a profile under the name Lexie Hall on each platform."

Noah stared at her, looking dumbfounded. "Lexie Hall? Why would Serena have profiles in Lexie's name? Did Lexie find out? Was that what the confrontation was about?"

"No, Mr. Paulson, Lexie did not know, and she and Serena did not engage in a confrontation on the night Serena was killed."

"How can you be sure? And how could Lexie not realize Serena was impersonating her?" Noah asked. "Or did she figure it out, was that why she set up a new email address?"

Richie had thought the email address was meant to be playful, a nod to their college days, but now that he knew Serena had been posting in Lexie's name he experienced that sinking feeling a person got just before the shit hit the fan and they were directly in the way. And he was sure he and Noah were about to get pelted.

"Lexie Hall is dead, Mr. Paulson," Agent Singh said.

THIRTY-SIX
RICHIE

A dense silence settled like a wet blanket over the four people present. Noah was visibly shocked and seemed even more broken, if such a thing were possible. Richie had also been blindsided. The two officers watched them intently, their gazes eager as they witnessed Noah's and Richie's reactions to the news.

"Lexie is dead?" Noah choked out at last. "Are you sure?"

"When did she die?" Richie asked, hoping against hope to somehow preempt the shitstorm that was about to engulf them.

"I'm glad you asked, Mr. Vaccaro," Agent Singh replied, but her attention was firmly fixed on Noah. "Lexie Hall died on July 17, 2022."

"Where?" Noah whispered.

"Phuket, Thailand."

"Cause of death?" Richie inquired.

"Undetermined."

"And Serena has been posting under Lexie's name all this time?" Richie asked. His throat had gone dry, and he fervently wished he hadn't agreed to represent Noah, who now had a very good motive to want his wife dead.

"Serena first started posting as Lexie once her body was identified, several days after it was discovered."

"They didn't know it was Lexie?" Noah cried, and Richie thought he still held out hope that a mistake had been made and the victim was someone else.

"Not right away. Lexie Hall's remains were found on Karon beach. There was no ID, and her phone and passport were never recovered. It took several days to identify the body."

"Are you sure it's her?" Noah exclaimed.

"Yes. The authorities were able to obtain her photograph from passport control in Bangkok once they had a name," Agent Singh said.

Richie had no doubt that the person discovered on that beach had been Lexie, but what he really wanted to know was how Lexie's death in Phuket related to Serena's murder in upstate New York.

"Are you suggesting that Serena intentionally removed Lexie's passport and phone?" Richie asked carefully.

"That is what we believe to have happened," Agent Singh replied. "Lexie was likely logged into the social media apps on her phone, so Serena changed the passwords on the accounts, then ditched the phone once she was able to log in from her own device. She probably disposed of the passport since, as far as we can tell, no one ever attempted to use it."

Noah looked like he was going to be sick, which actually worked in Richie's favor since at least he wasn't shouting or denying the allegations. He had the appearance of a man who wanted to die, which could look like guilt or extreme shock. Richie would be playing for shock and plausible deniability.

"So did Serena plan the reunion and send out the invitations?" Richie asked. He felt a bit sick himself. It was like he was trapped in a horror movie. *Turistas* came to mind, and he pushed the horrible images away, desperate to understand what exactly he was dealing with. Surely Serena would have mentioned if Lexie had been robbed and then murdered by a gang of organ traffickers, her body left on a beach once it no longer had any value.

"If she did, she didn't use any of her own accounts or her phone," Agent Singh said.

"Did you check with the owners of the Airbnb? Who made the reservation and the payment?" Richie asked.

"Lexie Hall. The reservation was made online using a credit card that belongs to Lexie and which was successfully charged. The same credit card was used to order the groceries."

"So, who was posing as Lexie?" Richie asked. "If Serena was contacted by Lexie and subsequently murdered, presumably it wasn't her."

"It may have been, to foster the illusion that Lexie was still alive, but the most obvious answer is that it was your client, Mr. Vaccaro."

"I had no idea Lexie was dead," Noah cried, and his pain was so raw, Richie felt tears sting the backs of his eyes. He blinked them away. The last thing anyone needed was a sniveling attorney.

"But what if you did?" Agent Singh suggested. "How would you feel if you were to find out that it was Serena who'd sent the text that ended your engagement to Lexie? And what would you do if you had discovered that Serena had been impersonating Lexie all this time, making you all believe that she was alive and well when in actuality she's been dead for three years, buried in a Thai cemetery no one will ever visit?"

"Agent Singh," Richie cut in. "Was Lexie's death the result of an accident?"

Agent Singh seemed poised to strike the final blow. Damn, the woman was good. "Authorities in Phuket ruled the cause of death undetermined, since they couldn't find any evidence to support an alternative conclusion, but knowing what we now know I would venture to guess that there's more to the story."

"What happened when Lexie died?" Noah asked. His voice was hoarse, and he looked like he was about five seconds from a complete nervous breakdown.

Agent Singh did not need to consult the folder. She must have memorized the details before she'd walked into the interview room, and determined that Noah was the most likely suspect and that there was sufficient cause to arrest him.

"Lexie's body was discovered at 12:22 p.m. on July 17, 2022. She was lying on her beach towel, wearing a bathing suit, sunglasses, and a sun hat that was pulled over her face, the same items seen in the photograph that was sent to all of you along with the invitation. It was when the couple who had been sunbathing next to her realized that she hadn't moved in several hours that someone finally checked if she was all right. She had been dead for approximately twelve hours. The police didn't find anything besides a tube of sunscreen and a silk sarong in the deceased's beach bag. It was only a tip from two Australian tourists, who had heard about the unidentified body and had thought it fit the description of a girl they'd met and had partied with several times during their time in Phuket, that led the police to the hostel where Lexie and Serena had been staying. When questioned, the manager said that Lexie and Serena had checked out on the morning of July 17 and were due to fly home later that day. He eventually admitted that it was Serena who had checked them both out. He had not seen Lexie but had assumed that she had gone outside to flag down a taxi that would take them to the airport. Serena had boarded the flight to New York. Lexie had not," Agent Singh concluded triumphantly.

"Is it your assertion that Serena murdered her best friend, then covered her tracks and returned home?" Richie asked. He was still processing everything he had heard and trying desperately to come up with an explanation that made sense, but there wasn't one. The truth was staring him in the face.

"A police pathologist carried out the autopsy on the body, but his findings were inconclusive. There were traces of ketamine in Lexie's blood, seawater in her lungs, and signs of pulmonary edema. She also had bruises on her shoulders that were consistent with carrying a heavy rucksack but could have been the result of someone holding her underwater. Ketamine is widely used as a date rape drug, but there was no evidence of sexual assault," Agent Singh stated.

"The pathologist thought Lexie might have died from secondary drowning, which can occur hours after water enters the lungs. Since there was no one who could verify if Lexie had experienced bouts of coughing, chest pains, lethargy, or difficulty breathing in the hours before her death, it was impossible to say for sure."

"So, it could have been an accident," Noah exclaimed. He seemed relieved, but Agent Singh quickly burst his fragile bubble of hope.

"It's true that Lexie might have drowned accidentally, but whatever happened afterward was very much planned and carefully executed. Even if someone had stolen Lexie's wallet, passport, and phone, how do you explain Serena checking them both out of the hostel, getting on a flight home by herself, and not telling anyone about Lexie's passing once she returned?"

"Maybe she didn't know," Noah cried. "They might have had a fight and gone their separate ways, and Serena thought Lexie would find her own way home when she was ready."

Agent Singh shook her head, her lip curling in obvious disbelief, but it was Sheriff DeVries who finally spoke. "Why would Serena remove Lexie's belongings from the room, check her out, hijack Lexie's social media accounts, and continue to perpetuate the lie that Lexie was alive? Serena's actions prove that she was either somehow involved in Lexie's death or used it to her own advantage."

"Why was no one notified of Lexie's passing?" Richie asked.

"The local authorities notified the American embassy in Bangkok, but since they had no proof that Lexie's death was anything other than an accident they simply informed them that she had passed. Lexie had no designated next of kin, and she had aged out of the foster care system, so the staff did not know whom to notify," Agent Singh explained. "Someone should have contacted Serena, since Lexie had been traveling with her, but even if they had, Serena wouldn't have told anyone. And the embassy saw no reason to pursue the matter further, probably because they had other, more pressing matters to deal with."

It amazed Richie that Agent Singh had found all this out in a matter of hours, but he supposed that, once Sheriff DeVries had pronounced Serena's death suspicious and alerted his higher-ups, the wheels had begun to turn. If the authorities had started to look into Lexie's whereabouts on the night of the murder, their inquiries would have led them directly to Thailand and the American embassy in Bangkok.

"What do you mean when you say that Serena used Lexie's death to her advantage?" Richie asked. He had a fairly good idea already, but he had to cast doubt on the motive Agent Singh had introduced.

"You were in love with Lexie Hall," Agent Singh said, addressing Noah. "You were engaged and planning a life together. Serena made you believe that Lexie had callously broken up with you via text and had gone on to date other men. Serena worked slowly and methodically to discredit Lexie and replace her in your affections. Even if you had moved on and were now devoted to your wife, to suddenly find out that Serena had done all that to destroy your happiness would make a compelling reason for murder."

Noah let out a strangled noise that could be interpreted as an admission of guilt but managed to regroup.

"You're right, it would be, but I didn't do it," he said. He was beginning to look angry now, the shock finally wearing off. "I had no idea Lexie was dead until today, and even if I had, how would I orchestrate all this? I didn't have Lexie's phone or her credit cards. And you can be sure I was not the person hiding behind SexyLexie69. You will find no trace of my involvement, Agent Singh."

"We only have your word that you were unaware of your wife's online activities, Mr. Paulson," Sheriff DeVries chimed in. "You could have found the posts on Serena's phone. She was surprisingly careless and didn't even bother to come up with a complicated passcode."

"We weren't like that. We didn't check each other's phones."

"Are you completely sure she never checked yours and hadn't perhaps discovered something you didn't want her to see?" DeVries asked.

"At this point, I'm not sure of anything," Noah stated, and his gaze shifted away from the sheriff and toward his folded hands on the table.

"Do you have an Instagram account?" Agent Singh asked.

"Yes."

"In your own name?"

Noah hesitated. "No," he admitted at last. "But it's not against the law to create a fake Instagram account. I never did anything but look." Noah's gaze was infinitely sad. "I missed Lexie. Is that a crime? I wanted to see what she was up to, but I couldn't admit that to Serena. She would have been hurt."

"And now she's dead. Murdered," DeVries reminded Noah cruelly.

"Agent Singh," Richie interrupted, addressing the higher-ranking officer in the room and firing off all his questions at once before he could be interrupted. "Do you have any physical evidence that connects my client to the murder? Can you show that he organized the reunion or sent the invitation? Can you produce the phone that was used to text us in Lexie's name? Can you place him at the dock at the time of Serena's murder? Do you have a single witness who saw Noah leave his bedroom and go outside after he'd gone to bed in the early hours of Saturday morning? Can you prove he knew Lexie was dead, or that he'd suspected Serena of impersonating her on social media?"

Agent Singh raised a shapely eyebrow, obviously impressed by Richie's objections and probably just realizing that he wasn't as green as she had initially assumed and she now had to rethink her strategy.

"Not yet, but we will," she replied.

"Well, until you do, you have no case," Richie stated with more confidence than he felt. "Release my client, effective immediately."

"We can hold him for twenty-four hours before we formally charge him," DeVries reminded him.

"Yes, you can, but you and I both know you have nothing, and the next twenty-four hours won't change that."

"All right," Agent Singh said as she leaned back in her chair and blessed Richie with a smile. "We will let your client go, for now, but we will require a DNA sample. We didn't get a chance to process him when he first arrived at the station."

"That is your right," Richie replied.

"I do have a few more questions before you go," Agent Singh said.

"Fire away," Richie said, still high on his victory.

"If you didn't kill her, who did?" Singh asked, fixing Noah with an inquisitive stare.

"I don't know," Noah replied.

"But surely you must have a theory. Someone in that house had to bear a grudge against your wife. Relationships are so complicated, aren't they? So many layers of emotion and shared history. And secret knowledge," she added slyly.

"There is nothing to know," Noah replied stoically. "What you see is what you get."

"Clearly not, since someone attempted to strangle Serena, then pushed her off the dock and stood by as she hit her head and drowned."

Noah winced and stared at his hands again.

"One of your friends has a restraining order against them. Did you know that?"

"Who?" Richie asked. He couldn't think of any reason one of his friends would have a restraining order taken out against them.

"Vince," Noah said under his breath.

"You knew about this?" Richie snapped.

Noah nodded. "But it has nothing to do with Serena."

"Not directly, anyway," Sheriff DeVries said.

"Who took out a restraining order against Vince?" Richie inquired.

"His ex-girlfriend, Nikki Glaser. It seems your friend became not only verbally but physically abusive toward her. Did you know that, Mr. Paulson?"

"Vince didn't go into the details."

"No, I'm sure he didn't," Agent Singh said.

"Are you familiar with the circumstances?" Richie asked.

Agent Singh did not reply. She pushed away from the table, the legs of her chair scraping the floor. "We will be looking into each and every one of you in the coming days, and I'm certain we'll discover some very interesting things."

"Again, that is your right," Richie reiterated. "It's your duty to discover who murdered Serena and why, but unless you have evidence against my client I think we're done here."

"I'll ask Officer Nunes to take Mr. Paulson's DNA sample," DeVries said, and stood as well. "She'll be right in. And then you're free to leave, but don't leave the county. Not until our investigation is complete."

Noah looked panicked at the prospect of a DNA test, but Richie gave him a nod. There was no way around it. Noah could either do it voluntarily or be forced to comply. DeVries would get it either way. As Richie watched Officer Nunes swab the inside of Noah's cheek, he thought only God could help Noah if the CSI techs had been able to collect the killer's DNA from Serena's remains and it was a match to his.

THIRTY-SEVEN
NOAH

When they left the police station, Richie unlocked the car and got behind the wheel without saying a word. It wasn't that he had nothing to say—he simply understood Noah's need for silence, and probably had thoughts of his own to digest. Noah couldn't even begin to articulate what he was feeling. It would take far longer than the ride back to the house to recover from what he had just learned. To say he was in shock would be a gross understatement. In the past twenty-four hours, his wife had been murdered—possibly by one of his closest friends—he'd lost a child he hadn't even known existed, and he'd discovered truths he would never be able to unknow about the two women he'd loved most in the world. The grief and shock pressed in on him so forcefully, it felt like a metal cage had been welded around his chest, and panic threatened to tip him over the edge. Noah shut his eyes, counted to ten, then did it again, forcing himself to breathe deeply until the pressure started to loosen, but the absurdity of it all tugged at his frayed nerves until a hysterical chuckle bubbled up in his throat. Richie glanced over, clearly assessing Noah's mental state. But he didn't seem alarmed enough to call for a psych hold, so he kept driving, his profile calm and composed.

Noah turned to look out at the street. Halloween decorations adorned the windows: fake cobwebs, pumpkins, plastic bats. All of it achingly familiar. Painfully normal. But nothing in Noah's life would ever be normal again. He thought about what it would be like to explain everything to his parents, to his coworkers. The shame, the speculation, the whispers. But that wasn't the worst of it. Richie had bought him some time, but what if he was charged with Serena's murder? What if he went to prison? His life as he knew it would be over.

Richie pulled into a Dunkin' Donuts drive-through and ordered two large coffees with sugar and cream. He passed one to Noah, placed his in the cupholder, and drove off as if they were just two guys on a road trip instead of a murder suspect and his attorney heading back to a house full of suspects. The coffee was hot, strong, and comforting. It reminded Noah of all the little things he'd taken for granted. But if Agent Singh could prove his guilt beyond a reasonable doubt, he'd lose everything—including his freedom.

"Rich, pull over," Noah said.

"You gonna be sick?" Richie asked, frowning. "Don't you dare puke in my car."

"I'm not sick. I just need to talk."

Richie nodded, slowing as he scanned the area. He spotted a park and coasted in, parking as far from the playground as possible. A handful of kids were running around while their parents hovered nearby. One little girl wore a unicorn headband over her strawberry blond curls, the sequined horn bobbing in the sunlight like a glittering antenna. She looked like Serena in pictures of her as a kid and he quickly looked away, crushed by the weight of his grief.

Two men with no kids loitering near a playground was never a good look, so Richie angled the Jeep away from the children and sipped his coffee, waiting for Noah to speak.

"I can't go back to that house," Noah said.

"Running away looks like guilt," Richie replied without emotion.

"Rich, one of those people either murdered Serena or helped cover it up."

"Quite possibly."

"You must have a theory," Noah snapped, his fear spilling over. "Come on, you're my lawyer—for fuck's sake."

"As your lawyer, I must focus on the facts, and just now the facts don't look good. Your prints will be on Serena's phone, and, if you found out about Lexie, that's motive. The fact that you didn't know Serena was pregnant? Also bad." Richie turned and met his gaze. "Why wouldn't she tell you, Noah? She had to have known."

"Maybe she wasn't ready."

"Who's going to believe that? The obvious conclusion is that she was afraid you'd lose it."

"I wouldn't," Noah said.

"This is me, bro. Be honest. What was really going on?"

"Serena was pressuring me to have a kid. I told her I wasn't ready."

"Yet she got pregnant anyway. That's motive, bro."

"I didn't kill her," Noah replied irritably. If he couldn't convince Richie, how could he possibly persuade anyone else? His only hope was to offer up an alternate suspect. "You think they'll talk to Vince? The restraining order shows he's capable of violence."

"We all are," Richie replied bleakly. He looked like he was about to put the car into gear, but Noah forestalled him.

"Aren't we gonna talk about the elephant in the car—Lexie?" he demanded.

Richie exhaled sharply. "Which part? The one where someone planned this whole weekend using Lexie's phone and credit cards? Or the one where Serena might have killed Lexie in Thailand and impersonated her for three years? Or the fact that Serena was murdered by someone who claimed to be Lexie? Because we've got a whole herd of pachyderms here, my friend."

"Serena didn't kill Lexie," Noah exclaimed. "No way. There

were drugs. Ketamine. Agent Singh said so. I think Serena panicked and ran. You know how harsh the Thai legal system is."

"Sure," Richie replied skeptically. "But how do you explain the rest?"

Noah felt the exhaustion hit him like a freight train. His body sagged with the weight of it. He was shattered. Every breath felt like a battle.

"If we don't figure this out, I'm going to prison," he whispered.

"The burden of proof is on the prosecution," Richie replied. "All your lawyer has to do is create reasonable doubt."

"Which you will, right? You can do that?"

"Noah, I can't represent you." The look Richie gave him said it all. Richie doubted him.

Noah glanced away, shattered by the magnitude of the betrayal inflicted by the one person he'd thought would remain in his corner. Richie put the car into drive and pulled out of the parking lot. It seemed he didn't have anything more to add, and now that he had recused himself Noah knew he was really and truly fucked.

THIRTY-EIGHT
RICHIE

Man, that was hard. Richie hated to cut Noah loose, but to represent him could be career suicide, not to mention a disservice to Noah. If he were charged, the news outlets would make much of the fact that they were friends and therefore Richie could not be objective. Friends coming to the rescue looked good in movies, but not so in real life. Besides, if he were completely, totally honest, Richie didn't know that Noah was innocent. It didn't matter from a legal standpoint, since Noah was still entitled to a fair trial, but as a friend he couldn't defend him if he were guilty. Everyone had a moral code they lived by, and, even though Richie's had always been pretty flexible, there were some things he had to draw the line at, like murder. He guessed Nonna Immaculata had instilled some ethics in him, even if he kicked and screamed all the way. She always told him he would answer to God, and Richie supposed in this situation, he couldn't afford to piss the Big Guy off.

And even though Richie hadn't been accused of anything—yet—he was also reeling. The news about Lexie. Man, where did he even begin? Richie had to admit, now that he knew the truth, or whatever passed for the truth at the moment—he was sure the situation was going to change as the Feds learned more—he thought on some level he always knew that something didn't add up. Lexie had her faults, as did they all. She could be too direct, way too eager to dive in and try to fix somebody, even if they didn't care to be fixed, and at times she was too needy to see that she had to give people their space and allow them to have some control in the relationship. But she was also the most sincere, caring person he had ever met, and Richie had felt her loss once she was no longer around.

When Noah told him Lexie had broken off their engagement by text and wouldn't take any of his calls, Richie had thought, *What did you do, bro?* It would take a betrayal of cataclysmic proportions for Lexie to walk away without a backward glance and not even have a conversation, if only to make her feelings known. She wasn't the sort of person to shy away from the truth, nor was she afraid to show vulnerability. If Noah had hurt her, she would have told him so, more than once. Lexie loved Noah with a fierceness that was both terrifying and enviable. If a woman Richie planned to make a life with ever loved him half as much, he would consider himself a lucky man.

It never occurred to him that the one to betray Lexie would be Serena. She could be vain and selfish, and Richie didn't care if it was wrong to speak ill of the dead; he had to be honest in view of what he'd learned—but he would never have suspected Serena of such unapologetic deceit. Richie knew she could be self-serving, but this sort of cruelty defied all logic. Why would she impersonate Lexie all this time if not to gaslight Lexie's friends and to torment Noah?

Whatever part Serena had played in Lexie's death, clearly no one was coming for her. The case was closed, the body buried, and the death certificate signed. Even if Serena didn't want to tell anyone what had happened, she could have just pretended that Lexie had blown them all off and gone her own way. Friendships ended all the time, and people sometimes grew tired of social media and went dark, at times, permanently. So why the ongoing charade? And who the actual fuck arranged this reunion? Could it have been Serena, maybe to punish Noah or to test his feelings for her? If that was the case, then the answer was clear. Noah somehow found out and lost his shit so spectacularly that he went for her, and when he thought she was dead he pushed her off the dock in the hope that the authorities would treat her death as an accident and he'd be off the hook. And if not for the bruises around Serena's neck, they would have. All the evidence would point to Serena having fallen, hit her head on the way down, lost consciousness, and drowned.

But if it wasn't Serena who planned this whole thing, and if it wasn't Noah who killed her—because let's be honest, no one saw him leave his bedroom after he'd passed out—then who was responsible for all this? Richie doubted it was Vince, but the revelations about him had come as a shock as well, and Vince had a room to himself, so who knew? Maybe Serena's death had nothing to do with Lexie and everything to do with her pushing someone too far.

Richie needed to speak to Remy, but he couldn't talk to him at the house, where anyone could overhear. And he couldn't be seen to unquestioningly support Noah, because if he did it could cost him. At this stage, Richie didn't trust anyone, not even himself, since clearly he knew nothing about the people he called his friends.

THIRTY-NINE
RICHIE

The rest of the drive back to the house was made in complete silence. Noah stared out the window, while Richie tried to act normal when all he wanted to do was drop Noah off and keep on driving. The prospect of seeing everyone and answering their questions set his teeth on edge, and he thought he'd claim client–attorney privilege even though he wasn't going to represent Noah in the future. What Noah decided to tell them was up to him.

When the Jeep rounded the house, Richie was surprised to find an official car blocking the parking area once again.

"They're back," Noah said.

Richie shook his head. "This is not the police. This is the Feds."

"I'm guessing that's not a good thing," Noah said morosely.

"No."

Noah looked understandably worried, probably thinking he'd get rearrested as soon as he got out of the car. Richie was worried for different reasons. The Feds were clearly looking further afield now, and all the guests were fair game. He parked on the side of the road, and he and Noah walked the rest of the way. The sliding door was partially open, and he heard arguing inside.

"No, you can't take it. I need it for work," Angelina screamed. There was the low rumble of a male voice, and then Angelina again. "I don't care. I'm not giving it to you."

"Ma'am, I have a warrant," a tall Black agent told her calmly as Richie and Noah stepped through the door. "You don't really have a choice."

"No," Angelina wailed. "Richie, do something," she begged.

Several laptops were stacked on the dining room table, and the two officers were in the kitchen, trying to wrest people's phones away from them.

"What's going on?" Richie asked, even though it was perfectly obvious.

"I'm Agent Locke, and this is Agent Roberts," the female agent said. She was around thirty-five with overbleached blond hair, cold blue eyes, and a stance like a brick shithouse. "We have a warrant that grants us the right to remove all personal electronic devices from the premises, including yours. Kindly set your phones on the counter, gentlemen."

"When will we get them back?" Richie asked.

To have his phone taken away was like having a hand amputated without warning. He was lost without it, and he had to be at work tomorrow. Thank God he remembered how to get back to the highway or he'd probably get lost without the GPS. And if he had to call in, he needed to jot down the number for the front desk and his boss, since he couldn't remember them by heart.

"Sir, we will process these items as soon as we can, but there's a backlog of cases, so it might take a few days."

"You mean a few weeks," Angelina said bitterly.

"It will take as long as it takes, ma'am," Agent Roberts said. He was tall, lean, and soft-spoken, and somehow all the more intimidating for it. "Need I remind you this is a murder investigation?"

"No, you don't need to remind us," Angelina said, and marched out of the kitchen.

"Are we free to leave?" Mia asked. She was still holding her phone, and her hand was shaking.

"You would have to speak to Agent Singh," Agent Roberts said. Mia looked confused, not recognizing the name.

"You will need to pick up your electronics once we've processed them. We don't deliver," Agent Locke said nastily.

"Why not?" Remy demanded.

"Because we're not Grubhub."

Remy didn't reply, but Richie could see the anger in his eyes and the effort it took to control his reaction. Remy had a hot temper, but he'd learned to hide it. A temperamental model was one thing, but no one wanted to work with a volatile photographer, at least not one who was still young and hungry for gigs. And a reputation meant a lot in his business. It meant a lot in all their professional lives, and to find themselves part of a murder investigation wasn't going to do them any favors if the news got out.

The Feds eventually left. Agent Roberts carried out a plastic bin filled with their computers and phones and deposited it in the back of the vehicle while everyone watched. Their gazes followed the car until it disappeared from view, and then they all stood there, as if they expected the agents to come back and tell them it was all a prank. Parents were probably less emotional when they sent their children off to camp, Richie reflected as he walked into the house and opened the fridge. He was always hungry when stressed, and there were still some cold cuts and cheese to pick at. Everyone drifted back into the kitchen and stood around, unsure what to do.

"Why would they take our computers and phones? What do they think they're going to find?" Angelina demanded as she angrily snatched a cube of cheese out of Richie's hand and shoved it into her mouth.

"They obviously think one of us murdered Serena," Mia said softly. "My God, how did we even get here?"

"Guys, there's something I need to tell you," Richie said, but Remy cut across him.

"Well, obviously they were wrong about Noah." He slapped Noah on the back. "Welcome back, buddy."

Remy was acting as if Noah had just come back from a doctor's office where he had been given a clean bill of health after some minor medical scare. And since Noah had been released and no one else had been asked to come to the station, everyone probably assumed that the tech check had been just a formality.

"It's not as simple as that," Richie tried again.

"Nothing will ever be simple again," Vince said.

"No, it won't," Mia replied angrily. She looked sad and worried.

Now that federal agents had come calling, the group were beginning to realize that Serena's death might have a long-term effect on their daily lives, and it would take longer than they had thought to put this tragic weekend behind them. Everyone except Noah seemed to be speaking at once, collectively venting their outrage at being kept prisoner in this house and lamenting the loss of their devices. Without their phones, they felt cut off from civilization and unsure how to fill the time, since now there were no electronics to hide behind when they needed personal space, no possibility of just putting in earbuds and listening to a podcast or an audiobook, or simply scrolling through their social media accounts.

"Shut up and listen, everyone," Richie hollered over the din.

Everyone went quiet and stared at him, their expressions ranging from surprise to mounting unease.

"What's up, man?" Remy asked.

"Lexie is dead," Richie announced.

He could have started from afar, but this was the best way to get everyone's attention and keep it for the duration of his explanation. He didn't have the emotional bandwidth to say it more than once and then deal with endless questions to which he had no answers. The news had to be brought out into the open and handled with grim determination and fortitude, much like a root canal or a colonoscopy. Noah sat with his head in his hands, but the rest of them stared at Richie, open-mouthed with shock.

"Lexie is dead?" Angelina echoed.

"Was she in an accident? Is that why she never arrived?" Mia asked. She was wringing her hands, and her make-up-free face looked pale and childish.

"According to the FBI, Lexie died in Thailand, in July of 2022."

"What?" A chorus of stunned disbelief filled the kitchen.

"What are you talking about?" Remy exclaimed. "Serena would have known if that happened. She would have told us."

"Serena did know," Richie replied, and took a deep breath. This was going to be the more difficult thing to explain, but it was also his only chance to catch everyone off guard and watch their initial reactions. "Serena is the one who has been posting in Lexie's name. And she may have been the one to organize this reunion."

"What? Why?" Mia cried. "Why would she do that?"

"It doesn't make any sense," Angelina said softly. "Why would Serena keep from us that Lexie was dead?"

"How exactly did she die?" Vince asked. He was a facts guy, and he needed to know the how and the why in order to arrive at a logical explanation.

"She drowned," Richie said.

"Like Serena," Angelina whispered.

She looked like she might pass out. Remy shoved a chair beneath her just as her knees buckled, and she sat down heavily, her fingers grasping the padded seat.

"My God," Mia said softly.

"There's more," Richie continued, "The coroner in Thailand thought Lexie's death might have been the result of secondary drowning, which can occur hours after someone has swallowed water. Lexie's body was found on the beach. She was lying on her towel, wearing her sunglasses, with her sun hat covering her face."

"So, it was an accident?" Vince asked.

"That's what they thought at first, but, in view of what happened to Serena and the fact that she had been impersonating

Lexie for more than three years, they now think the two deaths might be connected."

"Are you saying Lexie was murdered?" Angelina asked.

"That is a possibility," Richie replied.

"But you just said she died by secondary drowning," Remy said.

"By the time Lexie's body was discovered, which was just past noon, she had been dead for about twelve hours. She wouldn't have been lying on the beach with her sunglasses and hat on at midnight. Someone had laid her out, taken her wallet, passport, and phone, and left her body to be discovered. And Serena checked them both out of the hostel, took Lexie's things, and boarded a flight to New York later that day."

"Jesus," Remy exclaimed. "Are you saying she murdered Lexie and fled?"

"Lexie had ketamine in her system at the time of her death," Richie said. "Her death might have been an accident, but what Serena did afterward proves that she not only knew Lexie had died but must have had something to hide if she thought she needed to leave the country before she could be detained."

"But why didn't she tell anyone?" Angelina asked. She looked a little less pale but no less bewildered. "We would have believed her. We were her friends. Both their friends. We had a right to know."

"Serena must have believed she was still in danger," Noah said quietly. "She probably thought someone would come after her."

"But who?" Remy exclaimed. "If the authorities believed Lexie's death to be an accident…"

"Maybe whoever was actually responsible for Lexie's death," Noah said.

"You think someone else killed her?" Angelina asked.

"It's possible," Noah replied.

"But that still doesn't explain why Serena would pretend to be Lexie," Mia said with a shake of her head. "Whoever was responsible for Lexie's death would know she'd died. Fake posts wouldn't fool them."

"It had to be Serena who sent the text to Noah breaking off their engagement," Richie stated.

"How can you be sure?" Mia asked.

"Because I got the text the day after Lexie died," Noah choked out.

"Are you saying that Serena was the one to break off Lexie and Noah's engagement and then pretended that Lexie was still alive? Why, in order to torment him?" Vince asked. "Sorry, Noah," he muttered when he clocked Noah's stricken expression. It wasn't news to Noah at this point, but the implication clearly still had the power to wound him afresh.

"So it would seem," Richie replied.

"But why would she organize the reunion if she knew Lexie wouldn't show?" Vince asked.

"To test me," Noah said.

Richie thought Noah might mention the pregnancy, but he went silent, and Richie didn't think it was his place to share the news.

"How do they know Serena was impersonating Lexie?" Mia asked.

"The Feds accessed Serena's social media accounts. They found Lexie's profiles. She was managing them from her phone."

"Jesus," Remy said again, only this time he sounded bereft.

"So, is Serena's death payback for Lexie's?" Angelina asked.

"Given that it happened at a reunion supposedly hosted by Lexie, it'd have to be," Remy replied. "What do you think, Rich?"

"They've found no evidence that Serena was the one to organize the reunion, at least not yet. And even if she was, someone else killed her."

"So someone else knew," Mia deduced.

"That's the most likely explanation," Richie allowed. "And that's why the Feds are involved. This is way above DeVries' pay grade."

"Is that why they took our phones?" Vince asked. "They think one of us orchestrated this whole thing?"

Richie nodded and noted that Vince looked relieved. But just because he hadn't left an electronic trail for the Feds to follow didn't mean he was innocent. It was entirely possible that one person had murdered Lexie, another had arranged the reunion, and either of those two people or an unrelated third person had then killed Serena. All three things might be connected, or maybe only two events were linked and the third was a crime of passion that had nothing to do with anything that had come before.

"They're wasting their time," Angelina announced.

"Because you are sure none of us was involved or because you think whoever did this is too smart to get caught?" Vince asked.

Angelina gaped at him. "Because I don't think any of us were involved, obviously."

"So, what do you think happened?" Remy asked.

"Look, I don't know, okay?" Angelina exclaimed as she exploded out of her chair. "I can't even begin to wrap my mind around this whole thing."

"Me neither. I need some time to process," Mia said. She looked shaken, and her gaze kept shifting to Remy, who seemed to be avoiding making eye contact.

"Noah, are you all right?" Angelina asked gently. She bent over Noah and wrapped her arms around him, and Noah pressed his face into her shoulder. His shoulders were quaking, and it was only then that Richie realized Noah was crying.

Everyone's expressions were pained, and, except for Angelina, no one seemed to know what to do. After a moment of uncomfortable silence, Vince excused himself and left the kitchen, and Remy muttered something unintelligible and stepped out onto the deck. Mia followed his exit with her eyes but didn't go after him. Instead, she sat down next to Noah and laid her hand over his. Noah pulled his hand away and wrapped his arms around Angelina's middle. She rested her cheek against his head and held him close, her own eyes wet with tears.

Eventually Remy and Vince returned, and Noah seemed to get ahold of himself and let go of Angelina, who glanced around the kitchen, as if searching for something useful to do. Looking at the faces of his friends, Richie thought they all appeared genuinely shocked and saddened by everything that had happened, but, given the empirical evidence he had been presented with, he was certain that at least one of them had to be putting on an act.

FORTY

MIA

Fucking Remy. Mia could kill him. He was the one who suggested she use SexyLexie69 as her OnlyFans name when she had turned to him for advice. Mia had reminded him that Lexie had come up with that name, but he had just shrugged and said, "Well, it's not like she's using it." And it was the perfect name, especially since she couldn't seem to come up with anything on her own that didn't sound like a cartoon character. And it wasn't as if Lexie was ever going to find out, was it?

Mia should never have told Remy about OnlyFans, but he was the only person she could rely on to give her useful suggestions on what sort of content would garner followers without turning her into a porn star. She had to admit that his ideas were on point, but now that some federal agent might watch her videos Mia felt sick with dread. Remy had been the one to suggest that she play around with erotic asphyxiation in her pay-per-view content. She didn't actually strangle herself, but she did put on a studded dog collar and tighten it so that the viewers believed she was gasping for breath as she brought herself to a shattering climax. That video got the most views.

And if any of this came out, Mia's family would be sure to hear about it, and then they would say that everything they had warned her about and tried to protect her from had come true, and she would be forever used as a cautionary tale for other young girls who were struggling against the dictates of the cult she was raised in. The price Mia had to pay for leaving was the rift with her family, but somewhere, at the back of her mind, she had always known she could go back if she wanted to. She could still make peace with the mother who was happy to share her husband with two sister-wives and who unquestioningly accepted whatever edict her father, to whom she had been married at age sixteen and without her consent, had issued. Mia could still reconnect with her siblings and maybe not feel so alone in the world. But once the truth came out, those connections would be severed forever, as would be the bonds of friendship she had formed at school and relied on so heavily during those first terrifying years of independence.

Mia hadn't been overly worried when she thought the invitation had come from the real Lexie. If Lexie had found out about her alias, she'd explain herself and apologize for not asking for permission. Mia had actually thought Lexie would get a kick out of it. But Lexie was dead and had been for three years, and someone else had used the name only they knew about to lure them all to this isolated spot. And now Serena was dead as well, strangled like the Sexy Lexie in Mia's feed and then drowned like her namesake.

Mia was so scared, she didn't know what to think. The only person who could help her was Richie, but if Richie was representing Noah he couldn't represent her. That would be a conflict of interest, but Mia couldn't afford to hire an attorney to defend her, not if she was to take down the OnlyFans account. And who'd want to take her case anyway? They'd take one look at the evidence and think she was guilty as sin.

And what about Remy? Mia fumed. Did he suggest the name on purpose and then tell Serena all about it? Did he know all along that Lexie was dead? He couldn't have, but then Mia never would have believed Serena could be capable of keeping such an awful secret or intentionally perpetuating the vicious lie. Did Serena ever worry about getting caught, or had she enjoyed the power the lie had given her over everyone who had stupidly believed her?

And Mia sure as fuck never imagined one of her friends could be capable of murder. Possibly two of her friends, if Serena had been the one to murder Lexie. But as she looked at the stricken faces, she still couldn't quite believe it. Who? Why? How? And were they now done?

If God helped her through this, Mia swore, she would take down the smutty content and seriously consider becoming a nun. Or a sister-wife, which as far as she was concerned was far worse.

But she didn't want to go to prison. Or die.

FORTY-ONE
ANGELINA

"Anyone hungry?" Angelina asked once the initial shock had worn off and everyone just stood around, looking lost and unsure what to do, especially now that they didn't have their phones to distract them. "I'm sure I can put something together. It will make us feel better to sit down to a meal together."

"Not everything can be fixed with food," Noah snapped.

"I beg to differ," Richie said. "Things always look less dire after a good meal."

"Maybe to you," Mia muttered from her spot by the window.

No one was in the mood to go out, so Angelina opened the fridge and surveyed the contents. They were meant to have checked out by this evening, and there wasn't much left in the way of fresh food. There was still cream for coffee and leftover cheesecake, and several apples that were probably purchased by the previous renters. In the cabinet she found a box of bowtie pasta and a jar of marinara sauce, but when she checked the lid she saw that it had expired in April.

"We can't even order anything," she grumbled. "We don't have a single phone between us. How are we supposed to function?"

"There's a grocery store in town," Vince said, but no one

looked even remotely interested in going food shopping or preparing a meal.

"I have a phone," Remy said, and everyone turned to stare at him.

"How'd you manage that?" Mia asked, clearly impressed. "Did Agent Roberts not count how many phones he'd collected?"

"I gave him a phone," Remy replied. "But I have a separate phone for work. I don't like to give clients my private number."

"So, which phone did they take?" Vince asked.

"They took my personal phone, which is fine. They're not going to find anything incriminating."

"Would they find anything incriminating on the work phone?" Richie inquired, one eyebrow raised.

"They might," Remy said, but didn't elaborate. "Nothing to do with Lexie, though."

"You mean they might find the number for your dealer, or is it dealers, plural?" Angelina asked, spearing Remy with a judgy look.

"I don't recall you objecting too strenuously the other night," Remy replied, clearly irritated.

"Let's see the phone," Richie said.

Remy went upstairs and came back with an older-model iPhone. He handed it to Richie. "Here, see for yourself. There's nothing there. I wasn't impersonating anyone."

"You could have deleted all the apps," Angelina said, peering over Richie's arm as he scrolled through Remy's texts and checked his Instagram.

"Yes, I could have, but I didn't," Remy said petulantly. "And what reason would I have to impersonate Lexie or organize this shindig?"

Angelina shrugged. She had no answer to that. She couldn't see what Remy would have to gain. And as far as she knew, he didn't have money to burn. He probably earned a nice chunk from each commission, but he didn't have steady work, and to live in the Village wasn't cheap, even if you were lucky enough to sublet a rent-controlled apartment. Unfortunately for Remy, his grandparents' house had burned down to the ground, and there hadn't been an insurance payout, at least according to him. Whatever savings the Durants had had at the time of their deaths had to be gone by now, and Angelina couldn't see Remy blowing a couple of grand on a reunion he clearly thought pointless.

Except that it wasn't pointless. They had found out what had happened to Lexie and what Serena had been up to all this time, and, even though most of them would probably have preferred not to have learned the truth, it was out there now. For better or worse.

"None that I can see, so you probably don't have anything to worry about," Richie replied when Angelina remained silent. "Don't let them find out you have a second phone though, or you'll look guilty as hell."

"They won't find out unless someone tells them," Remy said. "I'd be happy to go get us some food," he offered once Richie had returned his phone.

"Are we seriously just going to sit here and stuff our faces?" Mia asked, her gaze sliding to Noah, who was staring into space, his eyes vacant.

"What else is there to do?" Remy replied. "We can't leave, so we may as well make the best of it."

"I'll come with you," Vince said. "I need to feel useful."

"Okay, then let's ride, Vinnie."

Remy typed a query into his phone and waited for the results to load. "There's Italian, Mexican, and Indian, all within a ten-mile radius."

"Italian," Richie replied without missing a beat.

"Yeah, that's fine," Angelina said.

Mia nodded.

"Noah? Vince?" Remy asked.

"I'm fine with whatever," Vince said.

Noah didn't reply.

"They don't have a menu posted online, but I'm sure they have the basics," Remy said once he'd consulted his phone again. "What does everyone want?"

"I'll have veal parm," Richie said. "And don't forget to get Italian bread."

"Yes, Master," Remy replied facetiously. "Girls? What can I get you?"

"Just a Caesar salad for me," Mia said. "I can't even think of eating something heavy. My stomach is in knots."

"Ooh, garlic knots," Richie mused. "Get those instead."

"Richie, can I share your veal?" Angelina asked.

"Get your own," Richie said. "I'm so stressed, I need to eat."

"Fine, get me grilled salmon over spinach, if they have it. If not, I'll take spaghetti with clam sauce."

"Noah?" Remy asked softly. "What can I get you, buddy?"

Noah shook his head, then stood and walked out. His footsteps resounded on the stairs, and then a door slammed as he retreated to his bedroom.

"We'll figure something out," Remy said.

"He likes meatball subs," Vince announced.

Everyone looked at him, surprised that he'd know that about Noah, but Angelina nodded in acknowledgement. Vince was right. Noah always used to order a meatball sub from Subway. Vince was not someone who said much, but he noticed everything and could usually connect the dots faster than anyone else in the room.

FORTY-TWO

ANGELINA

Noah refused to come down when Remy and Vince came back with the food. It was understandable that he'd want to be alone in view of everything that had happened. Angelina did take him the sub, though, and a can of Diet Coke. In case he got hungry. Noah just lay there on the bed, looking at the ceiling with that dead-eyed stare. Angelina set the plate and the Coke on the bedside table and let herself out. She didn't think he even noticed she was there, or didn't care.

It was too late for lunch and too early for dinner, but they didn't know what else to do, so they opened a couple of bottles of wine and dug in. Eating together and talking things over was a comforting thing to do with people Angelina had turned to for support for so many years, but by the end of the meal all she felt was fear and dark, bottomless grief. For Lexie. For Serena. For Noah. For the baby who never got to draw breath. And for Richie. He had told them about it over dinner. She could tell he'd been deeply torn between keeping the baby news to himself and opting for full disclosure, but he knew as well as they all did that the truth would eventually come out and it was best if they knew.

Mia seemed strangely relieved when Richie had also announced that he wouldn't represent Noah if he was charged with Serena's murder. It might seem disloyal, but Angelina could understand Richie's reservations. And he was right, Noah would need someone with more experience and fewer personal ties. Richie would make a fine second chair, but he wasn't ready to fly solo, especially not at the trial of his closest friend. Noah would never forgive him if he lost, even if he was guilty. And he would be found guilty, wouldn't he, because who else would have reason to murder Serena?

What would happen to Noah? she wondered. A plea deal? Life in prison? Angelina wouldn't have believed Noah was capable of such violence, but everyone had a breaking point. And if Noah found out about Lexie's death and what Serena had been doing all this time, it'd be understandable if he snapped. Everything he believed until now had been a lie, orchestrated by his wife. After three glasses of wine and bolstered by a dose of Dutch courage, Angelina mentioned her theory to the group, and they all agreed that it was possible, and Noah was the most likely suspect.

At least he now knew that Lexie had loved him until the end, and he had probably been the last person she'd thought of before she died, if she was even conscious. Angelina prayed she was not. She'd heard of secondary drowning, of course, but she had never come across anyone who'd been treated for it or had died from it. It was fairly rare, given all the other things people died of. But it was possible, and she wanted to believe that Lexie's death was an accident. But how could she justify the rest? Serena was Lexie's best friend, the person she trusted above everyone besides Noah.

Funny, but even at school Mia had said that Serena couldn't be trusted. In fact, Mia and Serena didn't really keep up with each other these last few years. Friday was the first time they'd been in the same room since Serena and Noah's wedding. And Mia kept her distance, especially later in the evening. It wasn't really obvious when they were all together and everyone was talking, but the chill was definitely there.

Did Mia know something? Did she blame Serena for Lexie's death? She could have told the rest of them if so, but would they have believed her? Everyone thought Lexie was fine, living her best life and documenting her journey on social media. There had been shots of her attached to the email, but Serena could have posted pictures they'd taken in Thailand that none of them had ever seen. And it was easy enough to say a photo was taken in India or Bali when all you saw in the background was a beach, palm trees, and tables at some outdoor café.

Angelina still found it hard to believe Serena could be that devious, but no one suspected the posts were fake. And why would they? Angelina would love to know what Serena thought when she received the invitation. If she hadn't sent it, she must have realized someone was on to her. Did she know who it was? Was that why she came to the reunion, to confront them and hash things out once and for all?

And was Mia really asleep when Serena died? She was when Angelina woke up feeling queasy, but Richie said Serena received a text at 2:17 a.m. Angelina woke up around 3:30 a.m. Serena might have already been dead by then, Mia back in her bed, sleeping the sleep of the just. Should she mention this to Richie?

FORTY-THREE

ALAN

Agent Singh looked tired by the time she finally emerged from Alan's office, which he'd been forced to vacate since she needed a private place to work. Asha had been on her laptop and phone most of the afternoon, and Alan had heard her raise her voice more than once as she berated some poor shmuck on the other end. She was an impressive woman, beautiful too, but not in an approachable sort of way. Alan didn't think she would respond favorably if he invited her to discuss the case over a meal, or even a drink. Asha was all business. Alan didn't have any romantic designs on the FBI agent; he was happily married. But he found that people worked better together in a relaxed atmosphere and could interact like individuals rather than a boss and their subordinates. He didn't really think of Asha Singh as his boss, but in this instance she was the senior investigating officer, and he had to follow her lead. And a good thing it was too, because he didn't have any suggestions worth mentioning.

Normally, Alan relied on the locals to point him in the right direction. In small towns, people knew things about each other, and even if a couple looked like the picture of domestic bliss their neighbors and the kids' friends could often tell a different story. With the murder of Serena Paulson, Alan had nothing to go on and couldn't rely on local intel. There were six houses on Witch Lake, and before the pandemic they had all been occupied year-round. But things had changed.

The house directly across from the property where Serena was murdered had been empty for nearly two years. The owner, a reclusive widower, had died intestate, and the house was still in probate, as was his boat. Two properties, including the one where Serena had died, had been converted into Airbnbs, and two more were for sale and had been on the market for months, currently unoccupied. But what if someone had been squatting at one of the vacant properties? Would they have cause to murder Serena if she had seen them? But seen them do what? Cook heroin? Stockpile explosives while they planned an act of domestic terrorism? Keep a sex slave chained up in one of the outbuildings?

It wasn't beyond the realm of possibility. Lord knew seemingly normal people got up to all sorts of crazy shit, but he would ask Linda Nunes to check out the properties before he mentioned his suspicions to the Fed.

"Were you able to find anything out?" Alan asked when Asha looked like she might be ready to head home for the evening.

"No. Yes. I won't know anything for certain until tomorrow," Asha replied with a deep sigh.

Alan waited, hoping she would fill him in without having to be asked. Serena Paulson had been murdered on his patch, and that, by extension, made Alan part of the investigation into the death of Lexie Hall as well. He shouldn't have to beg for updates.

Asha nodded and motioned for Alan to follow her into his office. There really wasn't anyone around to overhear their conversation, but she clearly didn't feel comfortable discussing the case in the open. Asha had the decency not to sit behind Alan's desk, and took the guest chair, while Alan heaved his bulk into his chair and leaned back a little, feeling like they were equals for the first time that day.

"We have several avenues of investigation to follow, but no real leads, not yet," Asha said. "I've spent the past few hours speaking to various officials about the possibility of exhuming Lexie Hall's body. I would like a second autopsy to be performed, preferably by an American pathologist."

"That must have ruffled a few feathers," Alan said.

"The issue is not who performs the autopsy but the order to exhume. When dealing with a foreign government, everything takes longer. There are more forms to fill out and more signatures to obtain. I don't think the Thais have an issue with the request, per se, but the wheels of justice never turn fast, and in this case the wheels are not even on the wagon. It might take months to see this done."

Alan nodded. He had never had to deal with foreign officials during the course of his investigations, not even the Canadians, but he knew enough about government agencies and the blight of bureaucracy to understand that this would take some considerable time.

"Do you think the original pathologist botched the autopsy?" Alan asked.

"Maybe. Or maybe he did a competent job, based on the facts that were available to him at the time. The authorities weren't treating Lexie's death as a possible murder, remember."

"Which makes no sense," Alan interjected. "Even if Lexie's death was accidental, the circumstances surrounding it are suspicious as hell."

"Suspicious but not criminal," Asha replied. "Serena could have said that Lexie had asked her to check out and had promised to meet her at the airport. When Lexie failed to show, Serena got on her flight. Thai authorities would have no cause to check Lexie's social media once Serena returned to the States, so, unless the pathologist was certain that Lexie was murdered, the police would have no reason to pursue the matter any further."

"I guess," Alan muttered.

He would have pursued the matter further had it been his case, but he supposed the police in Phuket were kept very busy with all the tourists that came through and got up to God knew what in a place they saw as their personal paradise. After Alan had seen the images of the tsunami that had obliterated Phuket in 2004, he couldn't think of Thailand without recalling the death toll and the devastation, but the young people who flocked to Phuket these days had probably been toddlers when the tsunami hit, and to them it was all ancient history that could never repeat itself.

"Since new information has now come to light, I think it's our duty to look deeper into what happened to Lexie Hall," Asha said, interrupting his thoughts.

"What about our suspects? We can't keep them here indefinitely."

"No, we will have to either charge or release," Asha replied. "The techs are working on the devices we collected this afternoon, but these things also take time. We need access to everyone's call and text records, but I'm not holding out much hope. Whoever planned this was devilishly clever. They wouldn't have used their own computer or phone to make the arrangements. There's another phone out there, Lexie's phone, but, even though the techs now have the number the texts came from and can request records from the provider, it has been disconnected. If I had to guess, I'd say the phone is probably at the bottom of the lake or buried in the woods."

"You don't think someone switched the SIM card?"

Asha shook her head. "It's not something you can do quickly with an iPhone. You need a special tool or a paperclip to open the card tray. And whoever had the cards would need to switch them several times throughout the evening."

"So, someone has a second phone," Alan concluded.

Asha nodded. "I'm sure of it."

"What do we do about Noah Paulson?"

"I've requested a few additional tests to be carried out on Serena's remains. With luck, we'll have the results by morning."

"You look like you could use a drink," Alan said carefully.

Asha smiled tiredly. "I could, but I must get home. My little boy is with my mom, and I would like to tuck him in and read him a bedtime story if I can tonight."

Alan didn't ask about Asha's domestic situation. It was none of his business. And it was time he got home as well. It had been a long and frustrating day, and all he wanted was a good meal, a beer or two, and a couple of episodes of *Breaking Bad* to take his mind off the investigation. He and his wife had only recently got into the series, and allowed themselves two episodes per night so they wouldn't get through it too quickly.

"Goodnight, then," he said. "I hope we have a breakthrough tomorrow."

"Don't hold your breath," Asha said as she got to her feet. "My guess is that we'll have to return the devices and allow them all to go tomorrow."

FORTY-FOUR
VINCE

Vince would sell his soul to get away from this place, but he had to stay. For one, if he left he wouldn't be there to defend himself if someone started throwing around accusations, and for another, he couldn't leave Angelina on her own. There was no car the night Serena was murdered. That was a blatant fabrication concocted by Remy. Vince would have heard it if there was. He was a light sleeper, and his room faced the woods and the road. No car, no mysterious killer. Serena was murdered by someone in this house, and, since he knew he didn't do it, it had to be one of the others.

Noah was at the top of his list, for obvious reasons. The fact that the police let him go didn't mean a thing. These days, police work was all about the probability of success. They had to have a solid enough case to go to trial; otherwise, it was a waste of valuable resources and the loss of favorable public opinion. All the speculation in the world would not sway the jury. Forensic evidence had to back up the prosecutor's arguments in order to get a conviction. The Feds might still find what they were looking for, so Noah was not in the clear just yet.

Mia wasn't a fan of Serena's, especially in recent years. She was always closer to Angelina. Vince liked Mia and always had, but she had a short fuse, and she got real nervous when Agent

Locke asked her to surrender her phone. People hid a multitude of sins on their phones these days, and, if Mia didn't think her phone data would be combed through, she might not have taken the time to delete anything that might appear incriminating. And she might have had reason to resent Serena.

Mia and Serena had been arguing on Friday night when Vince came inside to grab a bottle of water. He didn't hear exactly what was said, since the two of them were upstairs, but Serena's tone was threatening, and Mia sounded genuinely freaked out. Vince had no idea what Serena could possibly have threatened Mia with, but lately people didn't seem to care about the facts. An accusation was enough to destroy someone's life, and even if it was eventually proven false the stain on their character never quite went away, since people subscribed to the adage that there's no smoke without a fire.

Which was why Vince didn't mention the restraining order against him to the group or when questioned by the police. He didn't hurt Nikki. All he did was protect himself when she flew at him in a jealous rage. She would have scratched his eyes out if he hadn't grabbed her by the wrists, but no one was interested in Vince's side of the story once Nikki accused him of assault. Thankfully, his employers never found out, but now nothing was certain, and if erroneous assumptions were made he could lose his job and his good name.

Vince had spoken to Noah about the restraining order when it happened, which was a mistake since Noah had promptly told Serena, and now Vince was pretty sure Richie knew as well. Richie had given him a long, searching look when he returned from the police station, but Vince was grateful Richie didn't mention it to the others. He was sure Remy would latch on to it if he found out and make Vince out to be some unrepentant abuser of women. Remy always deflected attention from himself by turning the spotlight on someone else. He must have learned that trick from Richie, who wore his irreverence like a suit of armor. This weekend was the first time he had seen him drop the act and behave like a grown-up.

Remy and Richie, or, as he liked to think of them, Thing 1 and Thing 2, were high on his list too. They were both good-looking, charming, and outgoing, which made them attractive to both men and women. The women were attracted to their bad-boy vibe, but the men wanted guys like Remy and Richie on-side. They were more likely to succeed at work or with women when they were part of the proverbial cool crowd. What people didn't see right off the bat was that Remy and Richie were a lot smarter than the average pretty boy. They were always three steps ahead, and, if anyone could pull off impersonating Lexie to arrange this reunion, it would be one of them. Vince had yet to identify a motive for going to such lengths, but he wasn't close with either of them, so he couldn't begin to unpick what their objective might have been. The only thing he could think of was that Serena had something on one of them and paid for it with her life.

He was worried about Angelina; she had always had a blind spot when it came to Richie. That meatball could do no wrong where she was concerned. Vince wondered if she would accept evidence of Richie's guilt, but didn't think it very likely.

Vince was tired of speculating and wished he had his phone. He could go to his room and listen to some smooth jazz. He was tired of being around these people, and he needed time to think. Something had been niggling at him, but he couldn't seem to isolate that one important nugget of information. Something that had struck him while Remy and he were waiting for their order at the restaurant.

Oh, God. How could he not have realized it? Vince thought, brought up by the memory of what he had seen. It had been right there all along.

FORTY-FIVE
ANGELINA

The kitchen and the dining room were clean, the dishes were done, and Richie had taken out the trash. The others were watching TV in the living room, but Vince kept circling Angelina like a vulture. He'd asked her to go for a walk, sit out on the deck, or maybe light the firepit. Angelina appreciated his efforts to support her, but she wasn't really in the mood for a deep conversation right now, nor did she want to speculate about what had already happened or what would happen tomorrow. The only way she could keep this situation from overwhelming her was by staying busy. Unfortunately, there was nothing else to do, and it was too early to go to bed. How long were they going to be trapped there?

Surely the cops couldn't hold them there indefinitely. Angelina would google it if she had her phone, but, of course, the Feds had cut off their access to information. And she didn't want to ask Richie; he was tired of answering questions. And Remy hid away his secret phone as soon as he and Vince had returned from the restaurant. Angelina didn't know if using the phone would alert anyone to its existence, but she thought Remy just wanted to lie low. She wondered what his deal was. He'd definitely been keeping his distance from Noah. Was it because he thought Noah was guilty or because Remy had something to hide?

Angelina did wonder who'd be footing the bill for the extra time they spent at the house. Presumably, the owners wouldn't let them stay there for free just because the investigation was ongoing, and the police, or the Feds, or whoever was in charge, could hardly put it on Lexie's card. Would they have to pay the difference? That didn't seem fair, but she would gladly pay her share if they would return her phone and let her get the hell out of there. After everything that happened, she wasn't even sure she could remain friends with these people. Every time they would get together, they'd be right here, in this house, in this awful moment. And even if Noah was charged with murder, they would always be suspicious of each other, wondering who had known what and who had been covering for whom. Because someone always knew more than they were saying, didn't they?

Times might change, technology and science might advance by leaps and bounds, but human nature hadn't evolved since the first people murdered each other for food, drove someone defenseless from their shelter, not caring if they died of exposure, or forced the people they'd defeated into a lifetime of slavery. Those were human beings for you. Self-serving, power-hungry, and cruel. All you had to do to see evidence of their depravity was look at the news. Something unspeakable was happening in every part of the world, and, where someone was fighting for their very survival, someone else was profiting from the suffering of others and spewing falsehoods to justify their greed.

Angelina sighed with her whole body, desperate to release even a fraction of her anxiety. All this fear and sorrow was too heavy to carry. Maybe she could go outside to the firepit, where she could see Vince sitting, and hang out with him for a bit. She couldn't go out there alone; all she would think about was Serena, floating in that lake, her face as still and white as some martyr in a Renaissance painting. And that baby. Please God it didn't suffer when Serena died.

FORTY-SIX
MIA

Monday
November 3

Mia woke early. Normally, Angelina was the first one up, but she was still sleeping, her face relaxed and one arm folded beneath her pillow. This was the first time in a long while that Mia hadn't taken a sleeping pill, and it wasn't by choice. She hadn't been able to find her prescription bottle. It had been there yesterday morning, but when she went to brush her teeth before bed last night it hadn't been in her toiletry bag. With this crew, she wouldn't be surprised if someone had helped themselves. Maybe it was Noah. He was probably in hell, and lying awake in the middle of the night was the worst. She knew from experience that was when the scariest thoughts came and anxiety kicked in, sometimes leading to full-blown panic attacks. If Noah hadn't suffered from anxiety before, he was sure to start now. By this time next week, he could be in prison.

Did he do it? Mia wondered as she pulled on jeans and a sweater and tiptoed downstairs. She wouldn't blame Noah for lashing out, not if he'd found out what Serena had done. And although she hated to think badly of her friends she had to admit the truth: Noah was capable of violence. But so was Richie. Mia recalled a bar fight that broke out after a soccer game in which Noah, Remy, and Richie had played in their sophomore year. She had no idea what caused the argument; she'd been in the bathroom when the brawl started and then hid behind the bar to avoid getting hurt, but it had been an absolute free-for-all. Remy wisely stepped outside, but Richie and Noah went berserk, punching the guys from the visiting team until the floor was slick with blood and someone called the cops.

Everyone scattered before the police arrived, but when Mia saw Noah and Richie later that night neither was particularly remorseful. In fact, they were quite proud of themselves, and happily recounted the highlights for their audience. Could spontaneous violence be a prelude to something more deliberate in later years or was the fight a one-off, the result of teenage stupidity fueled by peer pressure and hormones?

And what about Serena? She could be catty and insensitive, but this? It was difficult to imagine that even Serena could sink so low. And for what? Why lie to everyone and keep the ghost of Lexie alive? There was only one plausible explanation. As long as everyone thought Lexie was out there, no one had any reason to suspect Serena had killed her.

Had she murdered Lexie? And if she had, had it been an accident or a premeditated act of brutality? The very idea that Serena could murder her best friend was unthinkable, but it was even more difficult to believe that Noah, whom Mia had always found too moody and uncommunicative for her liking, could be the motive. But Mia supposed people had killed for less. Sexual jealousy was one of the oldest motives in the world, and, for whatever reason, both Lexie and Serena had set their hearts on Noah. Had Serena truly loved him, or had she only wanted him because Lexie did?

Mia had twin sisters she hadn't seen since she had fled her family's compound when she was seventeen, but the two girls had fought incessantly while Mia was still there, always desperate to have what the other one had. It had nothing to do with the item but with the principle. Once they got what they wanted, they usually lost interest, but until it was theirs they were ready to do anything. And Mia had been made to referee because their mother hadn't had the time or the emotional fortitude to deal with their antics. She had been too preoccupied with maintaining her position in the family and making sure she wasn't overshadowed by a sister-wife, who'd then wield too much power and make her life a misery.

Thinking of her family forced Mia to confront her own problems. Would the FBI want to speak to her? Would it be today? Would they ask about her father? And would everyone find out about her upbringing and learn what she'd had to do to support herself? She'd almost confided in Richie last night, but changed her mind at the last minute. She may as well wait and see what happened today, then beg Richie for help if the authorities came for her.

Mia's thoughts were interrupted by the man himself, who came downstairs in a pair of lounge pants and not much else.

"Is there any coffee?" Richie asked groggily.

"I'll make some, but there are only two K-Cups left. And we don't have anything to eat for breakfast."

"I'm not hungry."

Two days ago, Mia would have made a crack about Richie's lack of appetite, but today she remained silent. She wasn't very hungry either, but she would have gladly made something and eaten it. Breakfast would have given her something to focus on and would introduce a semblance of normalcy into this warped new reality.

"Rich, do you think they'll give us our stuff back today?" Mia asked.

"We're dealing with a government agency, Mia. Have you ever known anything to happen quickly?"

"No, but how long can they keep us here?"

"We're free to leave."

"What?" Mia exclaimed. "Have you heard something?"

"On what? My *Star Trek* communicator?"

"So, how do you know?" Mia demanded. She wasn't in the mood for sarcastic comments. She was too wound up.

"The police can hold a suspect for twenty-four hours without charge. I believe the FBI has forty-eight hours, but then, unless there are extraordinary circumstances, they have to release them."

"Are these not extraordinary circumstances?"

"Yes, but unless a motion is filed with a court the suspect must be released."

"Are you sure?" Mia asked.

"I'm sure about the police. I've never had to deal directly with the FBI. There could be loopholes. But if they don't file a motion this morning, they'll have to let us go."

"But I need my phone," Mia wailed. "My life is on that phone. I don't even remember the attendance office's number at my school, much less anyone else's. And how would they let me know I could come get my phone if I don't have a phone?"

"They'll return the devices to DeVries. We'll have to call the station to find out if they're ready to be picked up. I'm actually thinking of leaving right now."

"Because of Noah?"

"I have to go to work. And yeah, because of Noah. I feel like shit, but I can't take him on."

"Because it would be unethical?"

"Partly, but also because I don't want to," Richie admitted with obvious reluctance.

"You think he's guilty," Mia stated.

"It doesn't matter what I think. It's not for me to pass judgment. I don't want to get involved, but I will help Noah to find a good defense attorney. I have several people in mind, but their numbers are all in my phone. I'll be able to contact them once I get into the office."

Mia handed Richie the first cup of coffee, then popped in the last pod to make coffee for herself. Richie took a carton out of the fridge, added a splash of cream to his coffee, and handed the carton to Mia. Then he walked toward the sliding door and looked outside.

"Holy fuck!" he exclaimed.

"What is it? What's wrong?" Mia cried. She dashed toward the door, and froze, her mouth falling open in horror. "Oh, Jesus," she whispered. "We have to call the police."

Richie slammed the mug down on the counter and raced upstairs, but Mia couldn't move. She was rooted to the spot, terrified yet unable to look away. Vince sat facing the patio door, the firepit before him filled with cold ash. Mia didn't need to go outside and check for herself to know Vince was dead. His eyes were closed, but he wasn't sleeping. His skin was as ashen as the cold cinders in the pit, and there was frost in his hair and around his mouth. He wasn't wearing a coat, and what looked like a vape had slipped from his limp hand.

It was only when hot coffee dripped onto her feet that Mia realized she was trembling. One death might be an accident, two a coincidence, although probably not in this case, but three deaths was a pattern. Even though she couldn't see any evidence of foul play, she didn't believe for a moment this had been a natural death. Three of her friends were dead, all under suspicious circumstances. Which one of them would be next if they didn't try to save themselves?

Mia turned away from the door, tears sliding down her face and dripping onto her hand. She had thought she had to fear the police, but at that moment she realized that whoever had killed Vince was vastly more frightening and unpredictable, and they were mere feet away from her at that very moment.

FORTY-SEVEN

RICHIE

"Remy, wake up," Richie cried as soon as he burst into the bedroom.

Remy opened one eye and stared at him blearily. "Let me sleep, man. It's not like we have anywhere to be."

"I need your phone."

"What for?"

"To call the police," Richie explained, and watched Remy grab for the phone, which was charging on the nightstand.

"You're not calling the police with my phone."

"It's an emergency."

"I don't hear anyone screaming, so, unless someone is hemorrhaging to death, you're not outing me to the police."

"Remy," Richie said quietly. "I need to report a death."

Remy's expression instantly turned into one of fear. "No. No. Who?"

"Vince."

"Please tell me he died of natural causes."

"I didn't examine the body, but I seriously doubt it."

"Does Angelina know?" Remy asked as he bolted out of bed and reached for his jeans.

"I think she's still asleep."

"Who found the body?"

"I saw him first. He's on the deck."

"How?" Remy choked out as he yanked the zipper with trembling fingers. "How did he die?"

"I don't know, and I don't want to speculate."

"Richie, what the fuck happened?" Remy choked out. "We all saw Vince last night. He was fine."

"You didn't come up until after midnight," Richie said, watching Remy for any hint of deceit. "Was Vince still outside?"

Remy shook his head. "He went up around eleven thirty. He said goodnight to me."

"I have to make sure no one goes near the body until the police arrive."

Richie pulled on a sweatshirt, then pushed his feet into sneakers, grabbed the phone, and left the room. Remy and Vince had been the last two people downstairs after Richie and the girls had gone up. And Remy and Vince had gone to pick up the food together that afternoon. Had something happened while they were alone? Had Vince begun to suspect Remy, and now he was dead?

"Fuck! What the hell is going on?" Richie muttered as he walked past Mia, stepped out onto the deck, and dialed 911 without looking at Vince. He couldn't bear the sight of another dead body, not when he could wind up being the next victim.

FORTY-EIGHT

ALAN

Asha Singh was already in the office when Alan walked in. She sat at one of the empty desks, her gaze fixed on a printout she was holding, a cup of coffee and a muffin from a local bakery on the desk before her. Alan took off his jacket, hung it up in his office, then settled at the desk across from Asha. She looked up and smiled, but despite the stretching of the lips she looked sad and tired, the smile more a grimace.

"Any new leads?" Alan asked, not sure how to take her response.

"Possibly."

"Tell me."

"Serena Paulson created a new Gmail account for Lexie on July 23, 2022. My guess is that Lexie wasn't logged into her email on her phone and Serena got locked out when she tried to log in. So she created a new, almost identical email address and used it to keep in contact with Lexie's friends Stateside. They, of course, assumed the emails were coming from Lexie as she traveled from place to place."

"Is that significant?" Alan asked. "We already know Serena was impersonating Lexie."

"It is because the email address the invitation came from is different."

"Which means someone wanted everyone to think the invite had come from Lexie, but since they couldn't create an identical address or log into the account Serena was managing, they created an email address with a name everyone in the group would recognize."

"Exactly," Asha said. "I'm certain none of them looked at the address too closely since they believed it to be from Lexie, but Serena would have had quite a shock if she wasn't the one to send the email. I believe this is proof that someone else sent the invitation for the reunion."

"So, why did Serena go to the reunion if she knew someone was on to her?" Alan asked.

"I don't think she felt she had a choice. She needed to find out who sent that email, no matter the risk. She probably thought they intended to blackmail her and had some sort of plan for dealing with the situation."

"But things got out of hand," Alan concluded.

"So it would appear. And there's more," Asha said.

"Oh?"

"Mia Olsen opened an OnlyFans account thirteen months ago. She goes by the name SexyLexie69."

"The same as the email address. Now that *is* interesting," Alan said. "Should we pick her up?"

Asha shook her head. "Not yet. The techs have thoroughly checked Mia's devices, and there's nothing to connect her to what happened to Serena. Mia did not send the invite, nor did she look for rentals in the area or place any orders with local vendors. The only time Mia accessed the Airbnb site was when she clicked on the link in the invitation email."

"That doesn't mean she's not involved."

"No, it doesn't," Asha agreed. "And it would seem that Mia Olsen is known to us."

"Really? In what context?" Alan asked.

"Mia's father is Jarom Young."

"*The* Jarom Young?"

"You know of any others?" Asha challenged him. "That man is guilty of multiple counts of statutory rape, tax evasion, incitement, and a litany of other offenses, but we haven't been able to arrest him for lack of evidence. If we were, he'd be serving a life sentence, like his idol Warren Jeffs," she said with disgust.

"So, how is it that Mia is living in the outside world unchallenged?" Alan asked.

"After she escaped from the compound, Mia found her way to a women's shelter in Salt Lake City, and a civil rights lawyer took her case pro bono. She was given a new identity in exchange for testimony against her father, but she didn't know enough to really help our case. Her birth name is Miriam Allred, and her mother is Jarom Young's second wife, Hannah Allred."

"Do you think Mia's friends know about her past?"

"I don't know. Maybe. I don't think that's relevant, but her OnlyFans alter ego is. And the fact that she grew up around a man who's avoided justice for years is not a detail to be ignored."

"She doesn't strike me as someone who wants to follow in her father's footsteps."

Asha scoffed. "Jarom's disciples are all men, but children absorb information by osmosis, and girls are rarely noticed in places like the one where Mia grew up. She could have learned how to cover her tracks just by observing. And Mia is the only one of a handful of women who managed to escape from the compound who didn't get caught and dragged back by the hair. She's living life on her own terms, and to me that speaks volumes."

"But what would be Mia's motive?"

"I don't know too much about her relationship with Lexie, but if Serena had threatened her anonymity that would be a solid motive for murder."

"But why would Serena threaten Mia?" Alan asked.

"If Serena found out what Mia had been doing, that would give Serena ammunition to blackmail her."

Alan nodded, but he wasn't swayed by Asha's theory. "The person who organized the reunion had a phone with Lexie's old number and they used it and Lexie's credit card to book the Airbnb and make all the arrangements. If Serena took Lexie's wallet and phone, then she would be the one to have both," he reasoned.

"And the only person who could gain access to said phone and wallet would be her husband," Asha replied with a nod of acquiescence.

"Which brings us back to Noah," Alan said.

"Yes, but without the phone or a credit card found in his possession our case against him is circumstantial at best."

"And the clock is ticking."

"We need to file a motion to extend the detention window for Noah Paulson," Asha said.

"I'll get onto the judge."

Asha was about to reply when her cellphone vibrated, and she held up one finger, presumably asking Alan to wait until she was done.

A panicked officer exploded into the room. "Sheriff, a 911 call just came in from the house on Witch Lake."

"Which house?" Alan demanded, already halfway out of his chair.

"Four Lake Drive. The one where Serena Paulson was murdered. You need to get out there right away."

"Was the caller hurt?"

"No, he wasn't."

"What's the nature of the emergency?" Alan exclaimed.

"There's been another suspicious death, sir."

"I'll call you back," Asha said into the phone, and ended the call. "I'm going to speak to the judge, then get onto the lab about the DNA results. I'll meet you back here, Sheriff."

Alan nodded. He didn't like to admit it, but he was glad Asha Singh wasn't coming out to the house. This was his jurisdiction, and he would look ineffectual if he was seen to be babysat by a federal officer. Alan and Linda Nunes were perfectly capable of responding to a 911 call, even if it had come from the address where another death had taken place only two days before. He would radio for back-up if he needed it.

FORTY-NINE
ANGELINA

Angelina was woken by a police siren and immediately sat up and turned to look for Mia, but Mia was gone, the comforter carelessly thrown over her bed. What was happening? Had the police come for Noah again? Angelina pulled on a pair of leggings and a long sweater and shoved her bare feet into Uggs. She was glad she'd brought them. It was cold, and no one had thought to turn on the heat last night. She was desperate to get downstairs and see what was going on, but first she needed to pee and brush her teeth. She had a terrible taste in her mouth after all that wine they'd drunk yesterday.

When she came down a few minutes later, Sheriff DeVries was in the kitchen, his expression murderous as he looked at all of them in turn. Officer Nunes was on the deck, standing next to a man who looked vaguely familiar. DeVries glared at her just as she remembered who the man was, then stepped outside and shut the sliding door behind him as he went to speak to the coroner.

"What happened?" Angelina whispered to Mia, who was white as a sheet, her hand icy when Angelina touched it to get her attention.

"It's Vince," Mia said quietly. "Vince is dead."

Angelina's hand flew to her mouth, but not before she let out a pitiful wail of distress. Bile pooled in her mouth, and she rushed over to the sink to get some water. The water was tepid, but it did help, and she took several long gulps before setting the glass on the counter. As soon as she felt better, Angelina turned to Richie, who stood silently behind Mia, the counter at his back. Noah occupied the same chair he'd sat in the day before, his gaze stony. There was no point asking him anything. He seemed barely aware of his surroundings. And Remy was looking out the window, all his attention on the coroner and DeVries.

"Richie, what happened?" Angelina asked hoarsely.

Richie shrugged. "Mia and I found Vince when we came down this morning. He must have died sometime last night."

"How?" Angelina moaned.

"I think he froze to death," Mia ventured softly.

"Froze to death?" Angelina repeated. "Are you kidding me? We're not in Alaska. This is upstate New York, and it's early November."

"It got really cold last night."

"Surely not cold enough to freeze." Angelina turned back to Richie, who wore a closed expression and refused to meet her gaze. "You don't think he froze," she spat at him. "I can see it in your face."

"No, I don't," Richie replied, but didn't elaborate.

"What did Vince ever do to anyone?" Angelina cried. "He wasn't even part of the group. Why would anyone want to—?" She turned to Remy, who was now watching her, but stopped herself from saying something accusatory just in time. She wasn't going to point fingers in front of the sheriff, who was just waiting for someone to give him an excuse to make an arrest.

Remy seemed confused by Angelina's obvious hostility, then looked at the floor. He backed away from the door when DeVries slid it open and came back inside.

"What happened?" the sheriff demanded, his demeanor

pugnacious and his eyes narrowed in suspicion as he looked around the group. "Can you not spend a night together without someone winding up dead?"

"Could Vince have frozen to death?" Mia asked. She sounded shaky but seemed determined to push her ridiculous theory.

"I very much doubt it," DeVries replied dismissively.

Angelina instantly felt defensive on Mia's behalf, but held her tongue. This wasn't the time to antagonize the sheriff, not when he looked like he was ready to haul them all to the police station, and she agreed with his assessment.

"First, I'm going to need an account of your movements last night. And then, I'm going to take this house apart piece by piece," DeVries said. "And this time, I will have CSI search through your belongings."

"I hope you have a warrant," Richie said.

"I do. The judge just emailed it over, Mr. Vaccaro." DeVries held up his phone so Richie could see the copy of the warrant. "If you'd like to examine the hard copy, you'll have to come to the station. Now, get dressed and wait outside. All of you. And leave by the front door. I don't want you traipsing all over the crime scene."

By the time the five of them filed outside, the coroner had zipped Vince into a body bag and, with the help of his assistant, maneuvered the gurney down the steps and toward the waiting van. They all stood in silence as the body was loaded into the back, and the doors were slammed shut with heartbreaking finality. Mia was crying softly. Noah had his hands in his pockets and was looking at his feet. Remy was staring at the lake, but Richie looked on, unflinching in the face of another sudden death. Angelina didn't want to watch, but she felt she owed it to Vince to bear witness. She hoped she would be invited to the funeral. She wanted to pay her respects to a man she had overlooked in life and could only love in death.

As soon as the coroner's van pulled away, the CSI unit arrived.

It was difficult to tell if it was the same team since the techs looked identical in their white suits and snug hoods that reduced their faces to pinched ovals. As before, they split up, several people heading up to the deck and the rest using the front door to access the interior of the house. Angelina glanced at the rest of the group. No one seemed to know what they should do or made eye contact. Everyone gazed toward the lake, since they clearly didn't care to look at one another. It was all too much, and Vince's death had hit too close to home.

"It's too cold to stand out here," Remy finally said. "Let's go to a diner. We can have some breakfast and hang out until they're finished and we can come back inside."

"How can you even think about food?" Mia screeched. She looked horrified, and, despite her overall pallor, the tip of her nose was pink with cold.

"We can't just stand here," Remy retorted. "This might take hours. And at least we'll be warm and there will be coffee."

"I could eat," Richie said with a shrug.

"God, what is it with you two?" Angelina cried. "Vince is dead. Do you not even care?"

"Not eating won't bring him back," Remy pointed out reasonably. "If you don't want to eat, maybe we can find a library or a park where you can wait in noble solitude. We'll pick you up on the way back."

"Fine, I'll come," Angelina exclaimed. She was angry and frustrated but didn't feel righteous enough to sit by herself in the library or freeze her ass off in some park. "Does anyone have their car keys?"

"Right here," Richie said, and dangled his keys before her. "Remy, give me the phone. I need the GPS."

"You may as well hand the phone over," Mia said. "You know they'll find it now that Richie called the police."

"I'm not handing it over till they make me," Remy said and passed the phone to Richie. "Come on, let's go."

Noah hadn't said a word, but, when Richie got in the Jeep and slammed the door shut, he suddenly pivoted on his heel and vomited into a nearby bush. He wiped his mouth with the back of his hand, then silently got in the car and turned to stare out the window.

FIFTY

ANGELINA

No one spoke during the drive to the diner. Only the perky female voice of the GPS could be heard guiding Richie toward the Corner Café. Angelina tried to hold back tears as she sat in the front seat next to Richie. Noah and Remy stared out the window, and Mia sat with her head bowed, her hands folded in her lap, clearly unable to look at any of them.

The diner was near the town center and looked like something from the 1950s, but, whereas some places intentionally recreated the retro vibe, this place had probably remained frozen in time from when it had been trendy and new. The diner resembled or actually had been a train car, and there were the obligatory red vinyl stools at the counter, matching booths whose seats were faded and cracked, and a black-and-white checkered floor. A few old-timers sat at the counter, nursing bottomless cups of coffee and chatting up the woman behind the counter. Two short-order cooks could be seen through the opening behind the counter, and two middle-aged waitresses moved up and down the length of the establishment, delivering food, pouring coffee, and exchanging news with the customers.

Everyone turned to gawk when the group walked in, the patrons' glances ranging from curious to hostile. This was a small town, and the locals must have heard what had happened at 4 Lake Drive. It took a moment for the woman who had to be the owner to decide whether she wanted to serve them, but her business sense prevailed and she sauntered over to the group, a smile of welcome stretching her thick, red-painted lips. She could have given the Joker a run for his money, especially since she'd completed the look with green eyeshadow, Angelina mused distractedly.

"Good morning. Will it be the five of you, or are you expecting one more?"

She wouldn't have heard about Vince's death, but she clearly knew who they were and where they'd come from.

"Five," Angelina said. "Can we take the booth at the back?" She couldn't bear to sit in the middle, where everyone would keep looking at them.

"Sure, honey," the woman said. "Go on. Your server will be with you in a minute."

The woman retreated behind the counter, but her gaze followed them as they walked toward the back and settled in the booth. Mia, Noah, and Angelina sat with their backs to the room. Richie and Remy sat facing forward. One of the servers, a tired-looking woman with faded bleach-blond hair, approached as soon as they were settled and set down menus that were sticky with use.

"Coffee for everyone?" she asked, looking around the group.

"Please," Richie answered, and everyone nodded.

The woman nodded and walked away, leaving them to peruse the offerings. She returned with a fresh pot of coffee, filled their cups, then left again, presumably to set down the pot before she returned to take their orders. Everyone pretended to be deeply absorbed in reading the menu, but they closed their folios and set them on the table as soon as the waitress came back. For a group of people who were grieving and in shock, they ordered a lot of food, and settled in to wait once the server stalked off, everyone intensely focused on fixing their coffee to their liking.

"Noah, did Serena keep in contact with Vince?" Mia asked, finally breaking the silence after several long minutes.

Noah shrugged. "I don't think so, but I'm clearly not the right person to ask."

"Don't beat yourself up," Angelina said. "You couldn't have known."

"Known what?" Noah asked belligerently. "That Serena knew Lexie was dead? That she might have been involved? That she lied to me for years? Or that she did everything in her power to drive the knife a little deeper with every post and every revelation about Lexie's new life?" His gaze shifted from one sad face to another. "The question is, what did Vince know?"

"Maybe he didn't know anything," Angelina said. "Sometimes people just die. They have conditions they're not aware of or an allergic reaction."

Noah turned to stare at her. "Are you seriously suggesting that two days after Serena was murdered, Vince suddenly suffered an allergic reaction that killed him?"

"I really don't think we should speculate until we find out the cause of death," Richie interjected.

"Why?" Noah demanded. "So you can decide whether you should distance yourself? It's okay. I get it, Richie. You need to look out for number one."

"Noah," Richie began, but didn't finish his thought since the waitress approached their booth, somehow carrying all their orders at once. She set the plates before them, asked if they needed anything else, then retreated behind the counter, where she muttered something to the owner. The woman nodded, her gaze sweeping over them, before she made a point of looking away.

"Guys, can we not make a spectacle of ourselves?" Mia asked quietly. "Everyone is staring at us."

"So, let them stare," Noah said. He turned to look at Remy. "Enjoying that omelet?"

"It's fine. Why don't you just eat, Noah," Remy replied coldly. "This is neither the time nor the place to talk about this."

"And what would be the right time, Remy?" Noah snapped.

"If you want to get into it, we can do that once we're back at the house, where we can at least speak in private."

Noah nodded and stared at his plate, which contained two slices of whole wheat toast, two packets of butter, and two plastic containers of strawberry jelly. He took a bite of his dry toast, then set it down again, his Adam's apple bobbing as he tried to swallow. It was obvious he couldn't get it down, so he took a sip of coffee and turned toward the window, looking out over the parking lot with that vacant stare that was becoming so familiar. It seemed his anger had burned out and now he wanted to be left alone.

In the harsh light streaming through the window, Noah looked pale and gaunt, his three-day beard making him seem unkempt rather than sexy and his weight loss suddenly obvious. He'd hardly eaten anything since Friday night, and his hands shook slightly as he set down his coffee cup. Seeing Noah's suffering made Angelina uncomfortable, so she turned to look at Remy and Richie, who looked unperturbed as they applied themselves to their breakfast.

FIFTY-ONE

REMY

Remy could feel the tension swirling around him. Noah shut his eyes and leaned his head against the wall, too depleted by his outburst to engage with anyone. But tortured as he might feel, his initial shock was beginning to wear off, and he was entering the anger stage of the grieving process. It was probably happening sooner than anyone would expect, but, given everything he'd learned in recent days, it was perfectly natural for him to feel hurt, betrayed, and angry. Remy could only hope that, when Noah finally did lose it, it would be in a controlled environment.

Mia was avoiding making eye contact with Remy, and Richie, who could always be counted on to break the ice in any situation, was inhaling his breakfast burrito and not speaking to anyone. Angelina was openly staring at Remy, the question right there in her eyes. *Did you kill Vince, and by extension Serena?* Remy could ask her the same question. In fact, he could ask it of any of them. Someone at this table had killed at least once, but who? Remy had known these people since he was eighteen. There were times when he really liked them and times when he'd hated their guts, but he couldn't accept that one of them was a remorseless killer.

And why Vince? Were revelations about what he'd been up to forthcoming? Was there more than had met the eye to mild-mannered, soft-spoken Vincent? Or had Vince figured it all out? The only person he would have shared his suspicions with was Angelina, but Remy saw her go up last night, and then Vince went up to his room nearly two hours later. What happened after he went to bed? Remy guessed the autopsy results would tell them more, but at this point they were all fucked one way or another. DeVries was not going to let them leave, not now that there had been another death. They were trapped, sharing an isolated house with someone who might feel driven to kill again.

Remy didn't often pray, but he was praying now. He prayed he'd make it out alive.

FIFTY-TWO

MIA

Mia ordered pancakes, but couldn't manage to swallow more than a few bites. The dough was sticking in her throat, and she felt like she was going to be sick. Her hands were sweaty, and her heart was racing. She needed to speak to Sheriff DeVries, but she didn't have a phone and couldn't approach him in front of the others. She had to tread carefully, or she might be the next one they zipped into a body bag.

Mia could tell Angelina thought Remy was somehow involved. She might be right. Remy and Vince were alone together for at least an hour last night. Remy must have said something that had tipped Vince off, and now Vince was dead. Poor, sweet Vince. Mia thought he'd loved Angelina. Not in that crazy, let's throw caution to the wind and ride off into the sunset kind of way, but in a quiet, dignified manner that lasted a lifetime, not a few sexually charged months or several volatile years. Vince had been a keeper, the sort of guy any woman would be lucky to meet.

What had Vince seen or heard that had suddenly made him a threat? Mia felt terrified, and didn't know whom to trust. She didn't think she could trust Richie. She was certain she'd seen him outside, giving Vince a small plastic bag, and there had been something watchful and stealthy in his manner. And then Richie came inside and went upstairs. A few hours later, Vince was dead.

How do I get to Sheriff DeVries without attracting the attention of the others? Mia thought desperately.

FIFTY-THREE

RICHIE

When the waitress brought over the check, Richie said, "I got it," and handed her a credit card, but she shook her head.

"You have to pay at the front, dear, but all the tips are in cash."

Richie tossed a twenty onto the table and stood. Everyone followed, walking like zombies toward the door. He thought it was probably too soon to go back to the house, but they had sat over breakfast for as long as it was bearable, and wanted only to be in a place where they could be safe from judgmental looks and whispered comments. At least at the house they could all hide in their rooms or go for a walk if they needed to be alone. Although, given the current situation, being on one's own could be detrimental to one's health.

Richie stopped by the register and handed his card to the hostess, who'd followed their progress to the door and had come out from behind the counter to take the payment. It was just as Richie replaced his credit card in his wallet that a police cruiser with the siren blaring pulled up before the diner. Everyone froze for a moment, then looked around, but no robbery was in progress, and no one was engaged in an altercation.

"They're probably just hungry," Mia said a tad sarcastically.

"That hardly requires a siren," Angelina replied. There was a tremor in her voice. This didn't bode well, and they all knew it, since all eyes were now fixed on them.

Noah silently walked through the door. The rest of them followed. Sheriff DeVries was already out of the car, and an officer they hadn't met was getting out of the driver's side. Nunes was by herself in a second car that had just pulled up.

"Gentlemen, I'd like a word down at the station," Sheriff DeVries said.

"Which gentlemen?" Richie asked.

"Mr. Durant and Mr. Paulson, and you as well, Mr. Vaccaro, as Mr. Paulson's legal counsel."

"I will not be representing Noah Paulson," Richie said. "I feel it would be a conflict of interest."

"You don't say," DeVries said, his lip curling with sarcasm.

"What is this about, Sheriff?" Richie asked. He tried to appear unperturbed, but it wasn't hard to see he was concerned.

"I think we should do this down at the station, don't you?" DeVries replied.

"What is it that we're doing, Sheriff?" Remy asked.

"Are you rearresting me?" Noah asked woodenly.

"Not yet, but I do have questions for you."

"I've already answered your questions, and I will not answer any more without an attorney present," Noah said.

"Fair enough. We'll be happy to call a public defender for you, Mr. Paulson. Would you care to represent Mr. Durant, Mr. Vaccaro?"

"I think it's best if I recuse myself from this case entirely," Richie said.

"Very wise decision," DeVries said with a nod.

"Look, what is this about?" Remy demanded. He pulled himself up to his full height, his stance defiant. He shot the sheriff a look of righteous indignation, which clearly irritated the man.

"All right, if you insist. Agent Singh requested further DNA testing, and the results have just come back," DeVries announced. He appeared to be enjoying himself, especially since he had a live audience that wasn't limited to his suspects. Diners were looking through the windows, their food forgotten as they watched the drama play out before them.

"And?" Richie demanded.

"You really want me to answer that in a parking lot?"

"Why not?" Richie replied. "Everyone may as well hear what you have to say, since what happened concerns us all."

DeVries nodded, a small smile tugging at his lips. "Some of you more than others, it would seem." He fixed his gaze on Remy, who appeared to be trying to work out how additional DNA testing might relate to him. "It seems you are the father of Serena's baby, Mr. Durant. So you can come voluntarily, or I can arrest you. The choice is yours."

The shock was unanimous, everyone staring at the sheriff as if waiting for the punchline that surely had to come. Noah made a sound that was difficult to classify, but had to be a combination of shock, pain, anger, and unimaginable betrayal. Angelina's hand flew to her mouth as she turned to look at Noah, and Richie shook his head in disbelief. He'd asked DeVries to share the news, but the fact that he had, and so publicly, was still as inappropriate as it was incendiary.

Remy stood stock-still, his mouth partially open and his gaze reflecting his incomprehension. He was so distracted, he did not notice Noah lunge toward him. Before anyone could react, Noah slammed into Remy, his roar of agony so raw and laced with such visceral pain, it had the power to chill anyone within hearing distance. And then Remy went down, his head hitting the asphalt with a dull thud as Noah threw himself on top and punched him in the face again and again. Remy gasped for breath as blood poured from his nose and mouth. He tried to protect his face, but the gesture only seemed to infuriate Noah all the more. He punched Remy on the side of the head and then, when Remy's hands jerked away, Noah hit him squarely on the nose. The impact slammed Remy's head against the ground again. There was the crunch of breaking bone, and bile and blood spilled from his injured mouth.

He managed to turn his head sideways to avoid choking on his vomit.

Richie and the nameless cop finally sprang into action and dragged Noah off Remy. The cop attempted to restrain him, but Noah was completely unhinged. He tried to free his arms and spewed obscenities at the policeman, who'd grabbed him from behind, all the while trying to kick Richie. The cop finally managed to cuff Noah and push him up against the sheriff's car. Richie, who'd taken a punch to the stomach, was bent over, panting as he rested his hands on his thighs.

"Noah Paulson, I'm arresting you on a charge of aggravated assault," Sheriff DeVries intoned.

He read Noah his rights, then pushed him into the back of the cruiser, while Officer Nunes radioed for an ambulance. Looking horrified, she fell to her knees next to Remy, who was gasping for air. Nunes laid her hands on Remy's shoulders and urged him to calm down, but Remy didn't appear to be paying any attention to her.

"The ambulance is on its way," she told him softly. "Try to breathe through your mouth. In and out. In and out."

Remy's chest heaved with the effort, and his legs jerked, but after a time he seemed to grow quieter, then went completely limp. His eyes fluttered shut and his head rolled to the side. His face was a pulpy mess, and his sweatshirt was covered in vomit and blood.

"He's passed out," Officer Nunes cried. "Where is the ambulance?"

It was another ten minutes before a siren pierced the air, and then an ambulance with the name of a local hospital on the side pulled into the parking lot. The paramedics jumped out and went to Remy, and checked his vitals before they strapped an oxygen mask over his nose and mouth and lifted him onto a gurney.

"Can I go to the hospital with him?" Mia cried as she lurched toward Sheriff DeVries. "He'll need someone with him."

DeVries shook his head. "Sorry, you can't go with him in the ambulance. But my officer will go with him, he won't be on his own." Looking down at Mia's desperate expression, he added, "You can meet them at the hospital if you like."

"Sheriff, I need to speak to you," Mia pleaded softly.

"Then come to the station, Miss Olsen."

Mia looked like a dog that had been kicked, but backed away, and stopped only when she reached Angelina. As soon as Remy was lifted into the back of the ambulance and the cop climbed in after him, DeVries got into the car and pulled out of the parking lot. Officer Nunes trailed the ambulance, and within a few moments all was quiet, the pool of blood and vomit on the asphalt the only evidence that a fight had taken place minutes before.

FIFTY-FOUR

ALAN

Once Alan returned to the station, he locked Noah in a holding cell, then placed a call to the Public Defender's Office. He thought he'd get a sandwich from the deli at the corner, since going back to the diner would result in him answering questions for the better part of an hour and he needed time to think. When Asha Singh walked through the door, he said, "I was about to get some lunch. Care to join me?"

Asha looked tense but shrugged and nodded. "Why not? It's always more pleasant to talk over a meal, and it seems we have plenty to discuss."

"We just brought in Noah Paulson. He jumped Remy Durant when he found out Durant was the father of Serena's child."

"I almost feel sorry for the guy," Asha said with a shake of her head. "Imagine how he must have felt hearing that bit of news after everything that had already happened."

"I sympathize, but I can hardly allow him to get away with aggravated assault, no matter how justified he might feel. Mr. Durant is pretty banged up."

"Do we know if he has sustained any serious injuries?"

"I'll give my officer a call once we get our lunch. He should know something by then."

They walked to the deli, ordered their sandwiches, then took the food back to the station, in case there were developments and they should be needed. The afternoon was pleasantly mild, the sunshine warm on their shoulders and the air wonderfully crisp. They decided to eat outside and settled at the metal picnic table, where they wouldn't be disturbed.

The earthy scent of sun-warmed grass mingled with the citrusy aroma of Asha's tea, and Alan wished they could just stay for a while, two people having lunch and getting to know each other rather than two law enforcement officers discussing violent death. It fully struck Alan at that moment how much he looked forward to his retirement and how desperately he wanted to solve this case before he went. Not because he was worried about his legacy but because three young people were dead. They deserved justice, and it was up to him and Asha to get it for them.

"Do you think Remy knew the baby was his?" Asha asked once she'd unwrapped her veggie panini and taken a small bite.

"I don't think so," Alan said. "He looked as shocked as Noah when he heard the news. The better question is, did Serena know the baby wasn't her husband's?"

"Impossible to tell, but it likely wasn't the product of an assault or she wouldn't be willing to spend a weekend with Remy."

"True," Alan conceded, but this new revelation just didn't make sense to him. "Every one of those people told us how much Serena loved Noah, so why would she have an affair with his friend?"

"Maybe she wasn't as happy as she claimed," Asha replied. "He clearly still loved Lexie."

Alan sighed. "It all revolves around Lexie, doesn't it?"

"It would seem so."

"Maybe Serena never told anyone about the pregnancy because she was going to have an abortion," Alan speculated.

Asha shook her head. "She had every intention of keeping the baby."

"How do you know?"

"Serena recently created a baby board on Pinterest and was in the process of pinning baby furniture and looking at strollers and infant car seats. She also spent a considerable amount of time watching pregnancy announcements on Instagram. That doesn't sound like someone who's about to have an abortion. And she would have had to have it very soon."

"Then she'd probably intended to pass the baby off as Noah's," Alan concluded.

Asha took a sip of tea, her expression thoughtful as she swallowed. "These days, it's not so easy to pass off another man's baby as your husband's. All it takes is one swab to learn the truth. I think Serena believed the baby was Noah's."

"The fact that she hadn't told him suggests otherwise," Alan countered.

Asha shook her head again. "Maybe she did tell him. Maybe she even confessed that she'd slept with Remy Durant."

"Which would give Noah a motive that had nothing to do with Lexie Hall."

"That supposition still doesn't rule Lexie out of the equation," Asha replied. "Someone arranged that reunion. And if it wasn't Serena..." She made the universal "beats me" gesture, then checked her phone.

"Any news out of Thailand?"

"Not yet," Asha replied distractedly. "But the results of Vincent Howard's postmortem just came in."

"And?"

"Vince died of an overdose, but they'll know more once the tox screen comes back."

"Could have been self-inflicted."

"Dr. Klein doesn't think so," Asha said as she scrolled through the report on her phone. "She found no evidence of systematic drug use, and the presentation didn't match what she would expect if Vince had taken the drugs shortly before his death. A drug overdose causes vomiting, rapid breathing and accelerated heart rate, tremors, seizures, and at times even full-blown psychosis. Surely someone would have noticed if Vince had experienced any of those symptoms."

"He was found outside," Alan reminded her.

"Yes, but Dr. Klein found no evidence of vomiting or cardiac distress. No excessive sweating occurred before death, and there's no evidence to suggest that Vince had suffered a seizure."

"What are you saying, precisely?" Alan asked.

"According to the results of the postmortem, Vince seems to have quietly slipped away."

"So, what made the doctor think the cause of death might have been a drug overdose?"

"She found a baggie of white powder in his jacket pocket."

"Cocaine?"

"Ketamine. Dr. Klein had the baggie dusted for prints, but it had been wiped clean."

"Did the search of the premises yield anything?" Alan asked. He was losing hope by the minute that they would unearth any helpful clues.

"Yes." Asha smiled for the first time since they'd sat down. "An empty prescription container was found in the garbage bin."

"Well, don't keep me in suspense," Alan exclaimed.

"It was for eszopiclone, which is a sleep aid, and it had been prescribed for Mia Olsen."

"Any prints?"

Asha nodded triumphantly. "Mia's, and Noah's."

"Mia Olsen said she wanted to speak to me," Alan supplied. "I asked her to come to the station."

"If she doesn't show soon, we'll need to pick her up."

"Think she wants to confess?"

Asha scoffed. "The more likely scenario is that she wants to tell us that her prescription has gone missing in order to deflect suspicion from herself should the bottle turn up."

"I think it's more telling that Noah's prints are on the bottle," Alan theorized.

"We'll have to ask him about that once his lawyer arrives."

"What are your thoughts?" Alan asked, his cheesesteak sandwich forgotten. This and the results of the DNA test and the postmortem were a real breakthrough in the case.

Asha took another sip of tea before replying. "Remy Durant being the biological father of Serena's baby is just one more strike against Noah Paulson. If he discovered that Serena was carrying on with his friend and was pregnant, he'd have a solid motive for murder. And now we have Noah's prints on the bottle of pills, which could very well turn out to be the murder weapon in the death of Vincent Howard. If he overdosed on sleeping pills, he wouldn't exhibit the usual symptoms but die quietly, without anyone noticing."

"But why murder Vince?" Alan asked. "You think he knew Noah was guilty?"

"Perhaps Vince had seen or heard something, or maybe he wasn't the intended victim," Asha said. "We don't yet know how the overdose was administered. It's entirely possible that Vince was killed by mistake."

"Could Mia be our killer? She has an OnlyFans account in the name of a woman who died under suspicious circumstances, and now her meds are missing."

"I think our killer is too smart to use their own pills and then simply throw the empty container in the trash for anyone to find. And who supplied the ketamine?" Asha mused. "Sleeping pills mixed with ketamine would be a lethal combination."

"You think someone took Mia's medication?"

Asha nodded. "I do. And they intentionally left the bottle where it would be found by the CSI techs. I think the killer was hoping to frame Mia or Noah for the murder of Vincent Howard."

"This killer is diabolical," Alan said.

"And most likely someone who has until now flown completely under the radar."

"Are you thinking Richard Vaccaro or Angelina Cabrera?"

"Angelina is a nurse. Her medical knowledge could be useful. But what's her motive?" Asha asked. "She wasn't particularly close with either Serena or Noah and hadn't seen either of them in person in months. She couldn't have known Lexie was dead, nor were the techs able to find any incriminating evidence on her phone."

"That leaves Vaccaro."

Asha nodded. "It does, doesn't it?"

"So, what would be his motive?" Alan asked.

"Maybe there was bad blood between Richie and Serena."

Alan considered this possibility. "Richie would be able to get away with murder, unless Vince happened to see something that might have incriminated him."

"My thoughts precisely," Asha said. "He's a criminal attorney and knows exactly what we would be looking for and how to avoid getting caught. Also, by first agreeing to represent Noah, he was present for the interview and now knows what we know. If you ask me, it's the perfect cover."

"But is there any physical evidence to link Richard Vaccaro to either murder?"

"Richie and Serena weren't in contact, but then he received a call from her last week. She left a message, which has since been deleted. The techs were able to retrieve it from the Deleted Messages folder."

"What did the message say?" Alan asked, really on tenterhooks now. They were finally getting closer. He could feel it in his bones.

"Serena threatened Richie, quite graphically, I might add. It seems she was afraid her husband would find out that she'd slept with him."

Alan screwed up his nose. "But is that really motive for murder? So they had a fling. It's amoral but not illegal. And clearly she was putting it about. But why kill her? And why murder Vince? Or Remy, if he was the intended victim?"

Asha looked thoughtful, as if she were trying to connect the dots. "Did Richie and Lexie ever date? Was he in love with her too?"

"I don't believe so, but maybe he's the sort who holds his cards close to his chest when it comes to matters of the heart."

"Could be," Asha allowed. "My theory is that when no one had spoken to Lexie in person for over three years, Richie grew suspicious and decided to do a little digging. With his level of access, it wouldn't be too difficult for him to discover that Lexie was dead and had been since her trip to Thailand with Serena. If he knew that, then he'd also know that the posts and emails were fake, and the only person who could have maintained an online presence in Lexie's name was Serena."

"So he arranged the reunion to flush her out," Alan supplied. "But was Serena's murder premeditated?"

"Perhaps Serena and Richie had a late-night confrontation that resulted in Serena's death."

"And was witnessed by Vince," Alan concluded.

"Exactly. I would even venture to suggest that Richie jumped in the lake and towed Serena's body to shore in an effort to explain his DNA on her body, if any was discovered, and also to check if the bruises on her neck were obvious. When he realized they were, he pointed them out to redirect attention from himself."

"So, when Richie realized his whole life was now compromised, he stole Mia's medication and somehow got Vince to take it," Alan continued. "What about the ketamine?"

"An extra layer of misdirection. As a criminal attorney, Richie is sure to know individuals who deal. He might have brought the drugs with him just in case he needed to frame someone, or make a death look like an overdose."

"But Richie and Noah go way back. Why would he try to frame Noah for the murder of his wife and then Vince?"

"People will do anything to save their own skin, Alan. As law enforcement officers, we know that. Perhaps Richie never meant for any of this to happen and only wanted everyone to find out what Serena had done, but then once Serena wound up dead he had no choice but to cover his tracks."

"And Richie was the one to call in Vince's murder," Alan said.

"Which means he has a second phone that he's kept hidden. I've already asked the techs to pull the records for that number. We'll see if anything incriminating comes up."

"Should Linda and I pick him up?" Alan asked.

"Not yet," Asha replied with a shake of her head. "Richie Vaccaro is not going to simply admit to what he's done because we present him with a theory. We need irrefutable evidence if we are to construct a case against him. We can hardly use one deleted message as proof that he had motive to murder Serena. Perhaps there's evidence on the second phone or on his personal computer. We'll have to obtain a warrant to search his apartment and seize his computer. And we have cause to pursue a case against Noah, especially now that his fingerprints are on the bottle and he attacked Remy Durant. Even if he's innocent of murdering two people, he is guilty of assault. We also have to conclusively rule out that someone we're not aware of visited the house. If we don't, the defense will try to float that theory."

Alan shook his head. "I had Linda Nunes and Officer Salter check the Ring camera footage. It's stored in the cloud for sixty days. No one is seen coming or going on the night of either murder. And the other houses on Witch Lake are all empty. Linda checked the properties and there's no evidence that anyone has been there in recent days. They're all locked up tight, and the real estate agents have not shown the properties to anyone since before the booking for the reunion was made."

"So it was definitely someone who was already in the house," Asha said.

"It had to be. I have a suggestion."

"I'm all ears."

"I think we should drag the lake. Not the entire lake, but the area within throwing distance of the dock."

"What do you hope to find?" Asha asked.

"Our killer is too savvy to toss a cellphone, laptop, or iPad into the trash or hide them in the woods. The best way to dispose of anything incriminating would be to throw it in the lake."

Asha nodded. "I also think we need to analyze every bottle taken from the house. If someone mixed sleeping pills into Vince's drink, there will be residue at the bottom, and hopefully both Vince's and the killer's fingerprints."

"Then we should also test every glass and cup," Alan said.

"If they used a cup, they'd have already put it through the dishwasher," Asha replied. "I know I would. But if they mixed the crushed pills into a water or beer bottle, they would have thrown it away so as not to attract attention."

Alan nodded. "Definitely worth checking. I'll ping the CSI team."

"And I'll put in a request for divers," Asha said. "We're going to nail this bastard."

FIFTY-FIVE

MIA

As soon as the sirens died away and they finally left the diner, Mia informed Richie and Angelina that she would be going to the hospital. She didn't mention that she would be stopping by the police station on her way to see Remy, and neither of them asked about her conversation with Sheriff DeVries. Mia thought Angelina might offer to come with her, but was relieved when she didn't. Angelina probably welcomed the opportunity to spend time with Richie and would make the most of having him all to herself, especially now, when she had to be grief-stricken over Vince and probably even more afraid.

  The drive to the house was tense, no one daring to comment on what had just happened and what it might mean. Mia was the first out of the car when they pulled up, desperate to leave as quickly as possible. Thankfully, the techs had finished with the house, but two white-suited individuals were still working on the deck, and a few people were searching the nearby woods. Inside, the house felt empty and hostile, the silence so dense it almost felt solid. The thought of spending another night under its roof made Mia's heart race with apprehension, and she thought maybe she could ask Sheriff DeVries if she might be permitted to leave.

  She packed the essentials into her backpack, then stopped by

Richie and Remy's room to collect a few things for Remy. He would need a clean T-shirt and sweatshirt, since the ones he was wearing were stained with blood, and he could probably use a fresh pair of jeans, underwear, and socks, in case he needed to remain in the hospital for several days.

Mia picked up the book Remy had left on the bedside table, a spy thriller she'd never read herself, but the sort he seemed to love, and stuffed it into the backpack. She looked around one last time, then grabbed Remy's deodorant and bodywash from his toiletry bag, in case he wanted to freshen up. She didn't think he'd be brushing his teeth, given his busted lip and swollen mouth, but she added the toothbrush anyway. Then she was ready to leave.

Angelina was standing on the dock, staring morosely at the house across the lake. Richie had just slammed the trunk of his Jeep shut and was walking toward Mia. Unlike Angelina, who just looked sad, Richie looked angry and seemed to vibrate with nervous energy.

"I'm off," Mia said. Richie nodded. "I'll pass on your good wishes for a speedy recovery," Mia added nervously. Did Richie realize she wanted to speak to Sheriff DeVries about him? Hopefully not.

"Don't," Richie snapped.

"Why not?"

"Because the way I feel right now, I'd happily finish what Noah started."

"Richie, Remy is still your friend, no matter what he's done."

Richie shook his head sadly. "I'm not sure I have any friends, Mia. Not anymore."

"What do you mean?"

"I thought I knew these guys. I trusted them and shared my thoughts and feelings with them without reservation. But it seems they never trusted me the same way. All this was going on behind my back, and I had no idea."

"I'm not so sure they knew it was going on either, if that makes you feel any better."

"I'm sure Noah suspected something was off. And Remy slept with Serena at least once that we know of. He never said a word."

"Surely you don't tell your friends everything," Mia countered.

"I do, actually," Richie replied. "Those I trust, anyway. Lesson learned, right?"

Mia nodded. She couldn't argue with that. She didn't think she'd be able to trust any of them after this, not even if they were all cleared of suspicion and life eventually returned to some sort of normal. Mia's neighbor, who moonlighted as a bartender on weekends and slipped her free drinks, always said that old friendships were one third nostalgia, one third resentment, and one third delusion, a bitter cocktail some people were addicted to. Mia now realized there was probably some truth to that. What did any of them have in common anymore besides their college years and the misery of the pandemic, when they'd clung to each other, desperate not to feel so isolated and lonely with nothing but Zoom for company? She'd keep in touch with Angelina, but she didn't think she'd ever see the guys again. It was time she moved on.

"See you later," Mia said.

Richie raised a hand in farewell and stalked off, heading away from the house. Angelina never turned around, not even when Mia started the engine.

A sense of relief settled over Mia as she drove down the narrow track, then turned onto the two-lane road that led into town. There wasn't much traffic, just the occasional car passing in the opposite direction. The asphalt was dappled with autumn sunshine, the trees that lined the road thick and tall, their towering canopies as wild and bright as a child's drawing. It felt wonderfully liberating to be on her own and surrounded by nature, and, although she had initially felt conflicted, she knew she had to do the right thing. Mia had been taught to protect her own, never to betray her family's trust, but, as much as she'd come to rely on this group of people who'd at one time felt like family, she couldn't justify sitting on evidence that could potentially crack the case. If Richie was innocent, he'd find a way to prove it.

And if he was guilty, then it wasn't her responsibility to shield him from the law.

Mia turned on the radio and found a local station that played music from the 1980s. She loved some of those old songs and had danced to them with her mom when she was a kid. That was when they had still been allowed to listen to pop music. Boy George crooned lyrics that were oddly appropriate to the situation and her surroundings, and Mia sang that loving would be easy if colors were like dreams, red, gold, and green.

She didn't immediately react when she heard a pop that sounded like a gunshot. It had probably come from the woods. Were people permitted to hunt so close to the road? Then the car suddenly lurched sideways, skidding off the road with a screech of tires. She gripped the wheel and tried to hold it steady, but the vehicle careened into the woods as Mia cried out in terror. The hood collided with the massive trunk of a leafy maple at full tilt. Her last conscious thought was that she should have put on her seatbelt, and then the vivid colors of the world around her faded to black.

FIFTY-SIX

ALAN

"Boss, an accident has been reported on Route 39," Linda Nunes called out through the mic on Sheriff DeVries' shoulder. "The driver is Mia Olsen."

Alan sat up straighter, immediately alert. Mia had to have been on her way to the station. "Is she hurt?" he called back.

"She's on her way to the hospital."

"Which hospital?"

"Kingston."

"Who's at the scene?"

"Jim Salter."

"What was the cause of the accident?" Asha asked.

"Jim says she went off the road and slammed into a tree. No other vehicles were involved."

"I want a forensic team on that car right now," Alan exclaimed.

He was already halfway out of his seat and shoving the remnants of his lunch into the bag it had come in. Asha was doing the same. Alan tossed his garbage into the bin near the entrance to the station and hurried toward the police cruiser, while Asha disappeared inside the building. As Alan got in the car, he was faced with a choice. He could go to the scene of the accident and see what had happened for himself, or he could drive straight to the hospital and speak to Mia. He decided on the hospital. Officer Salter was young, but he was a smart kid and could be trusted to preserve the scene until the CSI unit arrived. They'd take it from there. Perhaps Mia had become distracted, or maybe she'd spotted a deer, or had been drinking. Until he saw her for himself, Alan wouldn't know what he was dealing with.

When he arrived at the hospital, Alan headed directly to the ER.

"Mia Olsen was brought in about ten minutes ago," the triage nurse confirmed. "Dr. Lansky is with her now."

"Can I speak to her?" Alan asked. "It's important."

The nurse shook her head. "I'm afraid not. She's unconscious. Cracked her head on the windshield."

"Did the airbag not deploy?" Alan asked.

"I really don't know. If you care to wait, I'll ask Dr. Lansky to come and speak to you as soon as he's finished."

"Okay, thanks."

Alan took a seat and looked around. There were several people in the waiting area, but although a few were in obvious discomfort no one looked seriously injured. A little boy was crying that his stomach hurt, a man was clutching his arm, and a frightened older woman kept poking at her left cheek. Alan's mother had suffered a stroke two years ago, and he thought he detected a touch of paralysis in the left side of the woman's face.

Turning away, he pulled out his phone. There was a message from Linda. The CSIs were on the scene and examining Mia's vehicle. The crime scene manager, Mark Childers, would update him soon. Alan hated waiting, especially when he had nothing but endless speculation to occupy his mind, so he walked over to the shop, purchased *Fly Fishing* magazine and a Snickers, and tried to distract himself as best he could.

He was finished with the magazine and more than ready for another candy bar when Dr. Lansky finally came out to speak to him. Alan had met Robert Lansky before and knew him to be a thorough and compassionate man. He was tall, lean, and very attractive, in an impoverished European aristocrat sort of way, according to Linda Nunes, who read nothing but romance novels set in England and France.

"Is Mia conscious?" Alan asked. "Can I speak to her?"

Lansky shook his head. "Mia suffered a traumatic brain injury when her frontal bone collided with the windshield. Three of her ribs were fractured, probably by the wheel when she was thrown against it, and she has two broken fingers and a badly bruised clavicle. There's swelling to the brain due to intercranial bleeding, and we will have no choice but to put her into an induced coma if the situation doesn't improve within the next few hours."

"Will she be all right?" Alan asked softly. He felt genuinely sorry for the girl and hoped she would make a full recovery.

"It's too soon to call, but I'm hopeful. I had her admitted to neurology."

"Rob, was she driving under the influence?"

"There was nothing in her blood, and I didn't smell any alcohol on her breath," Rob replied.

"Could she have suffered a seizure or a cardiac event of some sort?" Alan asked.

"No evidence of either."

"Is there anything else you can tell me?"

"I'd rather not speculate. You are welcome to call later. Ask for Dr. Pass. He's head of neurology."

"Thanks. What about Remy Durant? How's he doing?"

"Better than Mia. He is severely concussed and has suffered a fracture of the zygomatic bone. That's the cheekbone in layman's terms. But otherwise, he's all right. We're keeping him for observation."

"Has he said anything to you about the case?"

Rob smiled and shook his head in obvious disbelief. "Alan, my job is to treat the patients, not to question them."

"Can I see Remy?" Alan asked.

"That's not up to me, since Remy is no longer in the ER. Maybe his treating physician will allow you a few minutes."

"Okay. Thanks, Rob," Alan said, and headed for the elevators.

FIFTY-SEVEN

RICHIE

Richie breathed a sigh of relief when the CSIs finally collected their equipment, piled into the vans, and left. He'd thought he might feel more at peace with them gone, but the house that had seemed so beautiful and welcoming only two days before now felt tainted and unbearably empty with just him and Angelina, who immediately began to clean. Richie could understand her need to keep busy—it was her way of controlling the chaos and imposing order on a situation that was beyond her comprehension—but Richie couldn't stand her furious banging or the sharp smell of the kitchen cleaner she used. He needed to think, and he always thought best outdoors and often took solitary walks late at night, when the streets were nearly deserted and there were few cars on the roads.

    He went outside, tore off the police tape that had been used to cordon off the deck and carried a chair that wasn't smudged with black fingerprint powder to the end of the dock, and set it with its back to the house. The lake was calm, the surface mirroring the cloudless sky above and the gently swaying trees. Nature didn't give a shit what people got up to. Their little lives were nothing more than fallen leaves, vibrant one moment, compost the next. But the leaves had their cycle, and humans should too. To die in your twenties, when you still had so much living left to do, was the ultimate waste. But before Richie could consider the weightier matter of untimely death, his thoughts returned to Serena and Remy.

What the fuck was that all about? And the operative word here was fuck. How could Remy be the father of Serena's baby? Richie knew they had been friends, but he'd always thought the only reason Serena had made an effort to keep up with Remy was because he was the closest Serena could get to the world of fashion and celebrity. Remy had clout, as far as Serena was concerned. He met famous people and was sometimes invited to the sort of events she could only read about online. As far as Serena went, Remy was a rock star. But Richie had never, ever imagined that Serena would want to sleep with Remy, or that Remy would be game. For one, Noah was Remy's friend, and some lines should never be crossed, and for another Serena had never had eyes for anyone but Noah. How and why had Serena and Remy got together, and how many times had Serena been unfaithful to Noah? Had Remy been the first? And had Serena threatened Remy as well?

This time a week ago, Richie would have had all the answers, but now he was ready to admit that he knew nothing at all. The revelations about Lexie's death had shocked him to the core, nearly as much as the possibility that Serena had known and might have had a hand in what had happened to her best friend. Had she murdered Lexie to get to Noah? In the course of his work, Richie met people who lied, schemed, and cheated, but it took a lot to murder someone, especially someone a person knew and had presumably cared about at some point. To look someone in the face and hurt them took not only guts but the kind of detachment Richie had never seen in Serena. She had been emotional and needy and always worried what people would think. Sure, it took all sorts of people to commit murder. Some of the most notorious murderers had been people you'd never suspect—intelligent, respectful, often charming individuals who were never on anyone's radar until their faces were splashed all over the news.

But if Serena had murdered Lexie, then who had murdered Serena, and who had killed Vince? Stunned as he had been to learn about Serena's part in Lexie's death, Richie simply couldn't accept that one of the people he'd trusted would intentionally harm Serena, or have it out with her in the middle of the night and then stand by and allow her to drown if she fell in the lake by accident. And what had Vince to do with any of this? They rarely saw him, and he most definitely had not been in contact with Serena. She'd never liked him, and had been annoyed when Noah had insisted they invite him to the wedding. If Vince had seen something that had got him killed, why hadn't he said anything to the cops? Had he tried to blackmail the killer and been killed himself because of it?

And could Noah really not have known that Serena was pregnant? He'd lived with her, for God's sake. Richie had always known when his girlfriends had their periods. Hadn't Noah noticed that Serena was very, very late? Had they not had sex on a regular basis? They hadn't been married that long. Surely it took longer than a year of marital bliss for the passion to cool.

And why would Serena not tell him? She'd made no secret that she wanted to start a family sooner rather than later, so why would she not share the happy news as soon as she found out? It didn't make any sense—unless she had known that the baby wasn't Noah's and had been terrified he'd figure it out. Had he? Was that why Serena was dead? Had Noah lost his shit when he found out? If he had and Vince had seen something, that would explain Vince's death, but then why had Noah gone apeshit this morning when Sheriff DeVries had named Remy as the baby daddy? Was it because Noah had been humiliated that everyone would now know the truth or because he had to act surprised in order to divert suspicion?

Richie sighed. Poor Vince. He had been innocent in all this, and would still be alive if he'd refused the invitation. The only reason he'd come was because he'd hoped to get back with Angelina, but it was clear she wasn't really into him. Angelina had seemed content with Jake and it was a shame they'd broken up. He had been the yin to her yang, or maybe the calm to her storm. They'd made a good couple, until Jake had traded her in for a newer, less complicated model. Maybe he was happier, maybe not. These days everyone seemed to be suffering from a raging case of FOMO. No matter what they had, they always thought something better was just around the corner.

Richie's grandparents had met when Immaculata moved with her family from Alcamo to Palermo at the age of fifteen. Immaculata and Matteo had married when they were seventeen, had four children in quick succession, and never looked back. Now, nearly sixty years later, they were still happy, in that insane, never-hold-back, passive-aggressive way of people who were raised by poor, uneducated parents in a time before couples' therapy and political correctness, and said exactly what they thought the moment they thought it. The things they said to each other were as outrageous as they were hilarious, but neither took offense, and once they vented their anger they simply kissed and made up, and never went to bed angry. Maybe that was the way to do it. Find someone you like and give it your all, without fear, reservation, or regret. And fight a lot so you can have incredible make-up sex.

For the first time in his adult life, Richie thought he might be ready for a serious relationship. He was tired of dating shallow, spiteful girls who were always on the lookout for something better. He wanted to matter to someone, to be loved. To be the one. And now that he had been reminded once again how fleeting life was, he suddenly wanted so much more. But the path to any goal began by taking the first step, and the first step was to leave this place as soon as possible, before the cops found evidence that would implicate him in these murders and the only person he'd have a meaningful relationship with would be his cellmate.

Getting to his feet, Richie strode toward the house, his decision made.

FIFTY-EIGHT

REMY

All things considered, Remy was comfortable. He'd been given Percocet for the pain and felt pleasantly weightless, as if his spirit wasn't tethered to his body. After he'd gritted his teeth through an MRI the nurses left him to rest, and the other bed in his room was empty, for which he was truly grateful. He didn't think he could bear someone who'd leave the TV on for hours or entertain noisy visitors. He wasn't even tempted to look at his phone, which was just as well since he'd never taken it back from Richie. All he wanted was peace and quiet, and the opportunity to examine his feelings now that he'd had a chance to absorb the morning's news.

At first, he'd thought what he felt was grief, then he'd understood it wasn't really a feeling of loss but deep sadness at the realization that nothing would ever be the same again. He'd miss Noah, since there was no way they could ever get past this, but he hadn't loved Serena, nor did he feel bad about the baby. The kid had been nothing but a tiny bean and wouldn't have felt any pain when Serena died. It had probably just ceased to exist, quietly and peacefully, without any distress or fear.

Had Remy known the baby was his, he would have insisted Serena get an abortion. He didn't want children, not now, not ever. He'd seen what fucked-up parents could do to a child, and he didn't want to be responsible for ruining anyone's life. No one deserved that, especially not an innocent child who only wanted to be loved and noticed. Pixie had never noticed him; she'd had more important things to think about. And his grandparents had never missed an opportunity to remind him that he was a burden, and they hadn't signed up to raise a child at their age. Remy couldn't say he blamed them. A person might do right by someone, but they couldn't force themselves to truly love another human being if their heart wasn't in it.

But now, for the first time in his life, Remy understood that the circumstances forced on him weren't his fault, nor was anything that happened a punishment. He had been as innocent as Serena's baby, and he didn't have to answer for the sins of his parents or the failings of his grandparents. He was free to choose his own life, and perhaps he was fortunate that he didn't have to answer to anyone if he made a mistake. He supposed now he could see why Serena had suddenly been so desperate to try for a baby with Noah. She had intended to pass the child off as his, since she clearly hadn't wanted to get rid of the kid or tell Noah the truth. Remy didn't think she would have got away with it, not when a simple blood test or a drop of saliva could tell the real story, but Serena had always had a way of twisting the truth to fit her own narrative and might have talked Noah out of any doubts if he ever suspected the child wasn't his.

Remy had never meant for anything to happen between them. He'd never even wanted to be friends, but Serena had latched on to him after coming back from Thailand. She was always calling, asking for advice, and confiding in him about her relationship with Noah. He had been happy to listen, since he quite enjoyed other people's drama, but he hadn't cherished Serena. Not as a friend and not as a woman. He had been lonely though, and Serena had filled part of the space Lexie had left behind. He suspected Serena had been lonely as well. She'd got her man, and she'd got him to put a ring on it, but somewhere deep inside she must have known that Noah had still loved Lexie. Maybe screwing Remy had been a way to get back at Noah for not giving her his whole heart.

Or maybe it had been a momentary impulse that she'd regretted almost as soon as it had happened. Remy knew he had. He should have never agreed to do the photoshoot or allow her to take her clothes off. Serena had wanted him to take a series of tasteful nudes that she'd intended to give to Noah for his birthday. Nothing trashy, nothing obvious, just erotic black-and-white images that could be classified as art. Unfortunately, Remy's libido hadn't been able to make that distinction, and Serena had got pretty turned on as she turned this way and that, showing just enough to get him hot and bothered.

Remy was accustomed to photographing beautiful, scantily clad women, but there were usually other people in the room, and the models rarely noticed him. He was there to make them look good. They were tools, like an extension of his camera. Serena had noticed him, and she had directed all her playfulness at him, making sure he'd been aware of her every gesture and facial expression. She might have regretted it later, but she had wanted it then. And she'd got it.

It had been quick, rough, and utterly devoid of any genuine feeling. Remy had taken Serena against the wall, and they had both been driven by blind lust that had burned out as quickly as it had flared. He had assumed Serena was on the pill, since she hadn't asked him to take precautions, and neither of them had ever mentioned it again. He had sent over the file containing the photographs, but he hadn't thought Serena was going to give them to Noah after the way the session had ended. But if Noah had found the pictures...

But there'd been nothing to indicate that he had, and Remy seriously doubted Serena would have come to the reunion if so. Noah had been as shocked by the child's paternity as Remy, and the uncharacteristic violence had been driven by the pain of betrayal by the two people Noah had trusted. Remy didn't even blame Noah for the beating. He deserved it and would gladly suffer the consequences if Noah would only forgive him, but that would never happen. Some relationships, once fractured, could never be mended, nor should they be. Without trust, what was there left worth saving?

And Vince hadn't trusted Remy either, he silently acknowledged. Vince had been quiet and weird on the drive back from the restaurant last night. He'd kept giving Remy the side-eye, but Remy had no idea what he'd said or done to make Vince wary. They'd mostly made small talk, avoiding any mention of Serena or Lexie. Vince had talked about his job, and Remy had told him about a work trip he'd taken. He'd even shown Vince a few photos on his work phone.

Remy's head began to throb as the Percocet started to wear off, and his hand went to his throbbing temple. The trip. It was something about the trip...

Remy didn't have a chance to finish the thought because Sheriff DeVries walked into the room. He pulled up a chair and settled next to the bed, looking at Remy and shaking his head in disgust. Remy wished he would leave, but the sheriff looked like he had a lot on his mind.

"You're a sight," DeVries said.

This observation didn't require a reply, so Remy remained silent.

"I'd like to ask you a few questions," DeVries said. "I was told you were the last person to see Vince alive."

"I'm not answering any questions without a lawyer present."

"It's not a formal interview, son," DeVries said.

Remy shook his head, which was a mistake since pain bloomed behind his eyes and a wave of nausea assaulted him. "Lawyer," he muttered.

"Did you know Serena was pregnant with your child?"

Remy yanked on the cord that told the nurses' station he needed assistance, then lay back against the pillows and shut his eyes. One careless reply and he could be charged with murder, and he wasn't about to incriminate himself. He had to stall for time. The longer it took, the greater the chance that DeVries wouldn't find anything that could connect Remy to the murders and would let him go once he was discharged. He'd suffered enough, as far as he was concerned, and he wanted only to go home.

A nurse came in. "I'm afraid it's time to go, Sheriff," she said. "He's clearly not up to speaking to visitors."

"I only have a few questions."

"Which will have to wait until tomorrow," the nurse replied firmly.

Remy heard the sheriff grunt as he stood and then the scrape of the chair legs against the floor as DeVries returned it to its place against the wall before finally leaving.

"Time for your medication, Remy," the nurse said cheerily, and that was the best news he'd heard all day.

FIFTY-NINE
ALAN

Alan called Mark Childers as soon as he got into the car. He'd waited long enough, and he needed to understand what he was dealing with. Mia's encounter with the tree could be a run-of-the-mill traffic accident, or it might be attempted murder, and until he knew which he had no idea which way the investigation was going to swing. What he needed to do now was rule suspects out rather than in. Mark didn't pick up, and, when Alan called back a few minutes later, the call went straight to voicemail once again. Alan was nearly back at the station by the time Mark finally returned his call.

"Alan," he boomed jovially. "Sorry, I couldn't pick up when you called. We're back at the lab, so I think it's safe to share a preliminary report."

"What are we dealing with here, Mark?"

Normally, they'd exchange a few friendly words. Alan would ask about Mark's son, who'd just started at Binghamton, and send his regards to Mark's wife, and Mark would do the same, but just then, Alan couldn't be bothered with the niceties. The afternoon was quickly slipping away from him, and he was losing his patience.

"The accident was caused by a blown-out tire, and, as far as I can tell, no other factors were involved. It wouldn't have been nearly as catastrophic for the driver if she had been wearing a seatbelt and the airbag had deployed. Without these safety measures, she was thrown headlong into the windshield when the car hit the tree at full speed."

"Was either tampered with?" Alan asked, his hopes rising marginally.

"The seatbelt is in fine working order, but the airbag was never replaced after the car was in an accident four years ago."

"How long ago did Mia Olsen purchase the car?"

"She bought the car nearly two years ago. It was a private sale that didn't go through a dealership, so we don't have any details on the condition of the vehicle at the time. I was able to obtain the accident report from 2021, but there's no way to know if Mia was aware the airbag was missing without asking her."

"So that's it? An accident?" Alan confirmed frustratedly.

"Hold on, buddy. I wasn't finished," Mark replied, and Alan could hear him smile into the phone.

"Do tell," Alan prompted, hopeful once again.

"The tire that blew out was pretty bald and probably hadn't been changed or rotated since before Mia purchased the car. We did find a puncture, however."

"Man-made?"

"I'm waiting on a tire expert to get back to me, but I believe so. Of course, it could have been made by a piece of glass or a nail, but it could also have been made by a blade. The location of the cut is suspicious."

"How so?" Alan asked.

"It was in the deepest part of the sipe, so pretty difficult to detect, especially in a tire that's been blown to shreds. And even if the vehicle had driven over broken glass, it's not likely that the inner groove of the sipe would be punctured. The glass would perforate the outer, more exposed area. A nail could cause a puncture in that spot, but the hole would be smaller and circular in nature."

"I can't believe you found it," Alan said, his elation on full display.

"The only reason we found it was because we were looking for it."

"Could a person have used a piece of glass to puncture the tire?" Alan asked.

"Yes, they could have, but it would be more difficult to make such a deep cut with a hunk of glass. Unless the person was well prepared and had a pair of thick gloves and a piece of glass long and sharp enough to insert between the treads, chances are they would have cut their hand, and the cut would be more jagged in appearance."

"That's something, I guess," Alan mused. It would be easy enough to check if someone's hand was injured.

"If someone punctured that tire intentionally, then they probably used a knife."

"And how would the expert know if it was intentional?" Alan asked.

"He will check if bits of glass, debris, or rust are embedded in the rubber. If the cut is clean, then it's probably man-made. I'll email the report to you by end of day tomorrow," Mark promised. "But I'll text if there are any developments tonight."

"Can you not get the report to me sooner?" Alan pleaded.

"Alan, if you want information that can stand up in court, then I'm afraid you're going to have to wait. You know how thinly stretched we are these days."

"Yes," Alan grumbled. "That seems to be the case everywhere."

"Be patient, my friend. Are you free on Friday? Maybe we can grab a beer."

"I'd like that," Alan said, and ended the call.

When he walked into the station, he was greeted by Asha, whose smile looked distinctly apologetic.

"What is it? More bad news?"

"I'm afraid so. My application to exhume Lexie Hall's body was denied. The medical examiner is confident that they will not find anything further, especially now that the soft tissue has decomposed and the pathologist would be working only with skeletal remains. And my request for divers was rejected as well. The powers-that-be don't believe the expense to be justified. Likewise, unless we have probable cause to detain anyone besides Noah Paulson, we have to let the others go. The judge won't authorize an extension."

Alan shook his head in disgust. He'd come up against bureaucracy many times over the course of his career, but this was truly ludicrous. No probable cause? One of those people was guilty. Possibly more than one. And if they could prove that Lexie Hall had been murdered, that would change the scope of the investigation. It was one thing to lie about a friend's death and impersonate them on social media; it was quite another to have murdered said friend. Serena could no longer answer for her actions, but, if whoever had killed her thought she'd murdered Lexie, that would certainly give them a compelling motive. And the damning evidence they needed to put that person away was probably resting at the bottom of the lake, unreachable now that they had no way to retrieve it. *Goddamn it!* When he came up against idiocy of this magnitude, he was doubly glad he was about to retire. He really couldn't deal with any more red tape or the stupidity of elected officials who had no clue what they were doing most of the time.

"Anything on Mia's car accident?" Asha asked after he'd remained silent for too long.

"The tire blew out. It might have happened on its own. It might have been tampered with. We won't know until late in the day tomorrow."

"The public defender has been waiting for two hours."

"Let's interview Noah Paulson, then," Alan said, and sighed heavily. He could feel the case slipping away from them.

But perhaps not all was lost. If new evidence was uncovered, the culprit could still be arrested, but if they were taken into custody near their home Alan would have no access to the investigation. The case would be handled by the local precinct, especially if there was no proof of Lexie's murder and so there was no longer reason for federal involvement and Asha was taken off the case as well.

Alan had done his best and had explored every angle. He could hold his head high in front of his friends and neighbors, knowing he'd done his job.

SIXTY

ALAN

Noah looked awful. His hair was tousled, his face looked pasty, and his eyes were red-rimmed. His clothes were rumpled, and there were bloodstains on his shirt, the blood most likely Remy's since Noah's face was intact. Alan went through the process of introducing everyone for the benefit of the tape, then turned to Noah.

"Mr. Paulson, did you know your wife was having an affair with Remy Durant?"

"No."

"Are you sure about that?" Alan asked.

Noah glared at him, his eyes glowing with anger. "Yes, I'm sure," he ground out. "And yes, I realize that knowing would give me a motive for murder, but I didn't. It seems I didn't know anything about her. And you know what? Now that I do, I'm actually glad she's dead. But I wasn't the one who killed her."

Mr. Warren, the solicitor, whispered something to Noah, probably urging him to keep from incriminating himself, but Noah didn't seem inclined to listen. He was clearly at the end of his tether and no longer cared what happened to him.

"You can charge me if you must, but I'm not answering any more of your questions. I didn't know about Lexie. I had no idea what Serena was up to. And I didn't kill anyone." He drew in a shuddering breath and continued. "I never had an issue with Vince. He was a good guy, and I'm deeply sorry he's dead. I did attack Remy, and I would do it again. He deserved it."

Noah seemed to have run out of steam and sat back, staring balefully at the interviewers.

"What about Mia? Did she deserve it?" Asha asked.

"Mia? What's happened to Mia?"

"She was on her way to the station to speak to us. Her car went off the road and hit a tree. Mia is in intensive care."

"Are you suggesting it wasn't an accident?" Noah asked.

Mr. Warren scribbled something on his legal pad but didn't comment. Alan was just about to reply when his phone pinged with a text. Normally he wouldn't read a message in the middle of an interview, but it could be important, so he excused himself and checked his phone. The text was from Mark.

> Got the results early. The puncture is definitely man-made. Most probably with a serrated blade.

Alan quickly replied, then turned back to Noah. "The tire was tampered with," he said. "It was punctured with a serrated knife."

Noah looked stunned, then shook his head. "I would never hurt Mia. No one would."

"Except that someone did," Alan pressed. "My guess is that they didn't want her to share whatever it was she was going to tell us."

"Your fingerprints were on the bottle of Mia's sleeping pills," Asha said. "We believe her medication was used to murder Vince. Perhaps Mia had realized that you'd taken it and was going to tattle on you."

"I took one pill, on Friday night," Noah cried. "I was going to tell her, but with everything that happened I forgot."

"Maybe she already knew," Alan said. "And believed you'd taken a lot more than one pill."

Noah's eyes brimmed with tears. "I don't know what Mia knew or what she might have believed. She never said anything, at least not to me. I'm sorry," he cried. "I feel like this is all my fault."

"Why is it your fault, Noah?" Asha was quick to ask.

Mr. Warren laid a warning hand on Noah's wrist, but Noah shook him off. "Because I should have known something wasn't right. I did know," he amended. "Inside, I always knew Lexie wouldn't just walk away. It wasn't like her. She never avoided difficult conversations or ghosted someone because she didn't have the guts to tell them outright she didn't want them around. I knew something was off, but I was so hurt, I just shut down for a while."

"Noah, did you love Serena?" Asha asked softly.

"I don't know," Noah whispered.

"Did you want to get back at Lexie by marrying her best friend?"

"I didn't think so at the time, but maybe some part of me did. Serena loved me. Or I thought she did. Now I see it was all a lie."

"Noah, we will need to take Serena's laptop from your home. We can obtain a warrant," Asha said.

"Take it," Noah said with a shrug. "I have nothing to hide, and I no longer care to protect Serena. Not that it matters. She's dead, so whatever you find will die with her."

"Not necessarily," Asha replied. "What we find might implicate other people. Your friends."

"They're not my friends. Not anymore."

"Not even Richie and Angelina?" Asha asked.

"Maybe Angelina."

"What about Richie?" Alan asked. He leaned closer in his eagerness to hear what Noah had to say, but Noah didn't reply immediately. He stared down at his hands and shook his head.

"I don't trust him anymore," he said at last.

Alan and Asha asked Noah a few more questions, but he replied with "No comment" to all of them. It seemed he was done talking.

"Either charge my client or let him go," Mr. Warren said once they'd reached a stalemate.

"As you know full well, we still have time, Mr. Warren, so we're not under any obligation to release him," Asha replied. "And we will be charging Noah with assault at the very least."

"I'll see you in the morning," the lawyer said to Noah before Linda Nunes came to escort him back to his cell.

"Can I get you anything?" Alan heard her ask as she led him away.

"Sleeping pills," Noah replied.

"I'm afraid I can't do that," Linda said. "Not unless you have a prescription from a doctor."

Alan didn't hear any more after that.

"What's your gut feeling on this?" Asha asked as she followed Alan out of the interview room.

"One of those kids is a murderer, possibly two."

"Unfortunately, they're smarter than your average miscreant and have managed to cover their tracks. Unless we find something that directly implicates them in the murders of Lexie, Serena, and Vince, they'll walk."

"What about the knife used to slash Mia's tire?" Alan asked.

"If I had to guess, I'd say that one of them used a steak knife they took from the house, and if they were smart they'd then run it through the dishwasher. Unless forensics can pull fingerprints from the tire, there will be nothing to connect the culprit to Mia's accident."

"I find it hard to believe that no one would have seen someone walk out with a steak knife, puncture a tire, then come back."

Asha chuckled mercilessly. "It's easily done. Push the knife up the sleeve, walk to the parking area, and pretend to look for something in your car. Then bend down, as if you've dropped it or need to tie your shoe, slash the tire, shove the knife back up the sleeve, and return to the house."

"You sound like you've done this before," Alan said.

"Show me a cop who wouldn't make a successful criminal. We understand how their minds work, so we're not so very different."

"Except we care about justice."

"Perhaps whoever murdered Serena cared about justice too. This was payback, pure and simple."

"And Vince?"

"Vince got in the way and had to be silenced."

"Remind me never to get on the wrong side of you," Alan joked tiredly.

"I settle my scores openly," Asha replied. "Oh, by the way, the electronic devices have been returned, and without an extension from the judge we can't hold Richie or Angelina any longer. Will you let them know they're free to leave?"

"I'll tell them tomorrow," Alan said. "I'm still hopeful the CSIs will find something we can use."

"Actually, the data from Remy's iPhone has just come back."

"Anything?" Alan asked, a kernel of hope blooming in his tired soul.

"Let's have a look. I have a feeling it might be illuminating," Asha replied, and waited for Alan to pull up a chair.

SIXTY-ONE

ANGELINA

Once the sun had set, the sky had turned pale lavender, the first stars just beginning to twinkle and a nearly translucent moon skimming the tree line with its rounded belly. It had turned cold, and the wind rustled through the trees, the branches beyond the window moving like the arms of a dancer. The house was silent, but unlike before, where the quiet had felt menacing, it was now welcome and soothing, a balm to the soul.

Angelina fitted herself closer to Richie, his bare skin warm against hers. She'd lost hope of ever getting close to him, but when he found her crying in the kitchen Richie had done his best to comfort her, and when she'd kissed him he hadn't pulled away. Angelina supposed he'd needed comfort too, but she had been surprised by the intensity of his passion and by the sweet things he'd said to her in bed. Richie might backpedal tomorrow and try to let her down easy, but she thought that, for the first time since they met, they'd made a romantic connection. And now that they'd crossed that line, she wasn't going to let him go so easily.

Angelina ran her fingers along his stomach, then dipped lower, but quickly withdrew her hand. Richie was asleep, probably the first solid sleep he'd had in days. She wouldn't wake him. She'd keep watch. At the moment, neither of them was in danger. Noah was at the police station, Remy was in the hospital, and Mia was probably still with him. It was the safest place she could be, so Angelina couldn't blame her for not rushing back.

Earlier, Richie had been worried about her and had even suggested they go to the hospital, but Angelina had talked him out of it. If Sheriff DeVries was any kind of detective, he'd find incriminating evidence as soon as he scrolled through Remy's personal phone, and then they would all be free. All they had to do was wait another day. Richie wasn't convinced and wanted to leave, but Angelina had urged him to stay, and it had been the right decision, she reflected with a smile as she pressed herself even closer.

Strange how none of them ever realized it, but Remy was funny when it came to sharing personal information. He always wanted to know the dirt on everyone else, but he was very private when it came to his own life. It was probably because his mother's life had been splashed all over the papers, and photographs of her dead body forever preserved online. Pixie Durant had been stunningly beautiful, but no one looks good in death, unless they had planned it, and Pixie clearly hadn't or she would have taken more care. Her face was chalk-white, with only a slash of red lipstick bisecting her cheek like a livid wound. Smudged mascara made her look like a racoon, and her hair was dirty and matted. The left side of her face rested in a pool of vomit, and her sequined spaghetti-strap top had shifted, exposing the underside of a pale breast. Pixie had been glorious in life and pathetic in death, so Angelina had never told Remy that she'd seen the photos. She hadn't wanted to hurt him.

But now she didn't care. She was glad DeVries had outed him in front of everyone and that Noah had got in a few good punches before Richie and the cop pulled him off. Remy deserved it for what he'd done to Noah, and for all the rest of it. Their friends were dead, and now the sheriff would know that Remy had to be the one responsible and arrest him. Remy had recently been to Thailand. Vince told her last night. He'd seen a photo of Phuket Big Buddha on Remy's work phone while they'd waited for their order at the restaurant. And Remy was sure to have pictures from his trip on his personal phone. He always took lots of pictures.

Vince had tried to warn her about Remy, and now he was dead. It all made a terrible kind of sense, and she hoped Sheriff DeVries would get there eventually. Lexie, Phuket, Remy. The death in Thailand a direct correlation to the two murders in upstate New York.

Remy had been the first one to arrive at the house. He'd let himself in and had accepted the deliveries of the supplies Lexie had ordered. He'd greeted the guests she had invited. And Remy must have been the one to confront Serena about what he'd discovered while in Thailand. Strangulation was more commonly attributed to male suspects in the deaths of women, since they were sure of their ability to choke the life out of their weaker victim. And now Sheriff DeVries and Agent Singh would finally work it all out. They had to.

Angelina wondered if she should share what she'd learned with Richie, but decided to wait. She didn't want to ruin this precious moment, and, since she knew for certain that Richie was innocent, there was no need to feel him out. She buried her face in the tender spot between his neck and shoulder and inhaled his wonderful scent. It was a mixture of bodywash, the cologne Richie always wore, Sauvage by Dior, and his own smell that she found wildly intoxicating. Was it wrong to be happy in the midst of so much grief and to dream about the future? But that was the essence of the human experience, wasn't it, the ever-present juxtaposition of light and dark, pleasure and pain, good and evil. There were highs and lows, life amid death, love that grew out of hate, and hope, even when there was little chance of a happy outcome. She had no reason to feel guilty. She had to fight for her own happiness, and, now that Richie had finally seen her and she had shown him how good it could be between them, she would do anything to ensure they had a future together.

Angelina sighed contentedly as she closed her eyes. In her daydream, Richie adored her, and they were finally together, two attractive, successful professionals building a life and planning a family. They would have a beautiful, romantic wedding, and honeymoon in Italy. Maybe Richie would want to go to Sicily and visit the places his family had come from. She wouldn't mind, not if it would bring him joy. She'd be happy just to be with him and have his undivided attention. And once they got back, they would settle into a life of domestic bliss.

Richie would be a devoted husband, and Angelina would be the perfect wife.

SIXTY-TWO

ALAN

"Will you look at that?" Alan exclaimed as he watched the images from Remy's phone populate the screen. "Now that is beautiful, and I'm not talking about the scenery."

"Remy Durant flew into Bangkok airport on June fifteenth of this year and flew out of Phuket International Airport July first," Asha said as she consulted an adjacent screen. She had been able to access Remy's travel itinerary, as well as his emails, both current and those that had been deleted.

"Did he travel alone?"

"No. His traveling companion is listed as Leyla Stan of Hoboken, New Jersey. The hotels and airfare booking are in both their names."

"Think we can interview Leyla via Zoom?" Alan asked.

"I don't see why not. We can hardly ask her to come here, and it makes no sense for me to go to Hoboken. I can have someone from the local office bring her in, but I'd rather speak to her myself."

"Don't trust your colleagues?" Alan teased.

"I started this case, and I will see it through," Asha said stoically. "I'm going to leave Leyla a message, and then I'll have the

Albany office put someone on Remy Durant, just in case he decides to check himself out and head to Canada. Are you planning to charge Noah Paulson with aggravated assault?"

"I can hardly let him go but, honestly, I can't blame the guy for losing it," Alan said with feeling. "He was justified."

"I know," Asha said sympathetically. "But he did give Durant a concussion and broke his nose and cheekbone."

"Let's see what shakes out, and then I'll decide which way to go on this tomorrow," Alan resolved.

Asha made a call, then stood and stretched. "I'm going on a coffee run to the bakery. You want anything?"

"I'll take a large latte and a slice of banana bread if there's any left. If not, a piece of coffee crumble."

"You got it." Asha reached for her jacket and purse. "See you in a few."

Alan finished scrolling through Remy's vacation snaps, then closed the file and leaned back in his chair. His gaze was on the screensaver, but his mind was firmly on the investigation. The interview with Leyla Stan could make or break the case. If she confirmed that Remy Durant had looked into Lexie Hall's disappearance while he was in Thailand, that would conclusively prove that he had known the truth. From there, it wouldn't be too difficult to establish that he had been the one to set up the reunion and send the invitations. And he would have been the one to reactivate Lexie's cellphone account, since it had never been officially closed, and send the text to Serena, asking her to meet him outside on the night she was murdered. The phone, or the SIM card, was most likely at the bottom of the lake by now, and the knife that had been used to puncture Mia's tire was probably squeaky clean, but a hazy picture was finally beginning to emerge, with Remy Durant at the center.

The only piece of evidence that didn't fully fit was Mia's slashed tire. Mia had told Alan she was coming to the station after Noah attacked Remy, so Remy would not have been able to puncture her tire since he'd been taken directly to the hospital. And as far as Alan could see, he would have no reason to go after Mia before then, unless Mia had made her intention known last night or this morning, once she realized her prescription was gone and correctly assumed that her pills had been used to murder Vince. If Remy had slashed her tire before the group had arrived at the diner, and the rest of the evidence checked out, then they would have an almost foolproof case against him.

And then there was the question of motive. It was possible that Serena's death had nothing to do with Lexie. Remy might have known about Lexie and decided to use the information to his own advantage, possibly to rattle Serena's cage if she had been making his life difficult. But perhaps the altercation that had ultimately led to Serena's death had been about her pregnancy and not Lexie's death. Alan didn't think Serena's murder had been premeditated, but he found it impossible to believe that Vince's death and Mia's crash had been mere accidents.

Which brought him back to Noah. If Remy had not known about Lexie's death, then the whole theory fell apart. But if Noah had found out what happened to Lexie, he'd have a solid motive to kill his wife, which would become even more powerful if he'd found out about the baby. Noah's fingerprints had been found on Mia's prescription bottle, and he could have slashed Mia's tire. If Mia had seen Noah take her pills, she would know that he'd been the one to murder Vince, and that would make her a target. Speaking to Remy and Mia might provide a few missing pieces, but, until Remy was released and could be interviewed under caution and Mia regained consciousness, they were still groping in the dark.

Alan looked up when Asha walked in, carrying a cardboard tray with two coffees and a brown paper bag that hopefully contained his banana bread.

"Leyla agreed to speak to me," she announced triumphantly. "Would you like to sit in?"

"Are you joking? Of course I would," Alan replied as he accepted his latte.

Asha handed him the paper bag, set her own coffee on the desk, shrugged off her coat, and checked the time. "We're on in eight minutes."

SIXTY-THREE

ALAN

When Leyla appeared on the screen, Alan thought she was very beautiful. She had dark almond-shaped eyes and pin-straight black hair that fell past her shoulders. Her make-up was expertly applied, and her hot-pink nails were filed into points. She smiled nervously. It wasn't every day that a person was questioned by the FBI. Alan left it to Asha to handle the introductions and explain the reason for the interview. Leyla was visibly uncomfortable, but nodded a lot and assured them that of course she was happy to help. Alan could just imagine what this poor woman had to be thinking. *I went on vacation with a guy who might have killed two people in cold blood. What will happen if they let him go and he finds out I assisted the FBI in their inquiries?*

"Leyla, Remy Durant will never learn this conversation took place," Asha said. This wasn't strictly true, since Leyla could be called to testify if the case ever went to trial, but Asha would keep that detail to herself, since it might never come to that and this interview could yield nothing.

"Okay," Leyla said. She didn't look convinced. "So, what do you want to know, Agent Singh?"

"How would you define your relationship with Remy?" Asha asked.

"We were seeing each other for a few months, but it was like, you know, super casual."

"Are you still seeing each other?"

"No, but we keep in touch on social media. We're friends."

Or we were friends seemed to hang in the air. Leyla would probably be blocking Remy on all platforms as soon as she got off the call.

"What did you do in Thailand?" Asha asked.

Leyla shrugged. "You know, the usual. We went sightseeing in Bangkok after Remy was done with his assignment and hit a few clubs in the evenings. And in Phuket, we mostly went to the beach."

They had probably done a lot more than that, but Leyla seemed to be playing it safe.

"So Remy was there to work?"

"Yeah, but the photoshoot took only one day. I really didn't mind."

"What did you think of Bangkok?" Asha asked. She was clearly trying to establish rapport, but Leyla looked like she was taking a test and expecting to fail.

"It was okay, I guess. You've seen one freakishly large Buddha, you've seen them all, right?"

"I've never been to Thailand," Asha said. "But I've always wanted to visit. Such a beautiful country. Did Remy stop into the US embassy at any point?" She had clearly hoped to take Leyla by surprise, but Leyla was instantly suspicious.

"No. Why would he?"

"To ask about Lexie Hall," Alan chimed in.

"Remy never mentioned anyone named Lexie."

"Did he ever go off on his own?" Asha asked.

"No. We pretty much hung out together the whole time."

"And what about while you were in Phuket?"

"I told you, we went to the beach. They have beautiful beaches in Thailand. Really stunning," Leyla said, a little more animated now.

"Did Remy go to the Pink Lotus Hostel at any point?" Asha asked.

"A *hostel*? No, not his vibe."

"Did he ever leave you on your own, Leyla?" Alan asked, exasperated by their failure to learn anything useful.

"Only when he went to the bar to get drinks. Look, Remy was super attentive. He's not like one of these guys who's all over you when you're alone and then treats you like you don't exist in public. Remy is a real gentleman."

"Why did you stop seeing each other?" Asha asked. "It sounds like you really liked him."

"I'm twenty-two. I'm not looking to settle down, and neither is Remy. We just wanted to have a good time, and we did. Nothing wrong with that."

"No, nothing at all," Asha hurried to reassure her. "So, Remy never left your side once he finished working?"

"Not really."

"Have you ever seen Remy lose his temper?" Alan asked.

Leyla shook her head. "Remy is pretty even-keeled. I've never seen him be rude to anyone, not even waiters or cab drivers. He treats everyone with respect. Look, I know you think Remy might be involved in these murders somehow, but I can't see him hurting anyone. It's not in him."

"That's very loyal, but how well do you really know him?" Alan asked. He was deeply disappointed and wondered if Leyla was lying to protect Remy, or by extension herself.

Leyla shrugged again. "How well do we really know anyone? You see stuff on the news all the time. A husband murdered his wife, or a mother killed her young children. And the first thing people always say is how shocked they are, and how nice and normal these people always seemed. I can only tell you what I saw for myself, and that was that Remy was cool. If he has another side, he never showed it to me."

"Thank you for your honesty, Leyla. We'll be in touch if we have any more questions," Asha said.

"Do you think she was telling the truth?" Alan asked after they disconnected the call. "She got defensive there at the end."

Asha sighed. "How would you feel if the FBI questioned you about a friend you thought you could trust when you were her age?"

"I take your point," Alan said. "But this takes us right back to where we started. If Remy didn't look into Lexie's disappearance while he was in Thailand, then it's more than likely he didn't know Lexie was dead."

"You don't need to go to Thailand to investigate someone's death. You can do it from the comfort of your own home," Asha replied.

"I know that, but we didn't find anything on Remy's computer. He never googled Lexie or tried to stalk her on social media. He posted the occasional comment, but most of his reactions were emojis."

"Noah stalked Lexie on social media," Asha reminded him.

Alan nodded. "But we didn't find anything incriminating on his phone or laptop either. Unless he has another computer or a second phone, there's no link."

"He has a work computer, doesn't he?"

"Good point. If he didn't want Serena to find out, it would be safer to use his work computer, even if he had a secret Instagram account," Alan said. "Does he have a work phone?"

"I don't think so," Asha said, "but it's certainly worth checking. I'll put in a call to HR tomorrow. I doubt anyone will still be there now."

"We keep coming back to Noah, don't we?" Alan said, his shoulders drooping with resignation. He had hoped they'd be able to build a case against Remy, but it wasn't coming together.

"Unless we're missing something, Noah had the most compelling motive, and, unless I'm very much mistaken, Vince's murder and Mia's accident were direct results of Serena's death."

"They would have to be. Why else would someone try to kill them?"

Asha sighed heavily. "We are not going to get an answer tonight, and it's time I went home. I've hardly seen my son these past few days."

"Have a peaceful evening," Alan said, and shut off his computer. If there was one thing he was sure of, it was that nothing more would happen tonight since both Remy and Noah were under guard.

Alan had just put on his jacket when his phone buzzed. The call was from Mark Childers, so he picked up immediately.

"Mark, what have you got for me?"

Mark sounded triumphant when he replied. "We were able to lift several fingerprints off the busted tire."

"And?"

"And they're a match for one of your suspects. And the same set of fingerprints was found on a water bottle that was taken from the house. Traces of chemical residue were embedded in the plastic."

Alan listened carefully, his heart racing as the identity of the killer was finally revealed.

"Got you," he said under his breath as his gaze locked with Asha's. She wouldn't be going home just yet.

SIXTY-FOUR
RICHIE

Richie folded his arms behind his head and watched Angelina as she walked toward the bathroom, her naked body silvered by the light of the rising moon. She'd changed since college. Then, she'd been all soft curves and shy smiles. Not really his type, but he could see the appeal for guys who were less confident and were attracted to quieter, needier girls. He'd always gone in for the ballbusters. That was probably why he'd hooked up with Serena. She would have gladly gone out with him; she had let him know as much in the days after he'd nailed her in the bathroom, but he'd never asked. Serena had been beautiful and very sexy, but there had been something calculating in the depths of her soul that had warned him he couldn't trust her.

Could he trust any of them? Richie mused as he got out of bed and pulled on his clothes. Sure, they were his friends, but would he tell them if he won a multimillion-dollar jackpot, was told he was sterile, or had done something illegal? No way. Not after this weekend. Maybe not before either. He hadn't been completely honest when he'd told Mia that he shared everything with his friends. He didn't. When it came to people he trusted his gut, and, although he had been steered wrong many times, his instinct was still the best tool he had for sussing out bullshit and protecting himself from unnecessary pain.

Richie's mom had been thirty-eight when she'd died, but her closest friends had been the girls she'd met in middle school. She'd always told Richie that people formed the strongest bonds before they learned to be guarded and competitive and were able to love people unreservedly and without judgment. Such devotion didn't last past middle school, but, as the friends grew older and faced more complicated problems, they were still able to be honest with one another and offer real, uncomplicated support, not just pointless platitudes and empty promises. Richie had taken his mom's advice to heart and had kept up with most of his school friends. He and Noah had even applied to the same colleges, but he no longer held the same rosy view of friendship as when he was in his teens. He'd been forced to grow up, but he'd always been real and honest. Well, except for not telling Noah he'd had sex with Serena, but other people held so much back. And maybe they were right to. Nothing was sacred these days, and once the information was out there was no way to get it back. Social media left everyone vulnerable and exposed, and he'd learned to keep his private life private and didn't share anything unless he meant for the world to know.

Richie was almost grateful Angelina didn't have her phone. She was just the sort to take a picture of him while he was asleep and post it just to spite her ex. Maybe that was why she'd come on to him. Or maybe it was because she genuinely liked him and hoped they could build something together. He wasn't sure how he felt about that, but he didn't have to decide tonight. Angelina understood that sex didn't obligate him to anything, and they could still be friends once this was all over without things becoming awkward between them. A one-night stand was nothing compared to having two friends murdered in the space of a few days.

Angelina turned on the shower, so Richie headed to the bathroom in the hallway and shut the door. He reached for Mia's toiletry bag and went through the contents, searching for the sleeping pills. He'd noticed the prescription bottle last night, but it wasn't there now. He checked Mia and Angelina's bedroom, but the bottle wasn't there either. Had Mia slipped the pills to Vince, or had someone else taken Mia's prescription? At this point, he wouldn't put anything past anyone.

And where was Mia? She'd been gone for hours. Surely she should have come back by now. Richie suddenly remembered that he still had Remy's work phone. He never gave it back when they got to the diner, since he knew he'd need the GPS to find his way back to the house. Surprisingly, no one had asked him for it, presumably because they had been distracted by the results of the DNA test the pathologist had conducted on the fetus. Richie retrieved the phone from his jacket pocket and was going to call the hospital when he realized he had no idea which hospital Remy had been taken to. There had been a name on the side of the ambulance, but he hadn't been paying attention, and there were several hospitals in the area. He would ask Angelina, he thought—she was sure to have noticed—but then remembered she was still in the shower.

Sheriff DeVries was bound to give him an update, so Richie called the station.

"Sheriff DeVries just left," the duty officer said. "Is there anything I can help you with?"

Richie explained who he was, then asked, "Have you heard anything about Remy Durant's condition?" He figured it was a small enough station that the duty officer had to know everything that had happened.

"The doctor's keeping him overnight for observation, and then he will be released into police custody." Richie was just about to ask on what grounds Remy was going to be detained when the officer added, "Mia Olsen is still in a coma."

"What?"

"She was in a car accident this afternoon. She has a brain bleed."

"Is she going to die?" Richie asked quietly.

"I really couldn't say, but they're doing everything they can for her," the officer said.

"What was the cause of the accident? Was there another driver?"

"No. Her tire blew out. It had been slashed."

Richie was holding the phone so tightly, his fingers hurt. He made an effort to loosen his grip. "Which hospital is she at?"

"Kingston. Same as Remy Durant."

"Can I call for an update?"

"You can, but I don't think they'll tell you anything unless you're a relative. Call back tomorrow. I'm sure the sheriff will know more by then."

The young officer should have known better than to divulge the details of an ongoing investigation. His indiscretion could lead to suspension or even termination of employment, but Richie felt no responsibility toward the man. He needed information and, if the policeman was happy to blab, it wasn't Richie's concern. He'd use the cop's inexperience to his own advantage.

"What about Vincent Howard?" he asked. "Did the results of the autopsy come back?"

"He likely died of a drug overdose. Sleeping pills most probably, but the tox screen won't be back for a few days yet. He had ketamine in his pocket." The cop seemed to realize that he'd said too much and hurried to correct his mistake. "I'm only telling you this because you're Remy Durant's legal counsel."

"I'm not actually, but thank you," Richie said, and ended the call. He didn't want the cop to claim that Richie had misrepresented himself in order to obtain classified information. Such a claim could get him disbarred, and he didn't need any more trouble than he could handle. But it seemed DeVries forgot to mention to his staff that Richie wouldn't be representing any of the group, and the omission had worked to his advantage.

Richie sighed, gripped the sides of the vanity, and leaned

forward to confront his tense reflection in the mirror. Remy was about to be arrested, Vince had died of an overdose, and Mia was hanging on by a thread. He wasn't going to tell Angelina. Not yet. He didn't want to upset her.

SIXTY-FIVE

RICHIE

Richie went downstairs to the kitchen but didn't bother to turn on the light. He peered in the fridge. There wasn't much left, so they'd probably have to go out for dinner, but he didn't feel like going anywhere. He was too anxious to feel hungry. The net was closing in and he needed a plan, but first he had to take care of business. He perched on one of the counter stools and used Remy's phone to text his boss, then sent a message to his grandmother to tell her he was okay and not to worry. He put the phone away when Angelina turned off the hairdryer and the house was plunged into silence once again.

She came downstairs, dressed in yoga pants and a black T-shirt with an outline of a white lotus. The caption beneath said

Ohm.

"Why are you sitting in the dark?" she asked, reaching for the light switch.

Richie was blinded by the bright light that flooded the kitchen. Angelina sat across from him and smiled softly.

"What's up?" she asked. "You look miserable."

"It just feels empty and weird with everyone gone."

"They're obviously keeping Noah overnight, and Mia probably decided to stay with Remy," Angelina said. "You know what a crybaby he is when something hurts."

Richie sighed and nodded, and Angelina reached across the island and took hold of his hand. "But it's nice for us to spend some time together. You know, I've dreamed of moments like this, when it would be just the two of us."

"Angie, why did you and Jake break up?" Richie asked. He knew why, but he wanted to hear it from her.

Angelina appeared surprised by the question, but replied after a small pause. "Jake left me for someone else."

"Just like that? I was sure he loved you."

"He didn't think I loved him," Angelina said with a shrug.

"Did you?"

"I don't know. I thought I did, but I never felt about him the way I feel about you," she admitted shyly.

Richie smiled warmly in acknowledgement of her brave confession. "What about Vince? Did you ever love him?"

"Why are you asking me this?" Angelina bristled. Bright spots of color bloomed in her cheeks, and she suddenly looked nervous, as if she thought Richie would be turned off by the knowledge that she had cared for someone else before him.

"Sorry. I was just curious," he said apologetically. "I didn't mean to pry."

"I'm not like you, Richie. I wasn't blessed with a passionate nature. I've always been more guarded, so it takes me longer to get close to someone."

"But you were close to Lexie," Richie said.

"Yeah. I was. Lexie was one of the few people who got me and who I thought genuinely cared. When you find a friend like that, you hold on to them for the rest of your life."

Richie nodded. "You're right. Lexie was unique. She showed up for people without expecting anything in return."

"Do *you* expect something in return for your friendship?" Angelina asked, looking at him with concern.

"I do," Richie admitted. "I think friendship should be a two-way street."

"Is it like that with you, Remy, and Noah?"

"I always thought it was, but I'm beginning to realize that I didn't know them as well as I imagined."

"We were all damaged, Richie. That's why we forged such a strong bond," Angelina said sadly. "We needed to create our own family. Lexie was a girlfriend to Noah and a friend to all of you."

"What was she to you?"

"She was more than a friend." Angelina's eyes brimmed with tears. "She was my soul sister. And I miss her. To find out she's died, and in such awful circumstances…" Her voice trailed away, and she shook her head in disbelief. "I still can't wrap my head around it."

"I hear you," Richie said. "It was definitely a shocker."

Angelina wrapped her arms around herself, as if for protection, and fixed her dark gaze on Richie. "Do you see a future for us, Rich?" she asked, her voice quivering.

"Right now, I can't see past today."

Angelina smiled sadly, and Richie knew the message had been received. He didn't want to hurt her, but he couldn't bear to lie to her. He didn't see a future for them. At this moment, he couldn't even see a future for himself.

"We really should wait for Mia to have dinner, but I'm going to make some tea. Join me?" Angelina asked as she slid off the stool.

"Is there any coffee left?"

Angelina shook her head.

"I'll have some tea, then."

"Would you mind getting me a sweater?" Angelina asked. "I'm suddenly really cold. There's a black hoodie on my bed."

"Of course. Be right back."

"Sugar?" Angelina called after him as Richie walked out of the kitchen.

"Two, please."

The hoodie wasn't on the bed, so Richie had to check the closet and the dresser before he found it in Angelina's bag. He didn't think she'd mind, but zipped up the bag just in case she should think he'd gone snooping through her things. He had noticed several pairs of lacy underwear and matching bras. Angelina either always wore lingerie beneath her casual clothes or she had been hoping to get lucky. He preferred to think it was with him rather than Vince, and it made him sad to think that Vince would never again experience any of the things that made life worth living. It saddened Richie to realize that one wrong choice, a decision that probably hadn't even seemed that important at the time, could result in untimely death. Poor Vince. If Serena had understood the risks when she'd agreed to come, Vince had been an innocent bystander who'd signed his own death warrant when he'd said something he shouldn't have. Such was life. A roll of the dice, and it was a one-way drive to the cemetery.

When Richie came downstairs with the hoodie, Angelina had already made the tea. She pulled on the sweater and adjusted the hood.

"Much better. Thank you, Richie."

"My pleasure. Is there any milk?" he asked as he wrapped his hands around the hot mug.

Angelina was closer to the fridge, so she went to check, and came back with a nearly empty carton.

"Thanks," Richie said, and added a splash of milk to his tea.

"I didn't know you take milk in your tea."

"Makes it taste more like coffee," Richie joked. He took a sip of tea and nodded. "This is good. Just the way I like it."

They drank their tea in silence for a few moments, each lost in their own thoughts as the night closed in around the isolated house. The wooden beams creaked and groaned as gusty wind tore through the trees, and the rowboat that had been re-tied to the dock after it had been processed by the techs knocked rhythmically against the wooden posts. The lake that had been placid that afternoon looked like a boiling cauldron in the light of the moon, and the homes on the other side stood like silent sentinels at the entrance to the forest. To Richie, it felt like he and Angelina were the only two people in the world, especially since he already knew Mia wouldn't be coming back to join them.

Angelina glanced at her watch, then looked up at Richie, her eyes glowing with emotion. "I really do love you, Richie," she said quietly. "I always have. But I know you will never be mine. I knew it as soon as I came downstairs."

"I love you too, Angie, but it's like you said, we are too damaged."

"So damaged that we can never be whole?"

"Do you think you'll ever be whole?" Richie asked.

"Under the right circumstances and with the right man, I think I could be."

"And are these the right circumstances, am I the right man?"

Angelina looked puzzled, and Richie sighed. He couldn't beat around the bush any longer. There wasn't time.

"Why did you do it, Angelina?" Richie asked.

"Do what?"

"Murder Vince, hurt Mia."

Angelina looked shocked, but there was no fear in her gaze, just resignation once she'd accepted that Richie had figured out the truth.

"I can guess why you killed Serena," Richie said. "You thought she deserved it for what she'd done to Lexie, but why Mia and Vince? What have they ever done to you?"

Angelina smiled wistfully. "Vince was convinced Remy did it. He saw a picture of Thailand on his work phone and decided that Remy had found out the truth. He thought Remy planned the reunion to expose Serena, but things got out of hand, and he wound up killing her."

"So you thought Vince's death would point the police toward Remy, especially once you told them that Vince tried to warn you?"

Angelina nodded. "I didn't realize Serena would have bruises on her neck. I assumed everyone would think it was an accident, and we would all grieve and get on with our lives. But once Sheriff DeVries labeled it a homicide and brought in the Feds, I had no choice but to try to deflect the blame."

"And Mia?"

"I didn't want to kill Mia, only put her on ice for a short while. I did it to protect you. She suspected you, Richie, because Vince had ketamine on him, and she knew it was yours. I think she saw you give it to him. But don't worry," Angelina rushed to reassure him. "I wiped off your fingerprints."

"I never gave Vince ketamine," Richie protested.

"So what did Mia see?"

"I gave him some weed for his vape. And how did you know Vince had ketamine in his pocket at the time of his death?" Richie asked.

"I put a baggie in his coat pocket, so the cops would think he overdosed."

"Why do you think Mia suspected me?" Richie asked calmly. Inside, he was reeling from Angelina's revelations.

"She told DeVries she needed to speak to him, and she ran as soon as she grabbed Remy's stuff."

"But that doesn't mean she wanted to speak to DeVries about me."

"Who else would she talk to him about?" Angelina asked, exasperated. "Noah was taken into custody, and Remy was in the hospital. And she was clearly afraid to remain here with us."

"I bet she never suspected you," Richie said bitterly.

"No, she didn't."

"And what about me? Did you think I'd suspect you?"

"I was so afraid you'd figure it out. You were always smarter than anyone gave you credit for."

"Is that why you fucked me? So you could accuse me of rape if things went south?"

Angelina shook her head, and her eyes filled with tears once again. "No. I did it because I'd always wanted to. And I'm so glad I did. I wanted to have something beautiful, a night I could cherish once you were gone."

Richie rubbed his eyes tiredly and pinched the bridge of his nose. "I'm not going anywhere, Angie."

"But I am. I'm going to take Remy's car and cross into Canada tonight. And if they catch up with me, I'll tell them you threatened me, and I was terrified you'd finish what you'd started."

"How did you figure it out about Lexie?" Richie asked. He finished his tea, pushed away the empty mug, then placed his hands on the island, where Angelina could see them. It was an act of surrender and proof that he didn't plan to do anything to hurt her.

Angelina's gaze slid to the mug, then back to Richie's face. "It was Jake who first noticed it. We were scrolling through Lexie's Instagram one night, and Jake said that her posts looked like stock photos. She wasn't in any of them. Once he'd pointed it out, I realized it was true. Lexie hadn't really posted any current pictures of herself." Tears slid down Angelina's face, and her mouth quivered with emotion. "Jake is a techie, so I asked him to dig a little deeper because I was suspicious. I had no reason to suspect any of you, but Serena was the last person to see Lexie, so I asked Jake to check the emails I'd received from Lexie. He compared them to the ones from Serena, and they all had the same IP address."

"Was that all? That was enough to tip you off?" Richie asked. He tried to suppress a yawn and noticed the watchful look in Angelina's eyes.

"Yes, but I needed proof, so I searched for Lexie. When I googled her, I got the usual stuff, links to her Facebook page, Instagram, X. There were a couple of posts she'd written during the pandemic when she'd started her own blog. Even stuff from school listing her as the winner of a scholarship and mentioning an award she'd received in her senior year. I kept scrolling, and eventually I came across an article from a Thai newspaper and used Google Translate."

"What did the article say?"

"It said the American tourist who'd been found dead on Karon beach in Phuket had been identified as Lexie Hall. I couldn't believe it. It didn't make any sense that Serena wouldn't know what had happened and would lie to us all this whole time. So I contacted the American embassy in Bangkok to make sure I had my facts straight. They confirmed that Lexie had died, but they said the cause of death was listed as undetermined. They had no reason to suspect foul play."

"Did they ask for your name?"

"No, but I would have given them a fake name anyway."

"Did you tell them about Serena?" Richie asked.

"What would be the point? What could they do, especially if there was no evidence of a crime?"

"But you thought a crime had taken place, and so you planned this reunion."

"Yes," Angelina admitted. "It wasn't difficult to get a phone and a credit card in Lexie's name. No one had reason to suspect Lexie was dead, and she'd used her birthday as a password on most accounts because it was easy to remember. Her only concession to security was to list it twice, so it was '6969.' She told me about it. So I walked into Verizon, got them to reactivate her account, then called the credit card company from Lexie's number and told them I lost my card. They asked me to verify the address and Lexie's mother's maiden name, which she always listed as Hall, and the customer service rep was happy to overnight the new card to Lexie's last known address and provide me with a tracking number. I waited outside Lexie's building until the FedEx guy showed up and asked him about my package. He handed the envelope to me and asked me to sign for it, which I did. The rest was even easier."

"Where did you get a picture of Lexie?"

"She texted me a selfie from Thailand. I attached it to the invite and hoped none of you would realize it wasn't a recent picture. The only thing I worried about was that you guys would make an excuse not to come, but who could say no to an all-expenses-paid weekend at a gorgeous lake house?"

"Why didn't you just confront Serena?" Richie demanded.

"Because I wanted to see how she would react to getting an email from Lexie and if she would think Lexie was somehow still alive. I knew she'd come. She had to find out what she was up against. I was going to tell you all on Friday, but then I decided to let Serena sweat it a little longer."

"But then you texted her from Lexie's phone, and you two had it out after we'd all gone to bed."

"Yeah," Angelina said. "I did. The anger had been building up in me all evening. I had to see her face and hear her say that Lexie was dead, and I wanted her to admit that she'd lied to everyone. But mostly, I just wanted to know why."

"And did she tell you?"

Angelina nodded. "She said I'd never be able to prove she drowned Lexie. Not if the police hadn't been able to. I asked her why she'd kill her best friend, and she said she was always jealous of Lexie's ability to get people to love her. Serena had wanted Noah, and she'd wanted Lexie's friends. It was as simple as that. She saw an opportunity and took it. It was easy, she said. Child's play. No one would come looking for Lexie, since she had no family and her friends would believe anything they read online."

"So, how did she do it?" Richie asked. "Did she tell you?"

Angelina nodded again. She looked angry and balled her hands into fists. "They'd been partying with some Australian guys, but the guys eventually left, so Serena convinced Lexie to go for a midnight swim. Lexie was high, and she'd been drinking. She didn't fight very hard when Serena held her down. And then she pulled her out of the water, arranged her on the beach, and took off with her phone, wallet, and passport. She was on a plane by the time anyone realized Lexie was dead."

"So you went for Serena, you strangled her, then pushed her in the lake."

"Yes," Angelina said simply. "I never intended to kill her, but I lost it, Richie. She wasn't even sorry. It was like Lexie was a bag of trash to be thrown away on some foreign beach."

"So it was all about Lexie?" Richie asked. He had a feeling Angelina had left some vital detail out of her account.

Angelina sighed, as if surrendering the last vestiges of her pride. "Serena laughed at me, Richie. She taunted me and said I was a loser who fixated on people and couldn't let go once they'd moved on. She said Lexie never wanted me to come to Thailand because she couldn't deal with my neediness. She wanted to have a good time and thought I would try to control everything." Angelina's look of righteous indignation would have given Richie a chuckle at any other time, but now he just felt sick to his stomach.

"Serena made me sound clingy and pathetic, and not worthy of love. She said you'd never want me because I'd make you feel managed and suffocated," Angelina moaned plaintively. "And at that moment, all I wanted to do was to wipe that self-satisfied smirk off her face. I mean, who the hell did she think she was? All she ever wanted was Lexie's boyfriend and Lexie's friends. And you didn't want her either, so talk about pathetic!"

"So what happened?" Richie asked.

"I didn't know what I was doing. I was so hurt, but then I realized that Serena needed to have water in her lungs for everyone to think she'd drowned, so as soon as she passed out I pushed her in."

"Lucky for you she hit her head on the way down, or she might have come around and swum to the shore."

"It wasn't luck." She smiled, seemingly at the memory. "I knew the boat was there. And if she didn't fall in the water after she hit her head, I'd have gone down and pushed her."

"And the phone you'd used to impersonate Lexie?" Richie asked.

"I threw it in the lake. I couldn't afford for someone to find it and start to piece it all together."

"You thought of everything," Richie said, his voice laced with feigned admiration. "And you put on quite a show when you discovered the body."

Angelina smiled, the vulnerability she displayed a moment ago replaced by an almost childish pride. "I had to."

"And what about Remy? Were you going to frame him all along?"

"No. I was going to wait and see what the police were able to find, but then I panicked."

"So you stole Mia's sleeping pills and put them in Vince's drink. And threw in the ketamine for good measure, in case Remy walked and you needed to frame me."

"Yes."

"But Vince was found outside," Richie reminded her.

Angelina shrugged. "He probably went outside to vape and then the pills kicked in. Doesn't really matter where he died, does it?"

"No, I guess it doesn't." Richie rubbed his eyes again. "I can barely keep my eyes open," he said with an embarrassed smile. "You really wore me out."

Angelina smiled wistfully. "I'm tired too, but I think it's time I was going."

"And you think I'll just let you leave?" Richie asked, and got to his feet.

"You won't be in any condition to stop me," Angelina replied.

She stood up as well—and grabbed onto the counter when she swayed on her feet. There was a moment of confusion, and then her eyes widened in horror, and her gaze flew to Richie's face.

"I switched the cups when you turned to get the milk," Richie said. "Were you going to kill me too, or just knock me out?"

"I would never have killed you," Angelina said, and Richie noted the past tense. Only then did it occur to him that they probably shouldn't have had this chat in the kitchen.

The sleeping pills had begun to take effect, and Angelina's movements had slowed just as her eyelids had started to droop, but the sudden realization that she was in danger had produced a surge of adrenaline, and suddenly she didn't seem sluggish anymore. She whipped around, her eyes scanning the counter for a weapon, until they alighted on the knife block next to the stove. She lunged for the knives before Richie could get around the island to stop her.

He was panting too, not only because he was in danger but because he now understood what Angelina was capable of. The sweet, shy girl everyone had thought harmless was a fucking sociopath.

Angelina grabbed a butcher knife and swung around to face Richie. She was breathing hard, and her eyes were open wide, her pupils dilated. She was struggling to stay alert. Richie had no idea how many pills Angelina had dissolved into the tea, but it had to be a few if she'd hoped to knock him out for several hours. The problem was that, once the fight or flight instinct kicked in, it could overcome the effects of the drug, at least temporarily. She would crash later, but at the moment Angelina was fighting for her life, and wouldn't go down without inflicting the maximum amount of damage. Richie couldn't waste precious moments calling 911. Besides, if he got the same kid as before, it would take a while for the baby cop to clue in and send help.

Angelina and Richie faced off, both entirely focused on each other and ready to spring into action. Richie prayed Angelina would come to her senses and put the knife down, but he could see in her eyes that this was going to be a fight to the death. As long as no one suspected her, Angelina had time and the chance to save herself. Once she crossed into Canada, she could avoid detection, as long as she had cash. A few thousand dollars could keep her afloat for months if she was careful, and then she could figure something out. She was resourceful.

Richie didn't have time to consider any other possibilities because Angelina let out a blood-curdling shriek and charged. The sluggishness she had clearly been experiencing a few minutes ago had been replaced by manic energy and old-fashioned bloodlust. It was either him or her, and Richie knew that, now that he'd tricked her, Angelina was prepared to kill. He pivoted out of the way, but she moved with surprising speed, cutting him off as he danced toward the patio door and backing him into a corner. Richie had to get outside. He didn't have his car keys on him, but he had the phone. He had recorded everything Angelina had admitted to, but would that evidence ever get to DeVries if Angelina killed him? He supposed they'd figure it out when they found his body, but it would be too late then, at least for him.

The forest was his only chance. It was cold and dark out there, but, if he could get away from this bright kitchen that was full of obstacles, he'd have a real shot. His grabbed for the door handle, desperate to unlatch it so he could access the deck, but Angelina slashed the knife across his forearm. Richie gasped, his gaze sliding to the long, narrow cut that had easily parted the fabric of his sweatshirt and the skin beneath. Dark red blood welled immediately and began to soak into the sleeve. Had Angelina cut his wrist? He wouldn't have long if she'd managed to sever an artery. Richie put all his weight on the wall at his back and kicked outward, and his heel caught Angelina in the lower stomach. She cried out in pain but didn't let go of the knife, and, instead of backing away as Richie had hoped, she threw herself forward.

Richie had nowhere to go. She had him cornered. He tried to maneuver out of the way, but Angelina wasn't about to allow him to escape. She looked maniacal, a cruel little smile playing about her lips as she considered her next move.

"Angie, please," Richie tried. "Just go. I won't try to stop you."

She shook her head, and her hair whipped about her face, making her look like some restless spirit. "I don't believe you. Not anymore."

Without a moment's hesitation, she thrust the knife toward his belly. It was by sheer luck that the blade pierced Richie's side instead of wounding him at the center, where it was sure to have perforated a vital organ. Richie let out a roar of shock and pain as the steel slid deeper and deeper into his unresisting flesh.

Angelina appeared shocked by what she had done; her eyes widened when she saw the blood that saturated Richie's sweatshirt within moments. Desperate to stave off another attack, Richie took advantage of her momentary distraction and grabbed her wrist, digging his fingers into her flesh until she cried out and her grasp on the handle began to weaken. Still, she wouldn't release the knife, and with a cry of fury she lunged forward again, this time stabbing Richie in the stomach.

He let go of her wrist, his hands going to his stomach as he tried to breathe, but no air inflated his lungs. He was gasping, his hands shaking as his knees buckled. The initial burning sensation was quickly replaced with agonizing, throbbing pain, and then there was a sucking sound as Angelina pulled the knife out and blood gushed from Richie's abdomen. He pressed his hands to the wound, doing his best to keep in the blood, and possibly his guts. He was panicking badly now, his mind racing as he searched for escape, but his feet were already slipping on the blood that had pooled on the ceramic tiles beneath his feet, and the bloodstained blade was mere inches from his heart.

Was this it? Was this how it was all going to end? He was too young to die. He hadn't done anything worth mentioning, and the only people who'd miss him would be his grandparents and Frankie. Dear God, Frankie, Richie thought woozily. He would be so sad and confused. He didn't really understand why people were gone forever when they died.

"Angie, please," Richie rasped, his pleading gaze fixed on Angelina, but her face was twisted with an emotion that seemed to be somewhere between hatred and fury.

He saw no pity in her eyes, no remorse, and no fear of the consequences. At this point she had nothing to lose, and she would make sure she got on the road as soon as she neutralized him. She couldn't allow him to call for help, so she would take the phone. And then she'd change, grab her bag and the car keys, and make for the border. All she needed was two hours. The border was only one hundred miles away and, as long as she had her ID, border patrol would have no reason to stop her. Richie didn't think either Alan DeVries or Asha Singh had considered the possibility of the killer escaping to Canada.

Blood seeped through his trembling fingers, and a strange lethargy began to take over, turning his limbs to jelly, but his mind still couldn't accept that Angelina, the girl he'd known, trusted, and kissed and caressed only an hour ago, would murder him in cold blood. Except the blood wasn't cold. It was hot and black and slippery, and the pain was growing more intense, probably because Richie's mind had finally caught up to what was happening to his body. His extremities were growing cold, and he was shaking with shock. A stomach injury could be fatal, but even if it wasn't, if he didn't get help in time he would die right here on the kitchen floor. It was only when the tears dripped into his mouth that Richie realized he was crying.

Angelina looked down at him, but there was no compassion, only detachment. As far as she was concerned, he was dead already. She drew her arm back, and Richie knew she was about to administer the fatal blow.

"This is my final act of love, Richie—a quick death," Angelina announced.

Richie gathered what was left of his strength and hurled himself at her. His intention had been to knock the knife from her grasp, but he slipped on his own blood and lost his equilibrium, crashing into Angelina and knocking her off balance. She screamed, and Richie felt the blade that was trapped between them but still in Angelina's hand. His head was swimming, and he could barely see. Sweat was pouring into his eyes even though he was freezing, and his mouth was so dry he couldn't even swallow.

Richie's vision dimmed at the edges, and he felt weaker and more untethered to life with every passing moment, but he forced himself to concentrate and managed to get his hand between their tussling bodies. Their hands were slick with blood, and the handle was slimy and slippery, but, try as he might, Angelina wouldn't let go of the knife. Richie knew he had a few seconds of consciousness left, and he meant to make them count. He managed to twist Angelina's wrist, turning the sharp end of the blade away from himself and toward her. Her hoodie and T-shirt had ridden up when Richie fell against her, and he could feel her bare skin against his quivering knuckles.

Angelina howled when Richie pushed down hard, and the

knife sliced into her belly. There was a fresh gush of blood, only this time it wasn't his. He angled the blade downward, aiming to do as much harm as he could before he passed out and she finished him off. Bright lights pulsated at the edge of his vision, and he released Angelina's wrist, unable to keep up the pressure. He could hear her screaming, but the sound came at him as if he were underwater. He no longer felt pain, only weakness and cold, and he pressed his cheek against the cool tiles. Angelina was still screaming, but what she seemed to be saying didn't make any sense.

"He attacked me," she shrieked. "He tried to kill me. Help me! Please!"

Richie barely registered the sound of breaking glass or the raised voices that swirled above his head. The kitchen was suddenly full of people, and someone was calling his name. They were telling him to hold on and speaking into a radio as they requested immediate medical assistance. Richie looked up into the worried face of Asha Singh, and then he let go.

SIXTY-SIX
RICHIE

Six months later

After a long, cold winter, spring had finally arrived, and the air smelled of flowers and freshly cut grass. The dusky sky shimmered lavender against the bright lights of the high-rises, and the Village was vibrantly alive as restaurants and bars filled with patrons and the cacophony of Friday night traffic drowned out the conversation and music that spilled from outdoor restaurants. Richie exited the train station and walked to his favorite bar on the corner of Hudson and Christopher. It was quieter inside, the dim lights, yeasty smell of beer, and music that flowed from the speakers instantly making him feel at home. He was the first to arrive, so he found an empty booth, slid his briefcase beneath the table, and ordered a Corona with lime. Then he settled in to wait.

If he were honest, he was nervous as fuck and hoped the alcohol would take the edge off before the others arrived. They hadn't all seen each other since that fateful breakfast at the Corner Café, and communication had been sporadic at best. By the time Richie had been released from the hospital, Remy had been back home, Noah had been cleared by the police, and Mia had still been in intensive care.

Remy and Noah hadn't been on speaking terms, but Remy told Richie that Noah had sent him a text once he was released. Noah hadn't said a word about Serena or the baby, but he had apologized to Remy for hurting him so badly and had thanked him for not pressing charges. As far as Richie knew, that had been the last time the two had been in contact.

Richie had thought they might all see each other at the trial, but Angelina's mother had hired Sarah Kendall to represent her daughter and, once Richie had heard the news, he had known a guilty verdict wasn't guaranteed, not even if the recording he'd made was played in court. He'd never met Sarah Kendall, but he had heard of her. She was a young Black defense attorney from the Bronx, and she was known for her fierce intelligence, refusal to be intimidated, and gutsy tactics. As an attorney, Richie had to admire Sarah's strategy. She had made sure the confession he had taped had been barred since it had been illegally obtained and was therefore not admissible in court. She had quickly dismantled the physical evidence against Angelina, claiming that her prints on the bottle that contained the sleeping pill and ketamine residue and on the blown-out tire were circumstantial. Angelina could have stumbled on the gravel and braced herself against the tire to keep from falling. And just because she had touched the bottle, it didn't prove she'd been the one to add the fatal mixture to Vince's water.

There was no physical evidence that proved she had tried to strangle Serena or that she had pushed her off the dock. Sarah claimed that Serena had stumbled in the dark and fallen, hitting her head and sustaining the injury that had rendered her unconscious and led to her drowning in the lake. There was no way to prove that the bruises on Serena's neck had been inflicted by Angelina.

Before she passed out, Angelina had claimed that Richie had raped, then tried to kill her. Since it had been just the two of them in the house and there was no one to corroborate his side of the story, the prosecutors had had to follow the evidence, which confirmed that sexual intercourse had taken place and that Angelina's tea had been laced with drugs. There was also the wound in her stomach, which she claimed she'd sustained when Richie attacked her. What she did to him was presented as self-defense. The taped confession, which although it couldn't be entered into evidence had been played for the judge in his chambers, had been the only thing that had kept Richie from being charged with sexual assault and attempted murder.

Last Richie heard, the charges against Angelina had been dropped and she had been released from the correctional facility in upstate New York where she had spent the months leading up to the trial. Richie hoped he'd never see her again as long as he lived. He was eager to see Remy, Noah, and Mia, but deep down he acknowledged that this meeting wasn't a reunion that would heal their wounds but an opportunity to say goodbye. They were all going their own ways. Remy and his new girlfriend were heading to Paris for the summer. Remy seemed different these days. More self-assured. It was as if he'd finally stepped out of the shadow cast by his mother's legacy and realized that no one really cared what Pixie got up to in the nineties or with whom. She was old news.

Noah had accepted a job in Pasadena and was in the process of packing up the apartment he'd shared with Serena. Richie thought the move was long overdue, but Noah had to go at his own pace after what he'd been through. Richie didn't think he'd hear from Noah once he moved, but he hoped they might reconnect one day, once the scars had finally healed.

Mia was house-hunting in Darien. She hadn't told Richie outright, but Remy had mentioned that she was seeing a woman. Richie couldn't say the news had come as a surprise. The fact that she had escaped from a religious cult had been much more shocking, but Mia didn't want to talk about her experiences or tell them about her family. She needed to move on, though waking from a coma and finding herself alone had to have been a painful reminder of how much she had lost. Richie hoped she'd create a new family, one she could be proud of, with whoever loved her for who she was.

It was as it should be, Richie thought as Mia walked into the bar and peered around in search of familiar faces. He'd moved on as well. He'd just been promoted, and he was dating a girl he really liked. Adriana was nothing like the women he'd gone out with before. She wasn't striking, busty, or self-obsessed. She was cute, a little overweight, and incredibly smart, and had an amazing personality. And she loved Frankie and never lost patience with him when he acted out from time to time. Adriana was genuinely giving and kind. In fact, she reminded Richie of his mom. He wasn't ready to confide in his estranged friends, but he thought he could see himself spending his life with Adriana. The thought of waking up to her for the rest of his days didn't scare him one bit. In fact, it made him happy.

Mia finally spotted him, waved, and made her way between the tables toward the booth. Remy arrived a few minutes later, followed by Noah, who looked like he might bolt at any moment. They all understood how hard this was for him, and left him alone until he felt comfortable enough to join in the conversation. It was awkward at first, and no one mentioned Lexie, Serena, Vince, or Angelina. It was all too raw and too painful. But this was a step forward for them all, and, even if they never saw each other after today, it would bring a sort of closure.

After a while, they began to relax, and the conversation finally shifted to more personal topics.

"I have something to tell you, guys," Mia said. She lifted her chin defiantly and looked around the table. "Some stuff is going to come out in the near future."

"What kind of stuff?" Remy asked.

"I've written a book about my escape from the cult."

"Are you self-publishing?" Noah asked.

Mia grinned happily and shook her head. "All I can tell you right now is that the manuscript was snapped up by a reputable publisher. It's going to be published in December, under my real name."

Noah reached out and laid his hand over Mia's. "That's really fucking brave, Mia."

"Maybe," Mia said thoughtfully. "Or maybe it's a decision I will regret for the rest of my life. Once the story is out, I will never be able to repair my relationship with my mother or my brothers and sisters. I'll be dead to them forever."

"Aren't you dead to them already?" Remy asked.

"I guess," Mia replied sadly. It was clear she didn't want to talk about the book anymore. "What about you, Noah?" she asked. "How do you feel about the upcoming move?"

Noah offered a tentative smile. "I look forward to the change of scenery. Too many memories on the East Coast."

"There are some smoking babes in California," Richie said and instantly regretted the thoughtless comment. It'd been less than a year since Serena died, and, even if Noah was ready to start dating, he might not want to discuss it with them.

Noah shook his head. "I have no interest in dating, at least not yet."

"Out of respect for Serena?" Mia asked. She seemed surprised that Noah would mourn Serena after everything that had happened, but refrained from saying so out loud.

"This is not about Serena," Noah said. "It's about me. I need to be on my own for a while, to figure out who I am and what I need. And when I get involved with someone, I want her to be a true partner, not an emotional crutch."

Remy nodded and said, "Good for you, man."

"What about you, Rich? Got any pictures of your new woman?" Mia chuckled. "Have you been tapped by the CIA or something? You never post anything on socials anymore."

"And I never will," Richie stated flatly. "I prefer to keep my private life just that—private."

"Is Adriana not allowed to post the occasional thirst trap of her boo?" Mia joked.

"She's a very private person," Richie replied.

"You look really good, Richie," Remy said. "Chiseled. Still off the carbs?"

"I eat what I want these days, but in moderation," Richie said. He no longer obsessed about his weight. He knew what was important and he would never again forget. "I'm focusing on the future."

And he was. This was the first day of the rest of his life, and he was ready for whatever the future might have in store. As they raised their drinks in a final toast, none of them paid any attention to the bleached blonde at the bar, who nursed a glass of Chardonnay as she watched them through the mirror mounted on the back wall.

SIXTY-SEVEN
ANGELINA

How chummy they looked, drinking and laughing together like nothing ever happened. They'd moved on with their lives, and they were probably happy and congratulating themselves on walking away unscathed. Angelina had managed to avoid a prison sentence, but her life would never be the same. She lost her job, her relationship with her mother was forever fractured since she knew the truth of what happened at Witch Lake, and she hardly recognized herself when she looked in the mirror. There was no more effective diet plan than prison food and the constant fear of being jumped in the showers, and there was no greater motivator than hatred. And she hated them all. Noah had moved on from Lexie before the body was even cold and married that bitch Serena. Remy had been ready to testify against Angelina if it came to a trial. And Mia had refused to take her calls when she only wanted to apologize and explain.

But most of all, Angelina despised Richie for breaking her heart. That was an unforgivable offense. The first man to break her heart was her father. He'd turned their home into a war zone, where everyone was forever walking on unexploded shells. Angelina's mother couldn't bring herself to leave him. She felt too guilty, even though he'd made her life a living hell. It was left to Angelina to free them from the misery and fear he'd subjected them to. Killing him was easy. No one was overly surprised when he overdosed on painkillers. He'd been in so much emotional pain, they all said. So tragic. So sad.

Angelina would never risk losing her freedom to get back at Remy, Noah, and Mia. They weren't worth the gamble. But Richie... *Oh, Richie will pay*, she thought as her hand went to the ropey scar on her abdomen that she could feel through the thin fabric of her top. Not today, not tomorrow, but one day, when he was happy and safe and thought he had nothing to fear. That's when she'd come for him. And everyone he loved.

Angelina got what she'd come for, so she saw no reason to hang around. She left a twenty on the bar and slid off her stool. She didn't look back. She didn't need to, even though she was tempted to see Richie smile just one more time. He wouldn't be smiling the next time they met.

"Richie, you're dead," she mouthed, and walked out of the bar.

A LETTER FROM THE AUTHOR

Huge thanks for reading *The Invite*; I hope you were hooked on the mystery of who killed Serena. If you want to join other readers in hearing all about my new releases and bonus content, you can sign up for my newsletter.

www.stormpublishing.co/irina-shapiro

If you enjoyed this book and could spare a few moments to leave a review, that would be hugely appreciated. Even a short review can make all the difference in encouraging a reader to discover my books for the first time. Thank you so much.

Thanks again for being part of this amazing journey with me and I hope you'll stay in touch—I have so many more stories and ideas to entertain you with.

Irina

irinashapiroauthor.com

www.ingramcontent.com/pod-product-compliance
Lightning Source LLC
LaVergne TN
LVHW031933070526
838200LV00076B/4530